GIRL, UNFRAMED

DEB CALETTI

Atheneum

NEW YORK LONDON TORONTO SYDNEY NEW DELHI

An imprint of Simon & Schuster Children's Publishing Division
1230 Avenue of the Americas, New York, New York 10020

For information about special discounts for bulk purchases, please contact
Simon & Schuster Special Sales at 1-866-506-1949 or business@simonandschuster.com.
The Simon & Schuster Speakers Bureau can bring authors to your live event. For more information
or to book an event, contact the Simon & Schuster Speakers Bureau at 1-866-248-3049 or visit our
website at www.simonspeakers.com.
Also available in a hardcover edition
Interior design by Tom Daly
The text for this book was set in Adobe Caslon Pro.
Manufactured in the United States of America
First Atheneum paperback edition June 2021
2 4 6 8 10 9 7 5 3 1

The Library of Congress has cataloged the hardcover edition as follows:
Names: Caletti, Deb, author.
Title: Girl, unframed / by Deb Caletti.
Description: First Simon Pulse hardcover edition. | New York : Simon Pulse, 2020. |
Summary: While spending a summer with her famous mother and her criminal boyfriend,
Sydney Reilly, age fifteen, finds love with Nicco, but her premonition of something
bad coming proves dreadfully accurate.
Identifiers: LCCN 2018048710 (print) | LCCN 2018041558 (eBook) | ISBN 9781534426979 (hc) |
ISBN 9781534426986 (pbk) | ISBN 9781534426993 (eBook) |
Subjects: | CYAC: Coming of age—Fiction. | Mothers and daughters—Fiction. | Celebrities—Fiction.
| Dating (Social customs)—Fiction. | Abused women—Fiction. | Mystery and detective stories. |
San Francisco (Calif.)—Fiction.
Classification: LCC PZ7.C127437 Gir 2020 (eBook) | LCC PZ7.C127437 (print) |
DDC [Fic]—dc23
LC record available at https://lccn.loc.gov/2018048710

Praise for *A Heart in a Body in the World*

A PRINTZ HONOR BOOK

A BANK STREET CHILDREN'S BOOKS
JOSETTE FRANK AWARD WINNER

A NEW YORK PUBLIC LIBRARY BEST BOOK
FOR TEENS OF 2018

A CHICAGO PUBLIC LIBRARY BEST BOOK
FOR TEENS OF 2018

A *BOOKPAGE* BEST BOOK OF 2018

AN AMELIA BLOOMER BOOK LIST 2019
SELECTION

YALSA BEST FICTION FOR TEENS 2019
TOP TEN SELECTION

"A book everyone should read right now."
—*NEW YORK TIMES BOOK REVIEW*

"A vital and heartbreaking story that brings together the #MeToo
movement, the effects of gun violence, and the struggle of
building oneself up again after crisis." —*ELLE*

"Equal parts heartbreaking and hopeful." —*BOOKPAGE*

"A moving, unfortunately timely, and gut-wrenching
story that will stick with you." —*BUSTLE*

"This is one for the ages."
—**GAYLE FORMAN**, author of the #1 bestseller *If I Stay*

"Caletti's novel dazzlingly maps the mind-blowing ferocity
and endurance of an athlete who uses her physical body
to stake claim to the respect of the nation."
—**E. LOCKHART**, *New York Times* bestselling author
of *Genuine Fraud* and *We Were Liars*

"More than bittersweet . . .
It will nestle inside your brain as well as your heart."
—**JODI LYNN ANDERSON**, award-winning author of *Midnight at the Electric*

★ "Remarkable." —*BOOKLIST*, starred review

★ "A timely novel." —*KIRKUS REVIEWS*, starred review

★ "Powerful." —*PUBLISHERS WEEKLY*, starred review

★ "Annabelle exemplifies persisting nevertheless." —*BCCB*, starred review

For my own mother and father,
and for theirs, and theirs, and theirs

CHAPTER ONE

Exhibit 1: Recorded statement of Sydney E. Reilly,
1 of 5
Exhibit 2: Aerial photo of 716 Sea Cliff Drive
Exhibit 3: Photo of Lila Shore, Giacomo "Big Jake"
Antonetti, and Sydney Reilly, Original
Joe's, North Beach, undated

I had a bad feeling, even before I left home. A strong one. If I'm here to tell you what actually happened, well, it started there. With a sense of dread. Like some pissed-off old ghost was going to haunt me until I heard whatever she had to say. It was eerie and unsettling like that. Urgent.

The feeling was there late at night, when I was alone in the dorm showers and the hot-water pipes creaked and groaned like a dying man, and it was there when I lay awake in the dark, watching headlights flash across the ceiling in a way that made me pull my covers up. But it was there in bright daylight, too, when Hoodean and Cora and Lizzie and Meredith and I went to Cupcake Royale and we made fun of Hoodean for getting vanilla (he always got vanilla). It was there on those last weeks of school, when the sky was blue and the sun was out and the air smelled delicious.

I tried to tell myself there were logical reasons for it. I didn't want to go to San Francisco anyway. I know it sounds crazy, since Lila lived in that Sea Cliff mansion perched above the Pacific. But I was happy at school—just being in class, or walking around Green Lake with Meredith, picking out what dog we'd want. Or sitting on my bed with Cora under my Frida Kahlo poster, playing our favorite songs to each other. Volleyball in the fall, crew in the spring, dim sum in the International District with Meredith's parents.

Leaving my friends for the whole summer—*that's* why I felt dread, I thought. Especially since things were getting so good lately. I felt like *IT* was about to happen. I didn't know what *IT* was, exactly, just something large, something that would change everything. Maybe *IT* was love, the passionate, all-encompassing kind, or actual sex, or maybe something else. Whatever it was, I wanted it bad, this something-big. I could feel it coming. I could feel it when my group of friends would be walking down the street, elbowing each other, laughing too loud, and people watched us with what I thought was envy. Or when we'd stroll into Victrola and the men would look up from their laptops to stare, even when Hoodean was with us. God, if I missed *IT* because I was stuck in a jillion-dollar house with my famous mother, I'd be heartbroken.

Which was another logical explanation for the dark feeling that followed me. Three months with Lila. She was a celebrity, and she was beautiful, but she was still my mother. The summer before, when I was fourteen, I wanted to tell her everything, to be best buds, to do stuff together. And then suddenly I didn't. Moms—they can be like a winter coat, helpful and warm and cozy, but then spring comes, and it weighs you down and maybe you just want to feel the cold anyway.

But I'm supposed to be telling you the truth, aren't I? And the truth is, Lila was never like that. She wasn't a warm and cozy mom like Meredith's, even if I felt the weight of her.

And the truth is, nothing made that sense of doom disappear—no explanations, no blue sky, nothing. It was persistent. It was spooky.

I didn't know what that feeling was. I didn't know which exact ghost from the past was trying to warn me. But she was real, and I didn't listen.

CHAPTER TWO

*Exhibit 4: Yearbook photo of Sydney Elizabeth Riley,
Academy of Arts and Sciences, Seattle*

A few weeks before I left, I tried to get out of going.
I was at Edwina's for dinner. "Hey, I could live with you for the summer!" I said. I made it sound like an idea that had just come to me, when actually I'd thought about it every night since the ghost started talking.

My grandmother scowled.

"I don't *want* to go," I whined.

But she was having none of it. "Sydney. Stop that. Of course you do," she said.

Of course I *didn't*. The weekend before, Cora and I had gone to her cousin Simon's baseball game. A cute boy had talked to me by the concession stand and played with my hair, and who knew what else might happen if I stayed for the summer. *IT* was everywhere, though maybe *IT* was just *more*.

"Pleeeease?"

Eye roll.

Because of my mother's career, and also because Lila wasn't exactly what you'd call maternal, Edwina pretty much raised me. You probably already know this. She lived with us wherever we went, from our first apartment, to Papa Chesterton's estate, to the modern house in Topanga Canyon. When I left for Academy in the fifth grade, Edwina came too, sitting beside me on the plane with her purse on her lap so no one would steal it. They chose Academy because Edwina used to live in Seattle when Lila was born, and she liked it there.

I passed their old house often. You picture Lila in *Nefarious* or in *What the Neighbor Knew*, and you'd think, *No way*. Now it was a tiny, crappy rental for university students, with a beat-up couch on the porch and a Huskies blanket covering one window. It was right next to a Wing Zone, which was pretty hilarious. Seeing that house—you understood why she changed her name from Linda Short to Lila Shore. A shore—all that wide space. Solid land on one side, the open sea on the other.

That night at dinner, in the nice craftsman house that Lila bought her, Edwina carried a big platter of ham to the table using pot holders that had seen better days. Ham for the two of us kind of cracked me up. It was probably on sale at Fred Meyer, since Edwina loved a good sale. My friends always liked going to Edwina's because she cooked big, old-fashioned food, food you barely saw in Seattle, stuff like *gravy*, like *roast*, and also because they thought Edwina was *colorful*. That's the word people use when someone has a big personality but you're kind of glad you don't have to deal with them yourself.

"You'd rather stay here with an old lady than go to that big, fancy place?" Edwina stabbed a slice and slapped it on my plate. I had a brief desire to become a vegetarian, because ham always has a way of reminding you where it came from.

"There's a new boyfriend," I said.

Edwina met my eyes, and our gazes played a whole film of the past.

"Well. You never know," Edwina sighed.

"Jake Something-Italian."

"She likes those tough guys. The Jets and the Sharks."

"The Jets and the Sharks?" I laughed. "What are those, made-up gang names?"

"You're kidding me. *West Side Story*? You never seen it?" She snapped her fingers, danced toward me like a gang-member grandma getting ready to rumble on a dark street.

"Ooh, scary, haha. Especially in those slippers."

That's how it was, you know? Lots of things were funny. I folded a piece of ham into a buttered roll. It was so good. I ate one and then another. I wasn't in that part of womanhood yet where your body was something you were supposed to keep one nervous eye on all the time, like a bank balance. I still belonged mostly to myself, but not for long.

"She's all gaga in love," I said with my mouth full.

Edwina waved her hand as if the new guy were a pesky

insect. "That beautiful house right on the ocean? You should've seen the Mission District, where I grew up. Six miles from there, but another universe. You're a lucky girl."

"All my friends are here." There was no way I could tell her how great things were getting lately, let alone about that uneasy feeling. The way it felt like the shutter of a camera, briefly opening, revealing a dark and gaping hole.

"Remember how much fun we had when we went to Mexico? It'll be fine."

"I was *eight*."

We did have fun in Mexico. We had an amazing time. I was a little kid, and I wanted nothing more than to be with Lila. She was the treasure you were only allowed to peek at, until one astonishing day you finally got to run your fingers through the pile of gold coins and try on all the gold jewelry and drink out of the golden goblets. Plus, she made whatever we did exciting. We sat under umbrellas and walked through markets and bought stuff and ate in nice restaurants and spent a lot of time staying out of the sun, even though sun is something Mexico happens to have a lot of. I could never really see her eyes in those sunglasses, but she held my hand and it made me happy.

I didn't know her as a person then. I knew her as a thing I didn't have in the way I wanted, though maybe that's true about most parents.

"Cora's taking a pastel workshop this summer. She wants me to go too." A last plea. I wasn't an amazing artist like Cora, but I loved my pastels—the colored dust on my hands, the way you could disappear into an image you created. "I'd be so busy, I wouldn't even bother you."

Edwina ignored me. "How about a haircut before you go? I'll make an appointment. Your hair is a big wall of blonde." This was how Edwina showed her love. Feeding you, buying you a six-pack of underwear at Target, watching the way you looked even if you didn't. Being brisk and bossy and occasionally critical. Sometimes you had to remind yourself it was love.

"I like it how it is."

"No one likes a big wall of brown."

I put my hair over my face. "I prefer to call it a waterfall of blonde." When I peeked through, Edwina was rolling her eyes again.

When you picture Lila Shore in *Nefarious* or in *What the Neighbor Knew* or in some article in a magazine, you can't imagine her growing up in a house like that, but you wouldn't have imagined *me* right then either.

I always felt too regular to be hers. I was just me, a girl. I was never beautiful. I was never desired.

And then I was.

CHAPTER THREE

Exhibit 5: Framed promotional film poster with
partially shattered glass, 27" x 41" featuring
Lila Shore in Nefarious

A week before I boarded the plane, Lila called. After
that phone call, I felt an actual pulse of worry, a skitter of anxiety under my skin, something more definite than the ghost
whisper. I almost didn't answer. The Mayor's Cup Regatta
was in two days, and I was about to go to practice. Coach
Dave gave extra crunches if you were late. The Mayor's Cup
was supposed to be just a fun, end-of-the-season thing, but
Academy was always competitive. We were good, and being
on that team mattered to me, like it mattered to all of us.

"Baby!" Lila sang. "So, here's the deal. Don't be mad. I know
I promised it would be just us, but Jake wants to come when I
pick you up at the airport."

"Liiiii-laaa," I groaned, because, well, typical Lila. A man, a lie. "I haven't seen you in months. And I don't even know the guy. It'll be weird."

"We'll have *plenty* of time alone. Plus, you two need to meet! You're going to be seeing a lot of each other."

She'd just contradicted herself, but whatever. The more important thing was, my head began to throb with tension. History was flashing before my eyes. The bad kind of history, where people do horrible stuff for generations, not the good kind where they learn and do better. "Just don't marry him before I get there."

"Oh, baby, don't. Come on."

She was exasperated. I could hear her nails clicking against a hard surface. It wasn't an unreasonable thing to say. As you know, she'd done that before. Lila and men—ugh. *Of course* I felt uneasy.

There was a long, strained silence. I looked out my window toward the Montlake Cut, the slender neck of the Lake Washington Ship Canal, where the crew team was already gathering. I could see the satiny blue and yellow of their uniforms, the same satiny blue and yellow I was wearing. Meredith would be knocking at my door any second.

"I've got to go. Practice is about to start."

"Oh, not yet! Don't leave mad. Please. Talk to me some more."

Lila, well, she could be a conversational hostage-taker, letting you free only after you met her demands.

"I can't."

"Syd! Don't be like that. Stay. Let me just read you this letter I got today. You'll laugh your head off. An actual *letter*. Who writes letters anymore? A *seventeen-year-old boy*, that's who."

She laughed, because we always laughed at mail like this. It was one of our things. But I didn't feel like laughing. I was fifteen, almost sixteen. I went to school with seventeen-year-old boys. I mean, yeah, the whole world watched her, but seventeen-year-old boys were sort of *mine*.

Right then, Meredith popped her head into my room, and I was so glad to see her, it was like I'd been stranded at sea for years and she was the captain of the tanker who spotted me. I waved madly and gestured for her to come in. Meredith had her Academy crew bag over her shoulder. She tapped her wrist where a watch would be if people wore watches anymore. "We're late," she mouthed.

"Meredith's here. I need to go."

"She can wait! What have I told you a million times?"

"Don't be the first one anywhere."

Meredith pretended to gag.

"Precisely. Oh, you should see the handwriting on this thing! So tiny and restrained! 'Dear Ms. Shore: I've never written anyone a fan letter, but ever since I saw *Nefarious*, you've tormented my imagination. That scene where you're on the ladder and Brandon Searing lifts your skirt and we see your legs and the white lace of your—'"

"Lila, I'm hanging up."

"Tormented his *imagination*! Isn't that a riot? I think he's got his anatomy mixed up."

"*Stop.*" I was pleading by that point.

"Oh my God! I'm late for my manicure. Baby, I have to rush out of here. I love you, I love you, I love you."

She waited for me to say it back. But I was irritated, plus all kinds of other things jumbled together like the pile of dirty laundry in the corner of my room. I didn't *want* to say it. I could hear what I owed just sitting in the silence.

"I love you, Lila."

Ugh! Whatever. I hung up. Meredith and I took the steps out of Montgomery Hall. "We better hurry," I said.

"You okay?" she asked. Mer was my best friend. She knew me. She knew the me I was then.

"Yeah," I said, even though I wasn't, not by a long shot. And that irritation I felt? It was going to get worse. A lot worse. Outright *fury*. "Hey, cute hair."

Meredith made the ends of her braids dance. And then we heard Coach Dave's whistle and had to run.

In the boat, out on the water, I looked down at my own, regular legs. I remember this so clearly, how I examined this one body part like it was the malfunctioning O-ring that might make the whole ship blow up. Those legs were long and skinny and ended with my feet in a pair of Nikes. My knees were as knobby as a couple of oranges. I had a scratch on my calf from when I missed the hurdle during the track unit in PE the week before. There were little golden hairs that shimmered in the sun.

The thing was, my legs were just plain old things to walk on. They had regular jobs. Like running to catch up. Like riding a bike. Like screaming in pain when they hit the sun-hot seat of Meredith's mom's car. Those legs would never torment anyone, I was pretty sure.

Here was my experience with desire right then: picking out the cutest boy in my class on every first day of school since I was five and admiring him from afar. That thrilling note-passing in the sixth grade, when Emma English told me that Jeremy Wykowski liked me. Middle school slow dancing, a probably-not-accidental boob touch. That boy from another school who suddenly entwined his fingers with mine at a basketball game, who I fantasized about for months afterward, probably because his real self wasn't there to mess things up. The last six months with Samuel Crane, involving phone conversations about stuff that seemed deep, kissing behind the metal shop building and a few times in his parents' basement, hands up a shirt, hands down pants, more like hunting around in your backpack for your phone than anything else. And most recently: the men looking up from their laptops in Victrola. A boy twining my hair around his finger, the smell of hot dogs and mustard around us.

Torment—I had no real idea about any of that, honestly. I wasn't sure I even liked Samuel Crane the way I should. He liked me, and it seemed like reason enough to kiss back. Obviously, there was some hidden door to the bigger world that I hadn't walked through yet. I heard about that world in songs and saw it in movies, but it wasn't mine. It was an intriguing mystery, or maybe an outright lie.

I could feel it stirring around in there, though. Desire. Or desire for desire. I wanted to feel deep, aching *want*, but I wanted to make someone else feel it too. That was maybe even more appealing—the power to make a guy want me, badly. I would never have admitted this. It seemed wrong, especially since my own mother had made a career out of being a sex object. It was a truth I kept buried, like a secret from myself.

"Syd-Syd!" Meredith called from her seat behind me in the boat. I looked over my shoulder. Meredith made a face, and I made one back.

"Sit ready!" the coxswain called. My hands gripped the oar and I buried the blade in the water. This was the moment we steadied the boat before we rowed like crazy, deep in the intensity and the speed and the high of the race. And these were the moments before I found the hidden door. Right then, I didn't have a clue where it was.

I would find it, though, as you know. Along with everything that lay behind it. And sixth grade was like two seconds ago, and my hands still had pastel dust on them, and Samuel Crane couldn't even drive yet.

One last thing. I should also tell you this:

We won the Mayor's Cup Regatta. And afterward, we squirted juice packs at each other and ran around screaming.

We were excited to win, but even more, school was almost out, and that's the best feeling there is.

I was so tired that night that I conked right off. That dark sense of being haunted, the ghost—there was no way she was going to keep me awake. So of course I had a horrible dream instead. Warnings are persistent, until they just plain give up on you.

I realize this sounds like something out of one of Lila's films, one of the scenes where a woman walks into a couple's shadowy bedroom and you see the glint of silver in the moonlight. But this is the truth: I had a dream about a knife. I woke up and my heart was pounding. It was the kind of terrifying dream that feels so real your hands shake. When I tried to explain it in the morning, though, it seemed silly.

"A horrible person got stabbed in the chest. It was you but it wasn't you," Cora repeated in the dining hall, as she chased some Cheerios with her spoon.

"It was so real," I said, but I could see the little smile at the corner of Cora's mouth.

CHAPTER FOUR

Exhibit 6: Set of Miyabi Birchwood kitchen knives on magnetic stand

Meredith and her mom, Ellen, drove me to the airport. They always drove me to the airport on school breaks, and picked me up, too. Now that I was finally underway, the ghost had gotten quiet. Then again, maybe I just couldn't hear her because Ellen had the music up loud, the way we liked it.

"Mer, Mer, Mer! Eight weeks until you come to visit!" I was bouncing all over the place. I was nervous, and the music was on, and back when I was packing my stuff, I convinced myself to get excited. *IT* could find me anywhere, and maybe my chances were even better away from home, where I could be anyone, not just the person my friends knew.

"I believe we've covered that," Meredith said. She was using her *You require a great deal of patience* tone, because I'd said the same thing about ten times already. She'd never visited me and Lila before, and eight weeks just seemed like forever. Man, I was going to miss her.

"We got you something." Ellen reached over the seat, and the car did a frightening little swerve.

"Mom, Jesus! Watch where you're going!"

"Don't say 'Jesus,' Mer. It sounds bad." Ellen tossed a plastic bag into my lap. It was probably one of the last plastic bags in existence in the entire Northwest. It maybe should have gone into a plastic bag museum.

"What's this?"

"Just a few things for the plane."

Ellen was always giving me stuff. They lived in a medium-size Craftsman in Capitol Hill, and Ellen sometimes spoke of *the sacrifices we make for a private school education*, meaning the day school rate at Academy. My mother rented a sixteen-million-dollar house and paid the full year of tuition and boarding in advance. Still, Ellen didn't seem to think I had what I needed.

I peeked in the bag. "You are so nice! Thank you! Oh, wow, jackpot!" Milk Duds, Reese's, Red Vines. A candy extravaganza. Plus that week's copy of *Inside Entertainment*. Also, a few mom-related things, like a package of Kleenex and hand sanitizer. Ellen was always on the front lines in the fight against germs. Hey, it was a dirty job, but someone had to do it.

"And I'm giving you this." Meredith handed me her copy of *The Deepest Dark*, by R. W. Wright.

"You finished!"

"God. It's soooo good."

"Look what I have for *you*," I said, and tossed her *The Night Dweller*.

We squealed. R. W. Wright was our favorite scary-book writer. We used to eat those up, even if all his books were the same. Vulnerable female and her friends stalked by a psycho. Saved by her last plunge of the knife. I'll never read him again.

"I brought *She's So Cold*, too." I rubbed my hands together in book glee.

"How do you girls even read those? Brrr." Ellen gave a fake shiver.

I reached over the seat and grabbed Ellen with monster hands and she shrieked. We rolled the windows down and the music blasted. My hair got all messy in the back seat. I didn't even care, because I was busy loving the song and thinking about how summer really did smell like sun and just-mowed grass. I was thinking about how much I'd miss home when I was gone. Home—there. Seattle.

These were the things we did. Ellen and Meredith, all of my friends. Regular things. Ellen driving us somewhere and dropping us off. Hanging out after Ms. Fiori's art class because she was the coolest and she spoke Italian and had a photo of her wife on her desk. Going on our Best Meatball in Seattle hunt, led by Hoodean. Cracking up over private jokes like "Tree Hugger" (don't ask). They all mostly forgot I had this other life, so I did too. I loved forgetting. I mean, I'd met some of those people in that magazine. But I loved being the me I really was. Not the me I was in relation to someone else.

"You have everything?" Ellen asked as we pulled up to the departures curb. I could hear the roar of planes taking off. Cars zipped in and out of the lanes. Taxis, too. People hugged each other good-bye.

"Phone. Charger. Candy bag. Pastels. Books." All the important stuff. "Check!"

"If you need anything, or if your flight gets delayed, you call me," Ellen said.

"Will do, chickadee." I loved Meredith's mom.

"*Mrs.* Chickadee to you. And if you use the airport bathroom, turn the faucets off with a paper towel. And the first stall is generally the cleanest."

"Is that true?"

Ellen shrugged. "I read it on the Internet."

I leaned over the seat and hugged Ellen, and then I hugged Mer. We'd done this lots of times. We'd done it since my first year at Lower Academy when I was ten when Meredith instantly became my best friend.

"Wait! Mom! We almost forgot." Meredith bent down, searched around for something.

"It's right there by your foot, Mer," Ellen said, and then Meredith popped up with a small wrapped box.

"For you. For tomorrow. Pretend it comes with a cake and candles."

"Aw! Thanks, guys."

"May sixteen be amazing," Ellen said. "And safe. Amazing but safe."

I smooched each of them hard and loud on the cheek. Big love. I zipped the box into my pack. And when I got out of the car, I felt hopeful. The slamming of trunks, and people hauling luggage onto the curb, and the planes rising in the sky— big things *were* happening, all around me.

"See you in eight weeks," I said to Meredith.

"San Francisco, here I come," she said.

I think a lot about that moment in the car, when we were driving and the music was on loud. How the wind rushed in. How Meredith's brown hair blew out the window, how she had one foot tucked up underneath her as she sat there in her shorts and her orange polo shirt. How the guy on the radio sang, *Hey, it's a summertime thing. Summertime thing . . .*

How I felt so light. How I felt so lucky. How the future was *right there.*

CHAPTER FIVE

Exhibit 7: Photo of Giacomo (Jake) Antonetti's yellow
Lamborghini
Exhibit 8: License plate of Giacomo (Jake) Antonetti's
yellow Lamborghini

The flight attendant did the safety dance, and I followed along on the plastic card because I wanted her to know that I was on her side in the event of a water landing. We took off.

Right afterward, in first class, we were offered orange juice and breakfast. Of course you know this, but if you're seated up there, they give you actual food and a cloth napkin and a real knife. They assume that people with money won't get violent, given the chance and the right cutlery. Well. God.

In the window seat next to me, there was a woman traveling for business. At least, I guessed she was, because she was wearing navy slacks and a silky shirt and had an efficient air, as if she were equipped to handle anything with calm certainty, even severe turbulence or a drop in oxygen levels. Her napkin was neatly placed on her lap, and she was making tidy cuts into her omelet, her fork in the superior upside-down position.

I felt her eyes on me. I felt the question. She was wondering what I was doing up here. Me, in my shorts and my Bazooka Joe T-shirt, my sandals. Chipped toe polish I painted on myself, which was pretty obvious. Breakfast already finished because I liked to eat on airplanes even if the food was gross.

Our empty trays were taken. The businesswoman tip-tapped on her laptop. I opened my magazine. I flipped the pages casually. And when I did, I saw Charles Falcon, at an event celebrating season four of *Gold Light Avenue*. I'd gone to his house a few times and swum in his pool before he got so huge, when he'd just been in *Nefarious* and a couple of beer commercials. I think he wanted to date Lila, but he was probably too nice for her. Naomi Meadows was also in there—a photo of her playing Tinker Bell on Broadway. She was in that failed TV pilot with Lila about the young dancer trying to make it in New York, where Lila was the sexy neighbor in the apartment next door. They were still friends. She'd come over and they'd drink gin and tonics and she'd call my mother Miss Lila.

I could forget about all this stuff when I was studying for finals or swimming with my friends at Matthews Beach or working the register at Jitters those Saturdays during the school year. (Edwina said a job would keep me from becoming an asshole.) Growing up, none of it had been all that important compared to which girl was being mean to me, or my spelling words, or losing my lunch box.

And then I turned the page. The image startled me. I did that confused *Hey, that person looks familiar* double take, like when you suddenly spot yourself in a department store mirror. It was Lila herself, in a Who Wore It Better? article. She was in a red gown with side cutouts, and her platinum hair had been crimped like a block of ramen. Her breasts (well, she was known for those, too) spilled over the top of her dress like . . . Okay, it's hard to avoid fruit analogies. The photo was of her at the Reel-to-Reel Awards, the kind of invitation she rarely got anymore. It was set next to an image of Ursula Tarby. Ursula Tarby had a thumbs-up by her photo, and Lila had a thumbs-down.

The hair was not her best look, but *really*? Thumbs-up, thumbs-down? On a *person*? I know, I know, there are ratings—stars and thumbs and bar graphs—on *everything*, from restaurants to Q-tips, but on actual *people*?

Nefarious came out when I was two, so I don't remember much about that time, when fans would mob her and photographers would aim their long lenses to get pictures of her sunbathing. But I knew about the clothes, the hair, the jewelry, the nails, the shoes. The teeth brightening, the wrinkle filling, all the stuff that supposedly made her beautiful enough to look at when she was already beautiful. I knew about the tension in the car before she'd appear in public, the nervous laughter, the vodka sipping, even though she was always careful not to be photographed with a drink in her hand.

I knew she'd hate the Who Wore It Better? piece. She'd feel humiliated, being judged like that. I felt bad for her. Beauty was her power, but what happened when your audience looked away? She'd feel like a failure for that thumbs-down. It would hurt her, but who cared? People forgot she was real. People forget that about each other a lot.

Still, there she was on that page. My very own mother. I left the magazine open on my lap. To send a message to the corporate woman. I ate my Milk Duds. I wiped my chocolate fingers on the real napkin that came with breakfast. I dared the corporate woman to notice the resemblance between Lila and me, though, honestly, I didn't know if there was one. Her hair was straight-up platinum, and mine was more the brown yellow of honey in a plastic bear. I was her height, and we both had blue eyes, but I always thought I looked more like my father.

Were we similar? Were we different? How much did it matter? (Answers: yes, yes, a lot.) Either way, I left that page open like a bold fact. *See?* This *is what I'm doing up here*, I tried to say.

Those were the times I knew I had a little Lila in me. When a sneaky part of me wanted to be regular but not *that* regular. When I wanted to be seen, too.

Of course, being looked at and being seen are two entirely different things.

And when you are looked at but not seen, you are an object. An owned thing. A napkin. A magazine. A knife.

CHAPTER SIX

Exhibit 9: Sworn statement of Jeffrey Douglas Reilly,
La Jolla, California

I expected Lila to be there outside the gate, beaming in a million directions like a lighthouse and wearing her huge sunglasses indoors. The sunglasses said: *Don't look at me, but look at me.* I wondered what he'd be like, the new guy, Jake. There'd been so many already that I knew her type. She liked a man with a big ego, good looks, charisma, the kind of stuff that seems like confidence until you find out it's actually controlling assholery.

Lila's dad, Hal, was supposedly this charming guy too, a ladies' man who was never around when things got hard or scary, when they were running out of money, or when Edwina lost her temper, or a tree blew down on the roof. But then he'd swoop in and lift Lila in his strong arms, and she'd feel like the light of his life. When he left for good, *poof*, the light blew out. Edwina's father—same thing. Charming but gone.

And wow, it was easy, really easy, for Lila to find the big, confident daddy-protector she never had. Lots of guys *loved* that idea. Men wanted to rescue her from whatever they thought she needed rescuing from—money troubles, a bad meal in a restaurant, other men. They wanted to wrap her in their strong man arms. And give her stuff. Jobs, presents, adoration, advice. They got to feel all manly and important, so they were *crazy* about her. I used to see the same thing at school all the time. If a girl was beautiful and vulnerable and had issues, guys dripped all over her like syrup on pancakes.

As I stood there in the airport with my pack on my shoulder, I felt a swirl of apprehension rising. Because, well, history makes more history.

You know about all of the husbands, right? Rex Revel. Guitar player and singer in the band Slay. Lila's first. They eloped on their first date. Stayed married for four stormy, cruel months. Moral of the story: Just because a guy looks good in leather pants and can scream the word "generation" eleven times in a row, it doesn't necessarily mean he's good husband material.

Jeff Reilly. My father. Owner of the Mockingbird restaurant chain (endless fries, place mats you can color), plus the upscale Sparrow in La Jolla, where he lived. They knew each other for three weeks before he asked her to marry him, which was twenty days longer than Rex Revel but hardly enough time to get to know important stuff, like the fact that he was still married. It was only after the ceremony, and after I was already a bundle of multiplying cells, that he told her. Way to be a player, Pops, you old dog, you! Gross. After he got divorced, he and Lila remarried to make me legal, but they stayed together only for another fourteen months. He appeared in my life about once a year, bearing gifts, same as Santa Claus. He was a ladies' man, a charmer, who could make you feel like the light of his life until he ditched you. Meaning: History is the sneakiest and most relentless monster there is.

Chase Chesterton. I know. His name sounds like a rich boy in a romance novel, but don't blame the messenger. He *was* rich, and romantic, but old. *Really* old. Do you know how old he was when they got married? Like, sixty-five, and she was twenty-eight. I knew him from age three to age six. They divorced after Papa Chesterton lost most of his money in a bad investment deal. He had long old-man ears and little fluid-filled moons of skin under his eyes.

I don't remember much about that time. Being a flower girl in their elaborate wedding. Itchy dress. Also, my huge bedroom in his mansion, which had a shiny floor that was fun to slide on in my socks. Lacy bed, also itchy. Bah-Bah, a stuffed giraffe that was tall as me. The firm line of Edwina's mouth when she came into my room to say good night.

My clearest memory is Chase Chesterton reclining by the pool, with his big white belly and old-man boobs, his stick legs in bedroom slippers that scuffed along the marble tiles. Something about this disturbed me even then. Maybe, you know, his old flesh and her not-old flesh. I didn't have words for it. I just thought he was icky. He looked like a grandpa. I tried not to breathe when he hugged me, even though he didn't smell bad. Bah-Bah vanished when they got divorced.

There were also various boyfriends. Ben Salvador. Super nice. He made enchiladas even a kid would like. Roberto-someone, who always remarked on what Lila ate and how she dressed. Something was always too tight or not tight enough. Trace Williams, who "had a temper." *Had a temper*, like it was a pet hamster. Erik. Derek. Enough that a few had names that rhymed.

Every time, it looked like this: Things would be going along fine, him being the big strong guy, her being the delicate flower, until she didn't *want* some controlling asshole telling her what to do anymore. She really didn't *need* rescuing, and the man arms just got suffocating after a while. His macho gallantry was actually domineering jerkdom. She'd speak up. She'd push back. Because, basically, she was strong. She was capable. She could get what she wanted. People forget that "feminine" doesn't mean "weak." Maybe she forgot that, too.

The *You be the little girl and I'll be the big, strong daddy* deal that the guy loved so much would blow up in his face. This would piss him off greatly. He'd wonder where his sweet, frail Lila had gone. She'd wonder how he didn't know she was more than that, way more, all along. Of course she was. She couldn't have gotten where she did if she weren't.

He'd feel pushed away. Rejected. A hole was blown through

the thin membrane of his ego. She'd stopped caring about his ego weeks before. Propping it up by letting him be bigger all the time had gotten exhausting. And, you know, that was why he chose her. To be the bodyguard of his ego.

That's when the trouble would start.

By "trouble" I mean divorces and slammed doors, money problems, you know. His car screeching off, unopened bills stacking up. Not the trouble that was coming as I stood in that airport.

Not danger.

Lila wasn't there.

I looked around the waiting area. A woman hugged a man in an army uniform. An elderly couple greeted a little girl. A guy in a suit stood around holding a Starbucks cup. But no Lila. I waited. Sometimes she was late. A lot of times she was late. *Late* gave you the spotlight. I wondered if I should go down to baggage claim and look for her there, even though I never checked luggage because I had most everything I needed at her house.

I tried to call. No answer. Just her voice on the recording: *Oh, just do the thing!*

"Where *are* you?" I said, and then hung up.

All of the fun excitement I'd managed to feel was vanishing fast.

I went to the airport bathroom and chose the first stall, and also used some paper towels to turn the faucet on and off.

I missed Ellen and Meredith already. So much. Also, Cora and Hoodean, and even our dorm supervisor, Mrs. Chen, who was kind of cold and bossy, but so what. I wanted to cry. I almost did. I actually wadded up some paper towels and put cold water on my face so I wouldn't.

When I came out of the bathroom, he was there.

Jake Antonetti.

I knew it was him instantly. And he was standing right outside, like he was sure I was in that bathroom.

I just took him in for a second. His stocky build. Really stocky, that kind of muscle-mass square body that meant he probably played football back in high school. His squarish head and hooded eyes and jet-black hair turning ever so slightly gray at the temples. His nose, which bent strongly to the left, maybe from a fist or an aggressive tackle. My first thought was, you wouldn't want to mess with him. Which meant, ugh, he was just Lila's type.

"Hey, sorry I'm late," he said. And then he hugged me. Ew. I didn't even know the guy. He had those squatty fingers that look like a row of wrestlers standing on a mat. I felt them pressing into my back. His cologne wrapped around me.

"Where's my mom?" I didn't say, *Where's Lila?* It was childish, but I wanted him to know who got there first.

"She hurt her . . . like, her wrist or hand or something. I guess the dog yanked—"

"Dog?"

"The German shepherd."

"We got a dog?"

"Nah, he's mine."

Lila didn't like dogs. Dogs jumped up on your dresses and snagged your silk blouses and did disgusting stuff like poop and pee and need you at the wrong times, kind of like kids.

I felt a little rise of hope, though. If I had to have Jake in my life, at least he came with a dog. We'd never had one with a dog before. Kevin-someone had a cat, and Papa Chesterton had horses, but that was the grand total of pets.

"Baggage?" he asked.

"Probably lots."

"I'll get a cart."

"It was a joke. You know, lots of baggage, haha?"

"Oh, hey. Yeah." He chuckled.

God.

I wanted to turn around and go home. The *IT* optimism I had when I was packing seemed stupid now. *This* was my life. We made our way through the airport to the parking garage. Somehow, he'd taken my bag and was carrying it. There was a corridor of awkward silence between us.

"I'm over here."

I followed. I realized as we were walking that I didn't really know anything about the guy. Lila usually spilled way too many details, but she'd been weirdly quiet about him. For all I knew, he might be a nice teacher. He could work in computer sales. Maybe he was a film producer, or a screenwriter, or a chef.

He pointed his keys in the general direction of the row of cars in the lot. A *bleep-bleep* chirped. I tried to figure out where it was coming from.

Then I saw it. A yellow Lamborghini.

He wasn't a teacher.

Even when we lived with Papa Chesterton in Hidden Hills, we didn't see many of those. The doors lifted like the wings of a praying mantis. I got in. I held my bag of candy on my lap. Back in the Milk Duds factory, those little chewy nuggets never imagined they'd end up here.

Neither did I.

Once he got out of the parking lot, Jake Antonetti hit the accelerator, and I held on.

And I held on and I held on. I held on until that rainy night in August.

CHAPTER SEVEN

Exhibit 10: Aerial photo of Sea Cliff Drive, east/west
Exhibit 11: Aerial photo of Sea Cliff Drive, north/south

I'd been to the Sea Cliff house only twice before, for a few days over Thanksgiving break and for a week at Christmas. I know that seems strange. People who live in one house their whole lives—like my friend Cora, for example—can't imagine it.

"How does it feel like *home*?" she asked.

"Home is where your family is," I answered, but this was a lie. I only said it because I knew the moving thing worried her. Honestly, the idea of home was confusing. If it meant what was most familiar, then home was there, in that dorm. With her and Lizzie, and our other friends, Hailey and Gia, and even Mrs. Chen. Home was Meredith's house, where we'd go and watch TV and Ellen would make us popcorn, and Meredith's sister and dad would come in and we'd throw pillows at them. Home was Edwina's, even if she told me to get my feet off the furniture, and said stuff like *Do you think I'm the maid? I'm not the maid*, and asked me if I'd met any new boys since Daniel. *Samuel*, but whatever.

If home was what you knew and what knew you, then home was the big evergreen out my window, and rainy, rainy days, where the needles would drip, and windy, stormy ones, where the boughs would bend and shake. Home was the curve of the Montlake Cut and the houses that followed its south bank. Home was Coach Dave, and the crew team. Yeah. Definitely them. Home was my favorite teachers: Terrence Oglio, English; Jayne Fiori, art. Or maybe, home was a longing for a place I'd never been.

It was hard to get attached, after all the houses. Papa Chesterton's mansion in Hidden Hills, the Spanish colonial a few blocks from the beach in Santa Monica. When Lila wanted to "escape pretension" (meaning her Papa Chesterton money was running low), there had been the smaller redwood-and-glass contemporary in Topanga Canyon. She sold that one a little over a year ago to rent the one on Sea Cliff Drive. Our family has a long history in San Francisco, which is why she moved there, Lila said. Edwina was raised in the city too. She told me a million times about her beautiful great-grandmother Ella, who survived the 1906 earthquake and fire. The story was, Ella fled with only her baby and her wedding photo, her cruel husband trapped in the blaze. Whether it felt like home or not, now that I was in that car with Jake, I couldn't wait to get there. Or maybe I just wanted to get out of that car. Jake wasn't much of a conversationalist, though I admit I wasn't exactly helping. I stared out the window as we drove down 101, turned onto busy Octavia Boulevard, and then finally headed down Fell, where I started to recognize things—the Painted Ladies (the row of Victorian houses on all the postcards), Golden Gate Park, with its big glass conservatory.

"You like the car?" Jake finally said.

"Yeah. It's nice." It sounded brattier then I meant. But then again, he was fishing for compliments, so yuck.

"Aventador," he said. I had no idea what that meant. It sounded like a character in one of Hoodean's video games. Maybe Jake was showing off his flair for languages. *C'est la vie, carpe diem, aventa dor.*

"I'll let you drive it if you promise not to crash into a tree."

"I don't even have my permit yet. And Lila doesn't want me to drive until I'm older."

"You're kidding me. The minute I turned fifteen, boom. No one took you to get it? All these years?" He was ready to be pissed at Lila or Edwina on my behalf, which, honestly, was kind of nice.

"It hasn't been years. I'm only fifteen now."

He seemed truly confused. He gave me that *Whaa?* look.

"Well, basically sixteen. My birthday's tomorrow."

He raised his eyebrows at me like this was surprising information, but I couldn't imagine Lila not mentioning either of these things. And then, I swear to God, his eyes went straight to my boobs, but maybe I was wrong, or just feeling uncomfortable in that small space. "Wow, well, you look a lot older."

This was news to me. I tried to sneak a glance at myself in his side mirror to see if he was right. It was hard to tell. I was used to myself. Maybe I did look a little older.

It was quiet for a while. And then, "So, you like school?"

"Yeah."

"What's your favorite subject?"

"All."

"All, huh?" He chuckled like I was a real go-getter.

After this, we ran out of conversation topics. Jake tapped his fingers on the steering wheel as he drove. I could tell I was making him nervous. I noticed the giant diamond ring on his right hand. It was one of those big, clunky kinds that look like college rings but aren't. Every time we hit a red light, he exhaled as if the world were against him.

We were on Twenty-Seventh—I was paying attention to street signs so I could learn my way around—when he started whistling. He looked over at me and lifted his eyebrows in some sort of question, only I didn't know what the question was. Then he grinned. I smiled back. I was supposed to smile back, but I felt uneasy in that hard-to-explain way, like when a certain man sits next to you on a bus. Or like that time Gia's brother drove me back to the dorm after her birthday dinner. You don't get the creeps exactly, just the pre-creeps. You start imagining how you'll roll out of the speeding vehicle if you need to.

I smiled back out of duty, but he must have thought we were pals now, because he reached over and squeezed my knee with his two fingers, in that place where it really hurts. He shook it a little, like we were playing a game. I think I was supposed to squeal. Instead, I said, "Ow," and he took his hand back, and I couldn't tell, but I thought he looked pissed.

The scenery was a disorienting mix of the familiar and unfamiliar, since the city was still newish to me. I was sure I recognized a street of tightly packed houses, but then again, it looked like all the other streets of tightly packed houses. Suddenly, though, the homes got larger and nicer. There was more space between them. And then, yeah, *those* I recognized—two cement pillars standing like guards on either side of the street, with the little metal plates labeled SEA CLIFF.

The first house through the pillars was a white wedding-cake mansion with a manicured green lawn. The street was wide and roomy, and the houses had actual yards, and the gray sky got brighter and larger, as it does when you get closer to the ocean. There were terra-cotta roofs and brick stairwells, hedges cut into fancy shapes. There were columned estates with large, curved white windows and embellished balconies and gated driveways. You felt the calm orderliness of money. You felt the way some people paid other people to clean up their messes. You felt . . . like there were lots of secrets hidden behind all that order.

The crew from a yard service swarmed a lawn like hedge-clipping ants. A leaf blower hummed, and the smallest gathering of leaves blew up like confetti. In between the houses, I spotted glimpses of the Pacific Ocean and the orange Golden Gate Bridge. We made a left and there it was: 716 Sea Cliff Drive.

You've seen it, I know, but for the record, Lila's house was a Mediterranean-style stucco painted a Tuscan orange, with a large stucco wall closing off the garden. It was maybe the fixer-upper on the street. At least, the garage needed a tiny bit of painting in spots, and the grass had a few rogue dandelions.

As Jake pulled into the drive, I was suddenly nervous to see Lila. This always happened. Even though she was ever-present, in texts and calls and magazines *right on my lap*, not seeing her for almost six months could make it feel like our first date. My stomach fluttered.

"All righty. Here you go," Jake said. He released the trunk so I could get my pack.

"Thanks."

Thanks. It was the wrong word. The very most wrong word. I forgive myself, because we say a lot of wrong things to a lot of wrong people. Still, when I think about it now, I want to spit that word right out of my mouth. I can see it landing in the dirt, feeding some ancient tree, one with the kind of big, old roots that crack sidewalks and lift foundations, same as an earthquake.

CHAPTER EIGHT

Exhibit 12: Floor plan, 716 Sea Cliff Drive
Exhibit 13: Photo of 716 Sea Cliff Drive, main entry

As I headed up the walkway to the door, I heard Jake's dog barking his head off. Actually, he sounded like he wanted to rip mine off. Visions of some adorable puppy vanished in two seconds.

"Max!" I heard Lila yell from behind the door. "For God's sake!"

I figured it might be better if I didn't just walk in. If Max thought I was an intruder, he might tear my leg off like I was the turkey and this was Thanksgiving. Jake was still in the car on his phone, so I rang the bell. The dog went insane.

"Knock it off, you idiot!" Lila shouted. When she opened the door, she had the dog by the collar. Or rather, the dog had her by the hand. He had the golden brown and black coat of a

German shepherd, and his teeth were bared, and his toes slid and skittered along on the marble entry like the most furious novice ice-skater you've ever seen in your life.

"Niiiiice puppy," I crooned.

"Jesus!" Lila was using every muscle in her body to hold him back.

But then Jake came up the walk, tucking his phone into his pocket, and before my very eyes, the dog transformed into an entirely different animal, the loving little angel in sweet reunion with his master. His limbs were his own again. He wound and bumped through Jake's legs as Jake kept walking, ignoring him. I actually felt kind of sorry for the dog—insulted by Lila, snubbed by Jake. He was like the bad kid that acted out in class because no one paid attention to him.

Jake kissed Lila's neck. "We're back," he said. But now Lila was doing the ignoring. The kiss was like a bee she swatted away.

"Hey, guy." I scruffed the dog's scary head and patted his large, intimidating body. "You're a beautiful boy," I told him. This was too much love too fast, because then he jumped up excitedly and we were staring at each other, eye to eye. I gave him a big shove down. In two seconds, I had dog hair all over me, but I didn't mind.

"Don't I get a hello?" Lila said. "Baby! I am so glad to see you. Come here."

I hugged her. She smelled like Lila—the gentleness of orange blossoms, the aggressiveness of spice. Of course she looked beautiful, in her white capris and a sleeveless navy top, her hair up in a stylish messy bun. Her wrist was wrapped in an Ace bandage. Lila was always getting injured or sick. Twisted ankles, broken fingers, mysterious stomach maladies. Little amber pill bottles lined her bathroom sink.

"What happened to your arm?"

"Damn dog pulled me right to the ground when the UPS man came. I'm sure it's a sprain. Baby, I missed you! Get in here."

Inside, the terra-cotta floors opened to a large staircase, which curved upward, like the inside of a seashell. The kitchen and the dining room were on the main level, and so was the centerpiece of the house, a large living room done all in white—white rugs, white furniture, white pillows. Lila called it the White Room, for reasons that should now be obvious. The entire back of the room was glass—windows that looked out onto the Pacific, and glass doors that opened to the patio, which perched scenically over the cliff. From there, an orange stucco staircase wound like a maze down to China Beach.

Lila told me she'd gotten a great deal renting the place, but this was hard to imagine. How could the word *deal* even sit in the same sentence with that house? That view. It took your breath away. Literally, like a sock in the stomach. Even when I knew what to expect, I walked in that day and wow. There it all was—the sea and the Marin Headlands, laid out like nature's most valuable work of art. And the Golden Gate Bridge, too, right there, looking close enough to touch. It shocked me, how beautiful that view was. It *pulled* me toward it. I went to the glass and looked out.

"You want lunch? I ordered all your favorites. Beecher's mac and cheese? Those lovely tomato basil paninis?" Beecher's mac and cheese was my favorite when I was six, and the tomato basil paninis were *her* favorite, but I didn't care. I was happy she'd thought of me.

"Sounds awesome. I'll just put my stuff away."

I should probably mention that Lila used to have a chef, but not anymore. She also had a driver and a personal assistant, in addition to her agent, Lee Miles, and her manager, Sean James. After *Rainmaker* lost so much money, though, and the pilot about the young dancer wasn't picked up, Lila was mostly doing commercials for companies in Europe. So she was down to a house cleaner who came in once a week, and we just ordered food in, or we'd go out.

"Oh, sure. Get settled. Make yourself at home."

Jake—*he* was the one who was making himself at home. I heard him toss his keys onto the long white counter in the kitchen, and then I heard the opening and shutting of a cupboard. There was the sound of rattling in a drawer, then a few moments later, the pop of a wine bottle opening. I actually heard the liquid glug as it went in the glass. It was pretty obvious that I'd stressed him out.

I carried my pack upstairs. On the second floor, there was Lila's huge bedroom and bath that looked out over the sea, as well as a media room, and a guest room with a view of the front garden. Up another flight was my room. Also, a second guest room and a workout space, which had a bunch of weights and equipment no one used. My room was smaller than Lila's, but it had the same view. I was the only one on the entire floor.

Up there, it was a little echoey, and I suddenly felt the kind of alone I did when I was the last one left in the dorm before vacation. I opened all the drawers of my dresser to see everything again. I got reacquainted with my stuff. Jeans! I remember you. Oh, right—*those* shorts and T-shirts and dresses.

And on my pillow was that stupid doll. It used to belong to Edwina's grandmother, the aforementioned baby who was carried from the burning building after the earthquake. Lila always put it there after I left. I hated it. The staring eyes scared me. I kept telling her that, but Lila loved dolls. I took it and tossed it under the bed in the guest room and I shut the door. I hoped it wouldn't haunt me from there, same as in R. W. Wright's *Glass Eyes*.

In my double-sink bathroom, with the stylish, retro octagon tile, I checked out all the cabinets. Hey, my old lotion from last time! There was the same half bottle of shampoo from my Christmas visit. Also, that enormous and stinky pine-scented candle Lila had set out as a holiday decoration. I stuck it under the sink.

The floor creaked, and I jumped. It was silly to be so jittery, but the rooms felt hollow, and cold, too, even in June, probably because no one had been upstairs in months. It was just Max, though, standing in the doorway. I was glad to see him. The house was stunning and beautiful, but it was old, and houses have stories, and I wondered what the walls knew. That stupid doll probably didn't help.

"Hey," I said. "Come on." I patted the bed, and he galumphed up. He curled his giant self into a doughnut. A very large doughnut. He was going to get hair everywhere and Lila would kill me, but I liked him there. I liked his warm body and the fact of his beating heart. The sea was so many gorgeous shades of blue outside those windows, but I was already feeling windswept.

My dream of some exciting, life-changing summer was floating away fast, like a piece of trash snatched by an outgoing wave. And if it weren't for that large doughnut dog, I'd be as lonely as I always was at Lila's. I remembered it then, that loneliness. Like my clothes and my old lotion, it was another thing I had to get reacquainted with.

CHAPTER NINE

Exhibit 14: Sworn statement of Albert "Lee" Miles, of
Stevenson and Miles Ltd.

At first I thought the television was on in the media room downstairs. The house was so large that it was hard to tell where noises came from. I heard the lifts and drops of conversation.

But then Lila's voice drifted up through the caverns of the heat ducts. This was how she sounded when she was displeased. Clipped, cold. Dismissive. Jake's voice was a low drone.

Shortly after, a full sentence burst through the vent like she was right there in the room. *So, she wasn't friendly! What do you expect from a* teenager?

God. The words made me feel instantly awful. My insides did the horrible curling-up of humiliation. I felt like I'd failed. The summer was already a disaster. And why was the word *teenager* so often an insult, when adults caused the biggest trouble?

I set my head on Max's side, and it bobbed up and down with his breathing like I was on a big dog boat. He sighed through his nose as if he totally understood, and my throat got tight with tears.

It was true that I hadn't been that friendly to Jake. But the thing was, I *had* been friendly. To Papa Chesterton and Ben Salvador and Roberto-someone and Mr. Henderson and Gerry H. and Jerry W. Every time she'd said *Hug Mr. Chesterton* or *Mr. Salvador* or *Mr. Williams*, I'd hugged Mr. Chesterton and Mr. Salvador and Mr. Williams, even if they were strangers that I didn't want to hug. I'd laughed when they tried to be funny. I'd disappeared when they wanted me to be gone.

I listened to see if it would turn into an argument. There was silence for a while. Everything was fine, I guess. I was hungry, but I didn't want to go down there.

When I heard footsteps on the stairs, I knew Lila was coming up. Max knew too, because he hopped off the bed and arranged himself on the floor like he'd been there all along.

"Hey, baby."

I didn't want her in my room. No. I didn't want *me* in my room. "What was that about?"

She sat down on the bed. "I never come up here! Someone could be living on this floor and I'd never even know it."

"Were you crying?"

"Do I have raccoon eyes? Stupid mascara. Oh, I'm fine. Really. It's just, baby, couldn't you have maybe asked Jake a few questions about himself? Been a little welcoming? He drove all that way to get you."

"I don't even know him."

"Well, he feels left out because we're so close." I didn't answer, and she sighed. She took my hand. "It's always just been the two of us, since *your father.*"

Maybe it was a new record, because I'd been there only, what, *an hour* before she said it. *Your father*—it meant *that asshole* and *the one who'd hurt her* and *the one who'd left her* and *the one I should never love as much as I loved her.* It meant *the loser parent,* compared to her. It meant *the enemy.* It warned me what a horrible traitor I'd be if I ever stepped into enemy territory or said anything nice about the enemy. It jammed me up close to her, because it also meant *we're on the same team.* Sometimes I heard the word *your* louder than *father,* and then I felt awful and guilty, like his badness belonged to me. Sometimes I heard the word *father* louder than *your,* and then I had to remember that that badness had made me, and that even an asshole-loser-enemy really didn't care about me.

I couldn't stand it when she did that. I was pissed at him, too, the way he treated me like a box to check off once a year. But I didn't want my anger to be forcibly bound to hers. I hated that game. I felt that hate rise up. And maybe I *was* acting like a teenager, because I wanted my hand back. I left it there, though, because I wasn't hateful, and I loved her, and I didn't want to hurt her feelings. Plus, it was easier to just play the game than not.

"Jake—*he's* a real man. He would never run off like a *coward*. We have another chance with him, baby, you know?" She was sitting right next to me now. She set her head on my shoulder. "I'm *so* glad you're home. My *person*."

I used to practically burst with joy when she said stuff like that. But at that moment, I didn't want to be her person. I wanted to be my person.

Lila lifted her head and gazed down. She tried to brush off her white pants. "Did you let that dog up here?"

"It's probably from me being hairy already."

"You have to watch him. Boys! They'll get away with whatever they can."

"For sure," I said, though I knew nothing about this. It was more stuff behind the hidden door maybe, because Samuel Crane was mostly shy. "He's very comfortable here."

"Jake lets him up on the furniture."

"I mean *Jake*. I thought you met, like, a month ago." I said it quietly. If I could hear them, he could hear me, too.

"Oh, no. We became *official* a month ago. But we met over a year ago. At Lee's pediatric AIDS gala." Lee, Lee Miles, Lila's agent. "Did I tell you that Lee and Adam adopted a baby from Ethiopia?"

"No. I can't imagine Lee as a dad."

"He says his partying days are over. Plus, Adam was *meant* to be a father. I told you that Jake is a real estate developer, right? That's how I got such a deal renting this place."

"So, what, he knew someone who knew someone?"

Lila laughed. "It's one of *his*."

"One of his? Like, this is his house? Is *that* why you moved here?"

"Syd, honestly. Our family is *from* this city. Your great-great-great-grandmother survived the *earthquake*. I spent so much time in this place as a kid! Edwina grew up, like, five miles away."

"I know. I just . . . It would seem weird if you did it for him."

"I returned to our *roots*. And how could I not love this city? It's so laid back! It's not all about fame and celebrity and *plastic surgery*. God, it's refreshing."

"But he's our *landlord*?"

She lifted her head from my shoulder. "Really, Syd. I don't know why you have to say it like that."

"I just mean, 'Never be financially dependent on a man.' 'Make your own money.' 'Your money is your freedom.'" She and Edwina always told me those things, and now I believed them too.

"You don't have to *judge*. You don't know the situation." Her jaw tightened. Her gaze turned cold. She stared out the doorway like something out there understood her much better than I ever would.

I didn't want her mad at me. Lila, well, you were either for her or against her, and the change could happen before you could blink. You were her everything until you did her wrong, and then every step and breath she took would speak of your crime. *You are bad*, the clip of her heel would say. *You are small*, her ignoring told you. *I can't stand you*, said her turned-away shoulders. Most of the time, I'd do anything to avoid that. When she shined her light on you, it was like a steady rain of glitter. That's the thing you tried for.

"I'm sorry. I'm just surprised. I mean, you knew him and he was our landlord last time I was here."

"Baby, relax. There was nothing to tell. And stop calling him our *landlord*. We're in a relationship."

Outside, I heard the hum of Jake's car starting up, and then the roar of the engine as he hit the accelerator.

"Did he leave? What about Max?"

"Oh, he stays. Jake likes me to have the dog for protection. I think he just wants that monster off his hands."

I looked down at the monster, and he looked up at me with sweet eyes. My heart melted. I died a little inside. We seemed to have a bond already, like the baby chick that imprints on a different species. I wasn't sure which one of us was the chick.

"So, Jake hates me now after one car ride?"

"He doesn't hate you! Do you know what he said? First thing? He said you were a very attractive young woman. That you look much more like me in person than you do in your pictures," she said. It was supposed to be nice, but it kind of creeped me out. "Baby, you *could* have been friendlier. This is important to me."

"I'm sorry."

"I know we planned to go to Tosca Cafe and have a movie night, but now I need to give Jake some TLC. His feelings are hurt! You can maybe order in and start the movie without me? I think we'll go for drinks and dinner. I'll be back before it's too late. You understand, right? Baby, we have a lot to thank Jake for."

I *didn't* understand.

Worse . . . I wondered why she needed him like that. Why *we* did. I wondered if Lila was having money troubles, more serious ones than layoffs of chefs and drivers. All at once, I felt different about the house. It was stunning and incredible, sure. But it made me nervous. The ghost reminded me that she was still there. I didn't really hear it before, the way the waves crashed outside and the wind whipped through the narrow corridor between house and sea. After that, I realized how exposed we were to all the elements.

CHAPTER TEN

Exhibit 15: Photo of 716 Sea Cliff Drive, rear
stairwell to China Beach
Exhibit 16: Photo of 716 Sea Cliff Drive, main living area
(the "White Room")

Before Lila left that night, I ate the Beecher's and a panini. I stuck the Beecher's in the microwave. I was eating it with a fork straight out of the box when Lila came downstairs.

She wore an off-white skirt and high heels and a gold, shimmery shell. Her blond hair was stacked high, swept up elegantly. Her heels were gold and sparkly. The Ace bandage was gone. She *radiated*. I don't know how else to say it. She was a star, but she actually looked like a real one, the kind in the sky. The bright ones that insist that you look.

"If you eat like that, you're going to lose that gorgeous figure you've gotten since Christmas," Lila said. "What happened after the last time I saw you? Are there hormones in the water there? You're a good two inches taller, my God. Um, *Miss Sexy!* I think we'd better bring you home."

"Haha, funny," I said. Sometimes Lila just said stuff. She always flattered people, even if what she said wasn't true.

"So innocent, in that tight shirt!"

I stopped eating. It was like she hit me. I actually felt struck. "God, Lila. That's real nice."

"It *must* be hormones, because you're awfully sensitive today."

I couldn't tell if she was teasing or not. But it all made me feel bad. I started pulling at my shirt, you know, to make it less tight. Maybe it was a little tight; I hadn't even thought about it. Maybe I was just being sensitive.

When Lila left, I didn't go to the media room to put in a movie. At least not right away. Instead, I snooped around the house as Max followed. I wanted to see what had changed since I'd been there last.

At night, in that glass house, everything was darkness and you couldn't tell if anyone was looking in. The sea was dark too. It was unsettling. At the slightest noise, Max would go tearing down the stairs, barking his head off, which didn't help matters. It put me on edge. He was like one of those smoke alarms that go off when you burn a piece of toast. I checked the security system, but I couldn't tell if the red light meant it was on or off. Lila always forgot to set it.

I wandered around, to the sound of my own footsteps.

There was a new painting in the White Room. I don't know how I could have missed it before. It was the only colorful thing in there, and it was huge—maybe four feet by four feet. It featured the head of a pop art blonde, her hair a cartoon yellow against a black background, her lips a blood red. With one elegant finger, she wiped away a single bright-white tear.

"Whoa," I said to Max. "Look. Gigantic crying woman."

He wagged. There was another new painting in the dining room. "Maybe you prefer this?" Max was keeping politely silent, but I thought it was kind of ugly. It had lots of triangles and squares at off angles, in angry shades of brown and red. "Whoa, it's a woman," I realized. "Ick."

In the kitchen, I spotted a shiny red mixer on the counter, and a set of expensive-looking chef pans and knives. "Don't tell me Lila's taken up cooking. You probably already know this, but she can't fry an egg." Max tilted his head as if trying to understand a foreign language, which I guess he was.

Other new developments in the kitchen: lots of booze up in the cabinets too. *Lots.* And a whole bunch of unusual spices—saffron, kokum. I sniffed one. "Gross," I reported to Max. It smelled like ancient copper pennies. "Who would eat this disgusting stuff?"

I made my way upstairs. I stopped on the landing, at the image of Lila hanging on the huge wall of the main stairwell. It was the framed film poster of that iconic scene in *Nefarious*, where she's naked and straddling Oliver Knight and you see the long curve of her backbone and her butt and her calves and her feet in those heels, as she looks over her shoulder and stares right into your eyes. It had been in every house I'd ever lived in. Papa Chesterton had hung it above the fireplace.

"Can you believe the shit I have to deal with?" I said to Max, and nodded toward it. His eyes were soulful pools of understanding.

I poked my head into Lila's room, but I didn't go in. I didn't really want to know what I might find. I saw the rumpled bed and a pile of shoes and that was enough. Next, I headed to the second-floor guest room next to Lila's.

The door was shut, so I pushed it open slowly. I peered inside cautiously, just in case there was another creepy doll on the bed, or maybe a whole bunch of them, which would make me scream my head off. Instead, I was surprised to see that the room had been emptied of all its furniture. Now, it was full of wooden crates. Large, thin crates of various heights, stacked against one another, lined up and leaning against the walls.

It had to be art. Paintings. What else had that shape? I was kind of excited, because *wow*. Jake was maybe some kind of art collector, and I loved art. Art was my thing! Actually, to be honest, I didn't know if art was my thing like it was Cora's. It was a passion for her, a piece of her brain and body she was born with, where maybe I just liked having a thing and pastels were fun. Still, this was an amazing find. "Cora would freak," I told Max.

I really wanted to see what was in those crates, but most of them were sealed tight. I carefully looked through the stacks, same as we'd flip through Hoodean's brother's vintage record collection, except the crates were really heavy. Some were so big that you'd need a couple of people to move them.

I finally spotted one that had been partially opened. The top of the wood frame was off, and the upper edge of all the layers of wrap and cardboard and foam were torn through. I wedged my fingers in so I could peek. I saw thick palette-knife swirls of yellow oil paint, hardened into layers.

It was old. Right away, I knew it was valuable. I don't know why I thought that. I could just tell.

"Is this weird?" I asked Max. "This is kind of weird, right?"

I mean, there were *a lot* of them. And why were they there? They should've been hanging somewhere, maybe a museum, not stacked up and *hidden* in that room.

I went back downstairs. I felt strange, a little hollow, same as that house. The sense of dread returned and knocked around inside of me. Outside the enormous windows of the White Room, I could see the orange glow of the Golden Gate Bridge, stretched across the water like a dragon in a Chinese New Year parade. The homes on either side of 716 Sea Cliff Drive glittered along the stretch of the dark shoreline. It was quiet, except for a clock ticking and the sound of the waves and the jingle of Max's collar tags. I went around turning on all the lights, but this made things worse. Now, I saw my own reflection in the black windows and nothing else. People had lived in that house since 1926, Lila told me, so I started doing all the wrong things, like wondering if anyone had died there.

I called Meredith.

"Eight more weeks!" I said when she picked up.

"Hey, Syd. I'm at Cinebarre with Cora and Hoodean and Sarah and Amy. We're meeting Cora's cousin Simon and some of his friends from baseball." I could hear Hoodean shouting "Syd!" in the background. "We're heading in."

"Oh."

"Are you okay?"

"Yeah." I was missing out, but even worse, it was just kind of creepy being there alone. That house was almost a hundred years old.

"I'll call you tomorrow! Hey, your birthday!"

"Big sixteen," I said.

After Meredith hung up, I opened the tall doors of the White Room, the ones that led outside to the patio. The night was cool, and I could feel a mist of sea spray on my face. It smelled great out there—salt brine and the deep, ancient ocean, plus something summer and celestial. Max thought so too—he lifted his nose and sniff-sniff-sniffed the dark night.

I gazed at the lights. Baker Beach and the Golden Gate Bridge were to the right. To the left—to the far left—Lands End, scene of shipwrecks and sheer, rocky bluffs, home of the Cliff House and the ruins of the Sutro Baths.

Down below, straight down, far down, was China Beach,

the protected cove that faced north toward the Marin Headlands. It got its name from the Chinese fishermen who used
to camp there in the 1800s, but on that night, it was just me,
leaning over that orange stucco wall. I leaned far enough over
that my feet lifted from the ground.

I decided to walk down to the shore. Enclosed in orange
fortified walls, the steps turned and switched back like a maze,
and ended up at that tide-pooled cove with waters that were
too dangerous to swim in. Lila had warned me about this last
time I was there. The sharks weren't the problem. It was the
rip currents you needed to fear. They were so strong that they
could suck you out to sea.

I could feel the sand on the steps under my bare feet, and it
got colder as I went down. Goose bumps trickled up my arms.
My lips tasted salty already. I looked up and saw Max still on
the patio, staying put and looking worried.

He was probably right. I changed my mind and turned
around. It was so dark that it seemed reckless. I could disappear out there and no one would ever find me. I tried to count
how many people would be sad, but that got depressing, so I
stopped.

The ocean crashed and roared, and no wonder. There were
those shipwrecks, and drownings, and the Chinese fishermen
in that cove, and the fifty years they were banned from being
there too, bashing with all that was coming. Because right
then, at that moment, Nicco Ricci was serving halibut and
Crab Louis to the diners of Sutro's as they sat at their candlelit

tables looking out over the Pacific. And on the terrace where I stood . . . well, you know what happened there.

I reclined in one of the stylish lounge chairs and petted Max with my foot. The waves thundered, but so did the thoughts in my head. Lila's words ran in an unforgiving loop. *You look much more like me in person than you do in your pictures. . . . If you eat like that, you're going to lose that gorgeous figure you've gotten since Christmas. . . . Miss Sexy . . .*

I wondered if I'd become someone different since I was here last. At least, she seemed to think so.

So innocent, in that tight shirt . . .

I thought about that boy at the baseball game, twining my hair around his finger. I thought about how I'd laughed too loudly at a joke he made, how I'd tilted my chin down and held his eyes, how I'd even shoved him teasingly, meaning *Go away, but don't go away.* I did it on purpose. I knew I was doing it. I wanted to make him do more than play with my hair, but now this felt like a dirty little secret.

And I thought about Cora. Just before school let out, some sophomores at Academy, Marcella Marconi and her friends, sent around a poll. Smartest guy, smartest girl. Funniest. Nicest. Cora was voted *hottest girl.* Marcella posted the results on a big sheet of paper outside the drama room and also online. Someone with the anonymous handle MizTaken wrote a comment: *Her? You must be kidding.* That day, I saw Cora sitting on the lawn, way out by the gym. Her eyes were filled with tears. *Am I supposed to feel proud or awful?* she cried.

Sexy was something you wanted to be. Sexy was something you should never be.

Right there outside, I took off my Bazooka Joe T-shirt, bra and bare skin out to the world. And when I got up and went back to my bedroom, I stuffed that T-shirt in the trash.

It seemed defiant, but what I really felt was ashamed.

CHAPTER ELEVEN

Exhibit 17: Sworn statement of Dirk Harley,
FirstLine Security
Exhibit 18: FirstLine Security alert records, 716 Sea
Cliff Drive

That night, I watched most of *The Middle After*. Lila and I had seen it maybe six or eight times together. It was our favorite. We'd hold on to each other and scream when the car takes the curves too fast. I stopped before I got to that scene, though. Lila could be dramatic and unpredictable and needy, but I also just missed her sometimes. Like, I wanted her to sit beside me and watch *The Middle After*. I wanted to brag to her about how well I'd done in Algebra II even though I hated it, or tell her about Meredith and me hiking all the way up Mount Si. Normal things. Missing something you never had should have its own word. It's a bigger missing than regular missing.

I brushed my teeth before bed, using the same half-empty tube of toothpaste from my last visit, gross. Max left my side to guard the front door. Poor guy. Dogs never get a day off.

Around one o'clock in the morning, he started to bark. I crept out of bed and tiptoed, in case a ghost or an intruder was coming down the hall to get me. I peeked out my bathroom window, which faced the street. It was just Lila home, finally. I saw Jake get out of his car. He opened her door for her. She got out too, and her white skirt and her platinum hair glowed under the streetlight.

And then Jake shoved her up against the car, and in two seconds, his hands were up her gold shirt. I didn't want to see that. I got back into bed and put my pillow over my head. I wished so hard that I were home. I'd have rather stayed alone in the residence hall for the entire summer than be where I was right then. I longed for home so bad, it felt like an actual ache in my chest.

After a while, I heard her come in. Max's toenails scurried around on the floor in excitement. "Be quiet! Be quiet!" she said, being way louder than he was.

A few moments later, she pushed open my door. It was an old routine of ours—Lila would return, wake me up, and tell me about her date, all giggly and talkative, like we were slumber party girlfriends. I wanted her to notice me so bad that I never cared if it was at two a.m. I wanted to be just like her—glittery, beautiful, adored.

But right then, I didn't feel like being the audience. I lay very, very still so she'd think I was asleep. Even with my nose tucked down in the covers, I could smell the alcohol-restaurant fumes on her clothes. "Baby?" she whispered.

I pretended to breathe in the regular rhythm of sleep. Finally she went away.

I turned my pillow to the cool side. Probably, I'll hate that booze-restaurant smell for the rest of my life.

In the morning, I woke up to the *bam-bam-bam* of hammering, and the *neeyroom* of an electric saw cutting through wood. I looked at the clock. Nine a.m. Outside, the fog lay along the sky in thick ribbons, but I could see the spots of blue that meant it would soon clear off. Good news, because it could be hours or even all day before the fog lifted.

Unless she was working, Lila always slept late. There were rules around this. Basically—don't even *touch* her door before noon. When I was little, at Papa Chesterton's and after, Edwina always made sure I never disturbed her.

I need my sleep, Lila would say. This is the kind of proclamation people make when they don't intend to change, like *I'm an emotional person* and *I'm just not organized* and *You know us Virgos—terrible with money.* I wasn't sure what I'd do for three whole hours, just waiting for her. But I hadn't seen her since Christmas, so I knew she'd want me to be there when she woke up.

"What do you do every day?" I asked Max. "Do you have to hold it that long?"

I watched him trot around the front garden, lifting his leg on various bushes. I filled his bowl with clean water. I found his big bag of food in the pantry.

Then I changed my mind. I took that really nice chicken breast from the fridge, one most likely meant for Lila's lunch. I removed a knife from that new set on the counter.

They were so sharp that I had to be extra careful. I chopped, tossed the chicken into Max's bowl. "That's for all your hard work being a guard last night. Also, because today is my birthday."

My birthday. Spent hanging around the house until Lila woke up. Meanwhile, last night, back at home, *IT* was happening to everyone else.

No. No and no and no.

The world was supposed to be my oyster, even if I hated oysters. Let's just say the world was my plate of fried shrimp, waiting for me and my fork. The world was all the stuff I was hungry for.

Max wolfed down the chicken, slopped water all over as he got a drink, looked up at me to see what we were going to do next.

"Hey, bud, I'm sorry." I patted his head. "But unless you know how to ride a bike, I'm going to have to leave you behind. Because I'm out of here."

I tucked a towel and a water bottle into my pack and went to the garage. The bike Lila got me last Christmas was still there, right where I left it. She thought I was crazy for wanting one. *You can just hire a car if you want to go somewhere!* she said. She couldn't believe I'd want to pedal up those hills when I didn't have to. But that's what we did in Seattle, especially when you didn't have a license. And on a bike, you could be right in the center of everything.

Lila had hidden it the garage. Every time I'd go by the door, she'd scream, *Don't go in there!* She wheeled it back inside on Christmas morning, and she was so pleased with herself that it made me really happy too. She was busy and beautiful and famous, but she'd planned that surprise for me. My father gave me a check inside a card that he must have sent to all his employees. *Happy Holidays*, it said on the front. Inside was his signature: *Jeff.*

"Hey, I missed you," I said. That bike was so pretty, with its metallic speckles. The tires were a little flat, though.

I hauled it to the front garden, along with the small repair kit that came with it. I leaned over and filled the tire using the air canister. When the tire was nice and fat, I stood straight again.

It was suddenly quiet. The hammering next door had stopped. I could hear a bird tweeting and a far-off lawn mower, but that was all. I looked over at the construction site. So far, the new house was only a poured foundation and the beginning bones of a structure. Last Christmas, an old mansion had stood there. It looked like a mini Roman temple, with enormous white columns and a huge entry, but it was gone now.

The new one was going to be modern, you could tell. There were lots of right angles and huge spaces for windows, where the sea and the sky showed through the skeleton.

And then I spotted him. You know, for the first time. A guy in jeans and a T-shirt, with a leather tool belt around his waist, looking at me from where he stood, high up, in that outline of a house. When he saw me looking back, he grinned. And then he whistled his appreciation for my ass, which had been in the air.

He was, I don't know, thirty? My first thought was, *Ick*. And then, *A construction worker, what a cliché.* And then, a whole bunch of thoughts that didn't go together.

That morning, I'd turned sixteen.

It was a number that mattered to me. It didn't matter so much to him.

CHAPTER TWELVE

*Exhibit 19: Photo of Baker Beach to China Beach,
with red arrow marking location of south
end cove*

*Exhibit 20: iPhone belonging to Sydney E. Reilly,
found at south end cove of Baker Beach*

*Exhibit 21: Silver locket w/ broken chain belonging to
Sydney E. Reilly, found at south end cove of
Baker Beach*

My favorite beach was Ocean Beach, next to the Cliff House and Lands End. But I decided to go to Baker, which was closer. On my last two visits, those beaches were cold enough to freeze your fingers into little fish sticks and make your eyes water. Now it was summer.

If you rode all the way down Twenty-Fifth, to the end of the big gated cul-de-sac, you could take a sneak set of stairs to the beach without going all the way to the parking lot another mile or so from there. I wheeled my bike out into the street, hooked a leg over, and got on. As I pedaled past the house next door, I swear I could still feel that guy staring, though I didn't dare check to see if I was right.

After that whistle, I felt eyes on me. No. The *possibility* of eyes on me. It was different from when the men looked at us over their laptops in Victrola. They were looking at *girls*, but this was me, one girl, my own self. I was suddenly aware of my body on the bike, my butt on the seat, my ass pointed toward any driver who might pull up alongside me at the stop signs. I wondered if my shorts were too short, or if my tank top, like my T-shirt the day before, was too tight.

But I also wondered if I looked good. Maybe I did. Maybe Lila was right, and I *had* gotten sexy or something since I saw her last. I was kind of pleased that the guy had noticed me, but creeped out. It was a compliment, but yuck. Sexy seemed sort of great but slightly dangerous. How were you supposed to tell if it was the good, exciting variety of danger, or the bad, frightening type? I thought for sure I'd somehow know, but an older guy seemed like both.

Either way, the whistle buried under my skin and became a permanent part of me. I had a radar for certain eyes afterward. It was a heightened awareness of the bad shit that could happen if I wasn't careful, and I could adjust the degree of it, but I would never be able to turn it off. His eyes on me like that—it also told me some terrible, guilty truth about myself, even if

I didn't have exact words for it. Mostly, that my body would always be an invitation.

I braked at the end of the street before crossing.

"Whatever," I said out loud, and pushed hard on the pedals. It all seemed pretty much out of my hands. Becoming sexy seemed to happen while you were minding your own business. Like, one day you weren't in the world where grown men wanted you, and then you were.

I reached the end of Twenty-Fifth and veered into the small lot. I locked my bike and took the stairs down to the shore. This beach was so different from the showy ones in Southern California lined with palm trees. It was more like a beach at home in the Northwest, with big rocks and roaring waves and sudden, misty sprays of seawater lifted by wind. One day, it would be blue and sparkly, and the next, dark and dangerous, like the friendly but moody uncle who drinks too much on holidays and starts a fight. Baker was supposed to be haunted, too. After dark, a woman supposedly walked the shore, and her voice was so hypnotic that she could lure you into the currents to your death.

I slipped off my shoes the second I reached sand. *Happy birthday to me*, I thought, because *look*. The bridge was scenic-postcard close, and the ocean smelled magnificent, and little kids were flying kites, and a cute couple was taking photos. A row of fishing poles stuck out from the sand, their owners lounging casually beside them.

That morning, the texts had rolled in, from Meredith and Hoodean and Cora, from Gia and Sarah and Ames, everyone wishing me a happy birthday. I decided to take some photos so that I could lie to them about what a great time I was having. I walked all the way down the other end of the beach to get a good shot of the bridge, and that's when I almost ran smack into a naked old guy wearing a Dodgers cap, with an allover tan and, oh, wow, wrinkled nuts hanging down like rocks in a hammock. And then I spotted another naked old guy sunning himself on a colorful towel, his penis curled up like a little pet he'd brought for a day at the beach. And then, bam, an old woman walking by the shore, with deflated-balloon boobs and woggly legs, the ancient crevice of her butt pointing up toward the sky as she bent down to pick up shells.

I'd forgotten that the far end of Baker was also a nude beach, though by the look of it, one for senior-citizen nudists only. Childishly, I got the giggles, then tried to take a selfie with one in the background so that I could send it to my friends, but then I felt bad about it and stopped.

The thing was, they were kind of great. That woman—she was wrinkled as an apricot, the opposite of what any Victoria's Secret ad would tell you beauty was, but she was fine with that. It seemed almost heroic, to be okay with who you were. To show the apricot to the world. She seemed to say, *Fuck you, my body is mine*, and once I got over the shock and my stupid, giggly nerves, I realized something else. There actually wasn't much to see. So what, breasts. Big deal, bare ass. Penis, whatever. They really didn't care about their bodies, so you didn't really care either. It was like . . . the body was a fact. I mean, who didn't have one?

It all made me so happy, and ridiculously hopeful. I decided to remember her, that old woman. She'd be my new role model. My sixteenth-birthday message. The confident whatever that I'd aim to have. The attitude I'd bring to *IT*.

This lasted maybe two minutes. Until the moment I spread out my towel and wiggled out of my cutoffs and took my tank top off. I lay there in my bikini. Every fault seemed to shout, *Don't look!* Every part that might be beautiful whispered, *Look*. Displaying faults or beauty seemed equally hazardous.

I propped myself on my elbows. I watched a kid dig a hole and try to fill it with water, and spied on a couple that seemed to be having an argument. The sun got warmer. I took out my lotion and rubbed it on my arms and legs, and dotted it on my face. I tilted my chin up and remembered that it was my birthday.

Far off, I spotted a guy making his way along the rocks. I watched him climb and edge down before hopping onto the sand. He kicked his sandals off. Closer now, I saw that he carried a pack and wore a faded brown T-shirt with khaki shorts. He swung off the pack, chose a driftwood log, and sat down with his back against it.

I liked his curly black hair. It was the kind of hair you'd want to put your hands in. He was close to my age, I guessed. There was something about him that felt familiar. Like someone I'd already met but didn't yet know. Like a book you think you've read before but aren't quite sure.

He unzipped the pack and took out a thin black journal. At least, I decided it was a journal when he also took out a pen and popped the cap off with his mouth. I wondered what he was writing in there. The city was kind of hipster, so maybe he was doing something hipster, like writing poetry.

The rock climbing, the journal, that hair—it gave me a story about him already, even if I had no idea what the actual sentences were. He was cute, too. Really cute. I should mention that. The sort of cute that ignites an awareness in you—of him, of your own self, of some potential energy between you.

It was my birthday, and the sun felt good, and a guy had whistled at me and I forgot the uncomfortable part of that and remembered the part where I'd made him want me. I started to imagine how my new sexiness would draw the boy over to me, and we'd talk. We'd decide to go somewhere, and I'd totally ditch Lila, and on my birthday, too. We'd be in his car and we'd drive, and Lila would be freaked out, would call and call, but I wouldn't answer. We'd stop somewhere and kiss and our hands would be all over each other and who knew after that. Mostly, I'd get whatever I'd been badly needing, and fun, life-changing stuff would happen, and I'd be transformed into who I was meant to be—someone powerful and sure, instead of the person who always cut her own hair and nervous-peed before every oral report.

I got up and brushed the sand off my legs. I walked toward

the ocean. I dipped my toe in, then bent down to scoop some water. I let it fall down my arms as if I needed cooling down. The guy was still writing in his journal. He hadn't even looked up.

I walked back to my towel. I tried to catch his eye, but nope. I stretched out my long legs. Reapplied the lotion. Took a long drink of water from my bottle. Propped myself on one elbow on my side. It was 100 percent Lila. A *Vanity Fair* article from ten years ago showed her in that very pose on a bed of glass shards that she told me were actually a soft, gelatinous plastic.

I snuck another glance. The guy was watching the little kid trying to fill the hole with water. Then he bent his head down and went back to writing.

God! It was frustrating. Confusing, too. I wondered if my new allure worked only on old guys, and not the ones my own age who I actually wanted it to work on.

I gave up. I opened my new R. W. Wright, *The Deepest Dark*. I got to the part where the bitchy girl was unbuttoning her blouse seductively, so you knew she was going to get it. And I realized, you know, that that's how it always went in his books. If a girl had sex with a lot of different guys—boom. Dumb blondes or women with big boobs were always goners. If she asked for it by taking nude swims at midnight or running alone through the woods, watch out. You only got to live, bloodied but triumphant, if you were nice and modest, pretty but not beautiful. Without desire. *Clean.*

I went for a swim. I felt irritated. When I got back, I let

things happen to that book that I never would have before. Water dripped on the paper. Sand got between the pages. R. W. Wright was kind of getting on my nerves.

"I can't believe you weren't here when I woke up! On your birthday, too!" Lila was all ready to go out for the day—white capris, black tank, white sunglasses on her head. She snapped her handbag closed.

"*You* ditched *me* last night. Because Jake had his *feelings* hurt."

"I told you, you really need to give him a chance. Look what came when you were gone." Her shoes clicked toward the entryway, and when she returned, she was holding a glass vase of pink baby roses. "Ah, *smell.*"

"For me?" The room filled with pink rose–iness. Even Max had his nose up.

"Yes, for *you.*"

I opened the tiny card. *Happy 16! Let's go get that permit, sister!*

Wow. "That was nice of him. Really nice," I said. It was so nice that I felt kind of bad for hurting him.

"See? Did *your father* even call?"

Ugh! "Not yet. I'm sure he will."

"I don't know why you always defend him." I stayed silent and took the blow, because I didn't know why I did either. Lila hunted for the keys to her Land Rover. "Baker, huh? Did you see a bunch of wrinkled snakes?"

"Yeah, but also this cool old woman who couldn't care less what anyone thought."

"Oh, baby, she cares. Her nonchalance is a different kind of caring. It's pretending-you-don't-care caring. Think how much attention she was getting."

"I think she just wanted to be herself."

"Attention is currency."

"Yuck," I said. "I hate that idea."

"Damn it. I swear they were right here." She tossed her purse on the kitchen table, started hunting under the mail on the counter. "Can you believe you're sixteen? Do you know what I was doing at sixteen? No, *fifteen*."

"Getting your first job with MGM."

"Getting my first job with MGM."

You probably know the story of how she was discovered, but they got a few things wrong. She wasn't at Langer's Deli eating a pastrami sandwich. She doesn't even eat stuff like that. She was at a plain old Peet's near her school, Crenshaw High, in LA, where Edwina had moved them in order to get Lila into acting. This was before Peet's was Peet's and Starbucks was Starbucks—they were just a couple of coffee shops. She'd skipped class and was sitting there drinking an espresso when Richard Mulaney saw her. He was so blown away by her looks that he arranged to have her meet Abe Daniel, her longtime agent before Lee. Rex Clancy gave Lila her first role, as the wayward daughter in *The Girl Is Gone*.

"*Working.* And partying my butt off, if I'm being honest.

Totally out of control." She was back to looking in her purse again. Unzipping the pockets she'd just zipped, unsnapping the compartments she'd just snapped.

"I don't intend to do any of that. Partying my butt off, I mean."

"Edwina has turned you into a priss."

"I like being a priss. I'm my own priss." I wasn't really a priss. Not in my imagination. If R. W. Wright could've read my mind, he'd have offed me, too.

"Oh my God, look!" She held up her keys. "They were right here all along. Let me tell you, Syd-Syd. You don't know what the year will hold for you. Anything could happen."

Well, she was right about that, wasn't she? Anything could. And everything did.

CHAPTER THIRTEEN

Exhibit 22: Visa statements, L. Shore, Jan.–Aug.

Exhibit 23: American Express statements, L. Shore,
Jan.–Aug.

Exhibit 24: Mastercard statements, L. Shore, Jan.–Aug.

Lila and I hit all the boutiques on Fillmore. It was my birthday present. Lila was excited about a surprise she'd planned for that night too. I could tell she was excited, because she was shopping as much for herself as for me. She was looking for something special. *I'll know it when I see it.* That's how I felt too, but not about clothes.

Right here, you can picture the scene in any of those movies where, well, it's usually some rich guy dressing up some less fortunate woman like she's a Barbie. She tries on various things for him to see, twirling and smiling shyly as he nods his approval or shakes his head to indicate it's not the outfit for her. He showers her with extravagance so she experiences the joy of feeling good about herself, all the while being the big man with money who gets to make sure she's up to his standards when she's on his arm.

This time, though, it was Lila and me, and maybe the same things applied. She talked me into this short white dress I'd never normally wear because it was way out of my comfort zone, all the while saying stuff like, *You gotta get out of your comfort zone.* Mostly, at home, I wore jeans and T-shirts like everyone else, crew gear, leggings and a sweatshirt. Now, same as those men in the movies, Lila nodded or shook her head.

But we left with lots of bags like in those movies too, stacked up along our arms. And it was not *un*fun to buy bunches of really expensive clothes that they wrapped individually in tissue paper and put into their own shiny bags with rope handles. It was not *un*fun to go anywhere with Lila. I remembered why I was excited to see her. And how great it could be when it was the two of us. She was spending time with me, and noticing me, and approving of me, and laughing at the things I said, and it sounds stupid to say this, but it was like she loved me. Then again, 95 percent of anything we do is probably to get that feeling.

Even though I preferred my comfort zone, I kind of liked her pressing me out of it too. Like she had confidence that I could be more than I was—sexier, prettier, shinier. *More* seemed like it would get me closer to my fated destination, whatever that was. Primarily, not where I was right then.

We went to Joie and then Alice + Olivia, and we got a few shirts and found Lila's *something special*—a short dress of silver sequins—and then went on to Paige, where I got a flowered sundress and a plain one, a pair of shorts, and two tees. They were the kind of places where there's a small amount of clothing in a very white, elegant space, nothing like the jam-packed H&M at University Village, where I usually went. Lila always said that you could tell the difference between a three-hundred-dollar T-shirt and a twelve-dollar one, but Edwina thought that was nonsense. Honestly, if you put two T-shirts next to each other and ripped off the tags, I doubt I could tell.

Lila loved the moment when she slid her credit card across the counter and the saleswoman recognized her name and made a fuss. I could see how my mother always held her shoulders back and pursed her lips in a waiting smile when it was time. At Paige, though, it didn't happen. The girl was a little older than me, and . . . nothing. She didn't recognize the name. She didn't recognize Lila. She rang up my clothes like Lila was anyone.

I could see Lila's mood turn. Her energy just kind of slipped, like a car downshifting.

"Done?" Lila asked.

"Done," I said. "Thanks. That was great."

It was late afternoon. We'd just split a salad at the Progress. It wasn't really that great and the service was slow, but then something awful happened. The waitress came back with the black padded folder. She leaned down as if whispering a terrible secret. "I'm sorry, Mrs. Shore. There seems to be a problem with your card."

Holy shit. And on top of that, the waitress had called her "Mrs. Shore."

Lila huffed and took out her wallet and gave the waitress another card, but in a few moments, the waitress was back again. "I'm sorry," she said, her voice a bit louder and more reprimanding. "Perhaps you have cash?"

I reached for my own bag, which only made things worse. "No, no, no," Lila snapped. "Put it away! There's something wrong with their fucking machine." She was making a big show of being upset, exhaling, rolling her eyes, like, *How could they treat me like this?* My stomach knotted. I had a horrible feeling in my chest. Horrible.

Something was very wrong. I was embarrassed, too. People were looking at us. Lila tossed a wad of cash on the table and the waitress had to gather it. In those movies, you never see that happen. No one's card gets denied. You never witness the guilt you feel afterward, bringing home the bags of stuff no one in their right mind should afford. There's only some song from the 1970s playing and the girl coming out from the dressing room in various outfits as the guy grins like his steak just arrived exactly how he likes it cooked.

"I'm glad *that's* over," Lila said when we got in the car. "Never going back *there* again." She made her voice bright and cheerful, but all of a sudden, her face looked a little tired. I mean, like, for two seconds. I saw maybe that she was under stress. A lot of stress. Her makeup, her foundation, had little cracks in it around her mouth. I felt sorry for her. I saw the burden she carried too, taking care of all of us—herself, me, Edwina.

I started to worry—about Lila and money. About us. I didn't know if we were okay. I wished I could make things better. I wanted to fix it for her. She was my mother, you know. That's how it works. You hate them sometimes, but then you'd do anything so they won't be sad. *Anything.* As a kid, you need your parent to be happy, or otherwise, God, the weight is huge. You feel anxious, as if you've failed. It's hard to deserve anything then.

The worry—it rattled me. It was that dread again. At first, it was like the unsettling chiming of crystals on a swinging chandelier, and then more like the clatter of teacups and china in a shuddering cupboard. Worse and worse. Getting stronger.

Tremors before the quake.

CHAPTER FOURTEEN

Exhibit 25: Chase bank statements, L. Shore,
      2010–present
Exhibit 26: Sworn statement of Sean James, manager,
      EML (Entertainment Management Ltd.)
Exhibit 27: Unsigned rental agreement, 716 Sea Cliff
      Drive

That night, as Lila and I got dressed in our new stuff, her excitement returned, so I tried to forget about lunch and the uneasiness that was trying to shake me with its long fingers. The money was a shadow worry; the ghost hovered around the ceiling. But I forced myself to feel all that shiny possibility again. Nothing bad was going to happen. Maybe things *were* okay. Maybe it *was* their machine.

Lila wouldn't tell me where we were going, or what we were doing. At 716 Sea Cliff, the windows of the White Room lit up with the twinkles of the city in the night sky, and Lila was twinkling too, in her sparkly silver dress. I had my white dress on, as well as a pair of Lila's really high platforms. *These!* she'd said. *It has to be these!* Most of the time I wore athletic shoes or sandals, and sixteen sounded so different from fifteen that I felt like someone else. Someone not me. Someone more like Lila, but definitely not Lila.

We took a bunch of selfies. We were so excited and high energy that Max kept jumping up. Lila seemed proud of me in my new clothes. I finally opened my gift from Meredith and her mom, a beautiful necklace with a silver heart, and I wore it with my dress, sending them a photo to say thank you. I think maybe Lila had had a drink or two by this point, because she was laughing a lot, and there was that alcohol smell, and when we went outside, she got her heels stuck in the grass. I was walking unsteadily too. I told myself it was only the shoes, but maybe it was more than that.

"Roll up that window, would you, baby? My hair," Lila said.

We were back in her Land Rover, and the window was down only the tiniest crack, but I did what she asked. We were heading in the direction of Fillmore again. I realized there was probably a reason she'd ducked into one of the busiest restaurants on the street while we were there that afternoon.

We pulled up in front of a small brown building with only the word *Provisions* above its windows. Lila smiled hugely and raised her eyebrows as if waiting for my response. I was supposed to understand the large thing she'd pulled off, but I didn't. "State Bird? Do you know how *long* it takes to get a reservation for this place, let alone for fourteen people?"

"Wow," I said. "Thanks, Lila." But I didn't know fourteen people in that city.

It was silly, but for a second I expected to walk in and see my own friends, maybe even Edwina or my father, who I hadn't seen in over a year, and who still hadn't called. But, no. Around the table were Lila's friends, many that I'd never met before— one of the writers from *Two Bros*, the Netflix show that was filmed in North Beach, and the director of the San Francisco Opera, even though Lila hated opera. Lila's old pal Louise was there too. Lila always called Louise her crisis manager as a joke, but it was pretty much true. I sat in the empty chair next to Lee, Lila's agent, who was there with his husband, Adam.

On my other side . . . well, holy shit. It was Jayson Little, the younger brother on *Two Bros*. *Jayson Little!* He was in his early twenties, but we were the youngest people there. I felt all blushy, and stupid things were coming out of my mouth, and Cora would die because she loved him. I was trying to pretend this was my normal life, because in some ways it was, but in more ways it wasn't.

Picture all this glittery candlelight and the vibe of money and important, interesting people in the room, and food that was so elegant that it was just plain wrong that the only future it had was heading straight for the waterslide of your intestines. Picture how it feels when you're pretending really hard, even though the little ball of nerves in your chest knows the truth.

At one point, Lee leaned over to me and whisper-shouted, "Look at your mom. That woman is a star, and she'll *always* be a star." And it was true, even if her biggest film was years ago. She radiated. She sparkled and air-kissed and got air-kissed and she said slightly shocking things that made people laugh. She held their hands and leaned in to hear them better. She listened like no one else was in that crowded, noisy restaurant. She might not have been in a successful film in eons, and she might have been best known for a scene where she parted her legs and nakedly straddled a man in a suit, but Lee was right.

"She looks happy," I said.

I wouldn't see her looking that happy for a long time to come, but that night she was.

Wine bottles kept arriving. At State Bird, they brought around carts of food same as dim sum, only it was food like ahi tuna with this puffed-up black rice, and pork belly with plum salad, and little pancakes with cheddar and some kind of ham. More and more plates stacked up. I thought about that credit card, but Lila didn't seem concerned. She drank and laughed and clinked glasses. She gave me one of her full glasses of wine and left it there in front of me.

I sipped. The liquid tasted sour and hot, but it gave me an easy, warm feeling in my body and a nice, swimmy buzz in my head. Jayson Little was telling me about a road trip he took when he was eighteen, and he was leaning very close to me, and I forgot all about who I was. I forgot all about who *he* was. It was a weird out-of-body experience, because I felt beautiful, and in my white dress it seemed like I was having some magical power over Jayson Little, even if the only thing I was doing was smiling and looking at him with awe as he told his stories. I barely spoke, but when I did, he laughed at everything I said, and he bumped up against my arm and touched my hand. It was kind of amazing, that power. The restaurant was getting noisy, and in order to hear, his head was so close to me, I could feel his breath on my cheek.

This was the sort of *IT* I had in mind. Maybe *IT* came with drinking or a man's warm breath, because I felt full in a way I hadn't before. My father had forgotten my birthday, but so what. I had a lame thought you hate yourself for, because I wished he could see me right then. From afar, where he wouldn't be allowed to come in. *Serves you right*, I said to the imaginary him watching through the glass of the locked restaurant door, where, from a distance, I was being amazing.

I was probably a little drunk on one glass of wine. The alcohol and the candlelight and the loud voices lifted me from myself. "Getting hot in here," Jayson Little whispered in my ear. This made me shiver, which made him grin. I fingered my heart necklace and thought stupid thoughts about love. I'm embarrassed to admit that, but it's true. I didn't really understand what was going on. I thought, I don't know. That he really liked me. *Me.* Jayson Little made a joke, then traced the neckline of my white dress with his fingertip and laughed. Oh my God. I couldn't believe it. I mean, Jayson Little was whispering in my ear and touching my neck. He was in his twenties and I wasn't, but I wanted to be near his energy and everything he'd already experienced and accomplished. Even if I was slightly terrified of his energy and everything that he'd already experienced and accomplished. I'd accomplished tenth grade, but he was so handsome.

He was *important* and magnetic. I wasn't. Or, I was right then, since he'd chosen me.

And then I looked up. Lila was standing over us. Standing? *Looming.*

"We never did have that drink, Jay," she said. Words stopped being secret whispers. Words got loud.

"Not yet," he said. He sat back in his chair, away from me. She gazed down at us, and there was some uncomfortable silence I didn't know how to read. There was the sound of silverware clinking against dishes. Voices shouting to be heard over the noise. Louise laughing wildly at the other end of the table, her head thrown back.

"Is Jake coming?" I asked. I'd just then realized he wasn't there. It seemed strange, after their night by the car, after my birthday flowers. Maybe the timing was bad, maybe it looked like I was trying to send her a message of some kind, but I wasn't.

She waved her hand at me. "This girl. So loyal. She thinks if you're dating, you need to be welded at the hip."

It wasn't true. I wasn't old enough to have theories about

dating. But that didn't seem like the point anyway. The point was to make me the child who didn't understand things. And, well, I didn't understand a lot of things.

Right then, Lila made eye contact with the waiter and nodded. It was time. A crew of waiters brought out trays of panna cotta with strawberries, and chocolate pots de crème. Everyone began to sing.

I felt suddenly awkward. Mortified. I felt a deep but confusing sense that something was very wrong, though I didn't know exactly what. I blew out the candle in my dessert. "Happy sixteenth, baby," Lila said, and kissed my cheek. She was still standing over us, me and Jayson Little. I forgot to make a wish.

"You're sixteen? Today? Like, you were fifteen a few hours ago?" Jayson said. I swear, he even scooted his chair away.

"It's my birthday," I said, as if that hadn't just been made very clear.

"You thought she was turning, what, *twenty*? You must think I'm *ancient*." Lila laughed, but it was a fake laugh. The knot of discomfort cinched tighter in my chest. I felt ashamed of how I'd smiled at him and how he'd touched me, and I felt like an idiot in my white dress.

"Well, hey, happy birthday," he said, and stood. He put his napkin on the table. "Early day tomorrow."

"No need to run off, Jay," Lila said. But he was already thanking her and saying good-bye. I couldn't eat that dessert. Humiliation just steals your appetite.

* * *

When Lila and I got to the car, it had the cool of night inside, and soon it filled with the restaurant-alcohol smell we'd brought with us. Lila probably shouldn't have been driving. On the way home, she said, "I hope you had a marvelous day, baby." She took my hand and shook it in the air a little.

But I only felt coldness now, and not just because it was a chilly summer evening and we were in sleeveless dresses. The warmth of her shine on me was gone. I felt alone. I remembered another night of a different summer. I was twelve. She lived in the redwood house in Topanga Canyon then. We'd gone out to dinner. I was wearing a sundress, and I'd painted my toenails and felt pretty. We had to walk through the bar of the restaurant, and I walked ahead, feeling my new straw purse bump along my hip. Behind me, I heard Lila hiss, "She's just a little girl, you pervert."

I turned around, and I saw a man in a suit, but I didn't know what had happened. She was protecting me from something, but I didn't feel protected. I felt embarrassed and dirty. I didn't know what I'd done wrong.

In that car, I had the same feeling. The white dress felt awful. I didn't understand the comfort zone or any zone, how to stay in it or step out of it or even know where the lines were. I felt bad for whatever I might have done. I wanted it back, the way it was when the brightness was on me.

CHAPTER FIFTEEN

Exhibit 28: Sworn statement of Louise Redwicker

I went to Baker Beach every morning. It was the one closest to home, and I tried to be back when Lila woke up. I was bored, and going to Baker was something to do. *IT* was beginning to seem like a stupid longing.

I'd bring a peanut butter sandwich and a water bottle, and I'd stretch out on my towel and read *The Deepest Dark* by R. W. Wright, where a psycho from the past punishes/kills every girl who drops her pants or opens her legs. I accidentally ripped a page. I wiped my dirty peanut butter fingers on another. I opened the cover as far as it would go and I bent it back.

I started to recognize the nudists. I gave them names. There was Chet, the old guy in the Dodgers cap, and Bill Sr., who had the long scar near his heart. There was also Quentin William III, who read British mysteries and ate those white round water crackers with bits of cheese he brought wrapped up in cellophane. And my favorite—Agatha. I really liked when she wore her sun hat. This seemed both ironic and stylish, since the rest of her was bare as a deflated balloon. She often had a City Lights book bag over one shoulder, where she'd put the good shells she found. Once, she had a friend along, who left only her shorts on, as if she were going one step at a time into the nudist waters. Every time I saw her, Agatha was her full, old self.

There were also a lot of the same non-nudists. A mom and her two boys. A group of teens who smoked pot and then left. But I never saw the boy with the journal again.

Not at Baker, anyway.

Those days began like this: I'd get on my bike. I'd roll it out the gate and fling one leg over.

And next door, the construction guy would stop whatever he was doing and watch. The other men kept sawing and hammering, hauling and drilling. But not him. He made a point of walking to the edge of wherever he was to catch my eye. He was a big guy, with big arms, wide shoulders, sandy-brown hair, and he'd just stand there and cock his head to one side, grinning. Or he'd shake it, like I was too much for his eyes to handle. And when he did this, I'd feel a slow burn crawl up my thighs and through my stomach and into some empty space in my chest. I didn't know if the burn was pride or desire or shame or powerlessness. I just felt the heat of it, and the way it rattled me. It was telling me to be afraid or to be fearless, only I couldn't tell which.

Sixteen was different. Or that summer was different. Or maybe I just started noticing. You know, men looking. It's strange to talk about. Girls can't even talk about these things to each other without someone saying or thinking, *Hey, she's not that hot*, or *Wow, she sure thinks she's special*, or *Why'd she keep walking past when she knew what was going to happen?* It's *bragging* or we're blamed for it, and how messed up is that?

Whatever, because this is a part of the truth I'm supposed to tell, the way I felt the eyes. And I felt those eyes in particular, his, the ones belonging to the man who worked next door. Some days, before I left the house, I'd hear that endless hammering, the sawing, and I'd think about the staring, and the way the house was just the bones of the structure without the skin of the walls, and I'd peek out the window to see if he was there, so I could leave without being seen. I tried to go the other way, up a different street and over, until I reached a dead end. Sometimes, I'd wear something new, something white that showed off my tan skin, and I'd think, *Go ahead and look. Have at it.* In order to be where I wanted to be, I had to go past him first. That was the thing, wasn't it? *Wherever* you wanted to go, you had to go past him.

It was like he thought I was his. Like I was a vase or a glass that he could admire or drink from or shatter, whatever he decided. I didn't get a say because vases don't talk and glass only reflects. I didn't know what to do about it. It seemed like it was just part of what you dealt with. Lila did. Cora did. Edwina did, in her day. I'm sure even our beautiful great-grandmother who fled during the earthquake did. That old mansion next door and all its history had been torn down. Something new was going up. But he was still the one holding the hammer.

Maybe ten days or so after my birthday, I was done with Baker. I was over it, going there just so I could hurry home to Lila. I felt pissed about it. Ever since my birthday, Lila had been in a mood. It was summer, and I was there so we could do stuff together, but even when she got up, she'd lie around, saying she didn't feel well. I tried to get her to go out for lunch, shopping, the gym, anything, but it was, "Baby, I'm just exhausted."

"What happened to Jake?" I asked.

"He's being an ass."

It was frustrating. Maddening. She'd asked me to be nice to him, and he'd given me those flowers, and she'd been so happy about him when I came that I kind of wanted him back, honestly. I was ready to give him a chance, if she'd only snap out of it. But she watched cooking shows for hours on end and had long closed-door talks with Louise, her "crisis manager."

God.

Every time I called Meredith (Seven more weeks! Six and a half more weeks!), I heard about all the fun they were having— bonfires, parties, swimming. I pictured eyes glittery from the light of a fire, beer in a cup, slick skin against slick skin underwater. I wanted it all so bad, my chest hurt with longing, but I was stuck in that house.

I got online and spent the birthday money my father sent

me. It had arrived a week late. It's hard to remember stuff like that—the day a daughter was born—especially when you'd wanted a son (according to Lila) and you were busy vacationing in Cabo. The enclosed photo showed him on a beach I'd never been to, with some friends I'd never met, wearing clothes I'd never seen, and holding the hand of his new girlfriend, who apparently had a kid that lived with them now. I bought some expensive new bathing suits and beach towels and other stuff I didn't even want.

And I took my pastels to China Beach or I read outside. Sun, warm, heat—restlessness. Lotion on legs, tan skin, the great feeling of sea air, with nowhere to put it. I finished *The Deepest Dark* and tried to go on to *She's So Cold* but couldn't finish. Suddenly, I badly wanted the loose girls, the easy girls, the sluts, the forward ones, the ones who made the first move and were hungry and who *needed* things, to stay alive, but they never did. One day, I stuck my gum in the cover and never opened it again.

I felt empty and anxious. And alone. I was missing out on everything a summer could bring. That house, even with all its large windows, felt gloomy. Those enormous paintings of women stared from the walls every day. I'd get the mail, and there were more bills. Lila never looked at them. They stacked up like a tippy building on uneven ground. The dread just waited, the ghost floated around, and my anxiety spiked whenever she tossed another envelope to the pile or poured a drink too early in the evening.

I finally decided to go hang out at Ocean Beach and walk around Lands End, just past it. If Lila woke up and I wasn't there, too bad. Maybe I'd stay the whole day. Maybe she'd have to wonder where I was for once.

"I'm sorry to leave you in this house of doom all day," I said to Max.

He looked sad.

Then I had a great idea.

"Forget that. You're going to get depressed if I don't get you out of here. You'll catch it like the flu, bud. Come on."

I called the car service number that Lila had given me. When the car arrived and I went outside, I tried not to glance next door. But I heard the pounding. I felt the eyes.

"Ocean Beach," I told the driver.

"The dog, too?"

"Yep."

The driver sighed.

Max rode in the seat like a proper gentleman. "Don't let him make you feel bad," I said to Max after I signed the bill and we got out. "I'm sure you're way more polite than a lot of people."

I'd been out that way before, when Lila took me over Christmas break. I loved everything about it—the big, wide sand of Ocean Beach, the mysterious and beautiful Lands End, the ruins of the old Sutro Baths. The baths used to be this enormous labyrinth of saltwater swimming pools, filled by the tides. Back in the 1930s, the pools had slides and trampolines and *trapezes*, but now only their cement outlines were left. There was a cave down there too, where the waves rushed in so hard, the roar was an explosion. And then there was the Cliff House—the big white restaurant perched on the bluff. It had been there forever, all different styles over the years. Long ago, it was even this amazing eight-story Victorian mansion. It burned down twice, and was once destroyed when a ship carrying dynamite crashed on the rocks, but they just kept rebuilding it again and again.

The minute I stepped from the car, I felt better than I had in ten days. I could breathe out there, and I had a friend with me. We took the sandy stairs, and Max ran down them like he was a newly freed prisoner escaping his old life. He sniffed and peed on tall stuff. He raced to the beach, dying to do every awesome dog thing, like splashing in the water and chasing seagulls, rolling in gross beach junk and sniffing the butts of all the other dogs. His joy made me feel joy.

It made me realize how lonely I'd been. How that house felt seriously haunted, even if the only ghost was the one I'd brought with me.

After we'd been at the beach awhile, I clipped Max's leash to his collar. "Wait till you see what's next," I said.

We walked to Lands End, and I took him out by the crumbling walls of the ruins, where the old baths were filled with disgusting, algae-thick water, which he of course wanted to go in.

"Yuck. Stay on task," I told him. "It's worth it, I promise." We hiked around the rocks, which were kind of slippery and hard to navigate, but he didn't seem to mind.

Then we arrived. The little cave. I waited until the people ahead of us left, so we could be in it alone. Inside, you could see through a rocky corridor and out an open end, where the waves crashed. When a wave broke, there was a boom that sounded like the earth breaking in half.

"Wow, huh?" I shouted. Max just stared toward the open end of the cave, as if taking in the majesties of our universe.

"All right. I knew you'd love that. Shall we go?" We headed back to Ocean Beach. I removed the cereal bowl I'd brought in my backpack and filled it from my water bottle. Apparently, butt-sniffing and taking in the majesties of our universe makes you pretty thirsty. Max lapped for a good long while. When he stopped, water dripped from his chin.

"Now that's what I call beautiful," a guy said.

I wheeled around to face the voice. I thought it was another pervy man, but I was shocked to see the boy with the journal. Stunned. It was him, the same guy, and how was this possible? It seemed like one of those coincidences that happen only in the movies. It had to be fate, right? Maybe this was *IT*, magically happening. Well, actually, seeing him out there was pretty much a guarantee, but I didn't know that yet.

He was wearing dark pants and a white shirt, an outfit way, way too hot and dressy for that summer day. A uniform, I realized. A waiter's uniform.

"Really beautiful," he said.

But he didn't mean me. He knelt down and looked Max right in the eyes and scruffed his big, thick neck.

It was the first thing I learned about Nicco Ricci.

He was not the kind of guy who'd turn his head at every attractive female. Who'd leer and remark and gawk. But, man, he couldn't keep his eyes off dogs.

CHAPTER SIXTEEN

Exhibit 29: Sworn statement of Mrs. Doris Brawley
Exhibit 30: Sworn statement of Joshua K. Brawley

"What's his name?" the guy asked. His white sleeves were rolled up to his elbows. His dark, curly hair seemed to have a mind of its own.

"Max."

"Hey, Big Max. Look at you, huh? You're a real head-turner, aren't you? Purebred?"

"No idea."

"A mystery dog. I like that."

"This is going to sound weird, but I think I've seen you before," I said.

"Yeah?"

"At Baker? I'm pretty sure it was you."

"Oh, probably. I live right by there. And I work here." He hooked his thumb up, toward the Cliff House. "On break, in case you couldn't tell by the socks and father shoes. I'm here pretty much every day. Or sometimes Baker."

So much for fate. And then . . . well, I lost all words. My brain slammed shut. Centuries of silence passed. I couldn't think of anything to say. I wasn't the confident girl at the baseball game, flirting. I wasn't even the girl who'd stretched out on the towel, trying to get him to look. I blushed. I blushed so hard, I felt the flames in my cheeks.

"Well, hey, gotta get back," he said. "Good to meet you, Big Max. Maybe I'll see you around."

He didn't give me his name. He didn't ask for mine. He just wanted to pet my dog. I'd taken a long drink of water at Baker that first time I saw him, and he'd barely noticed me. Max took a long drink of water, and boom.

That day when I got home, there was a truck in the driveway. Two guys were taking big crates out of the back, bringing them into the house.

It was the first time anything like that had happened. At least, the first time I'd seen it. I know the date is important, but I'm not sure. I don't know exactly. I could look back at a calendar and try to guess.

But I paid my driver, and Max and I went inside. I had to haul him by the collar because he wanted to jump all over those guys. The doors to the patio were open.

I led Max through the White Room. I couldn't believe it, but Lila was out there, smoking a cigarette.

"What are you doing?" I asked. I was so mad. No one with half a brain smoked anymore. I felt like she was standing there waving a pistol in the air. "Why are you *smoking*?"

She exhaled with her lips pursed toward the sky. She wore an emerald-colored sleeveless jumpsuit and sandals lined with blue stones. "Nervous habit."

"Well, put it out. I don't want that cancerous stuff in my lungs."

"Don't be such a prude," she said, but she took a last puff, and tamped it out on the stucco edge of the staircase.

"What's going on with that truck?" I asked.

"Jake's storing some stuff here."

"I saw. Paintings, right? Artwork."

"Yeah."

"More? I mean, it seems like he has a lot of them already. A real lot."

"Well, he's a dealer," she said, as if this were obvious. "An art dealer."

"I thought you said he was in real estate."

"He's in both. He's in a lot of things."

"Ma'am?" one of the men called.

"Yes!" She became the flowing, bright, and brilliant Lila as she headed inside. I stood on the patio and pretended I wasn't listening.

"Mrs. Brawley said you'd have a check?" the driver said.

"Oh, I know nothing about *that*," she said. "You'd have to ask Jake."

"We were supposed to get payment today."

"I'm just the girlfriend."

"We can't leave the stuff, then."

"Take it back. It doesn't matter to me."

The guy's voice was tense. Pissed. Max stood at the end of his leash, watching. His ears were pointed up, alert. He heard the tension too. I stopped pretending that I wasn't listening and watched them. The men—they were, like, *immovable*. Arms folded. Big refrigerators of men. One of them stepped outside to make a phone call. I sat down on the end of the chaise longue and held the leash. "It's okay," I said softly to Max. I was trying to be reassuring, even though the whole thing was making me nervous.

When the guy came back, he said, "Fine. We're outta here."

Lila shut the door behind them. I heard her exhale. When she came back outside, she seemed almost giddy.

"Well, that's done! Oh, baby, did I mention? Jake's coming over tonight to take us out to dinner. Fun, right? God, I thought he'd never forgive me!"

They'd been fighting. That's why she'd been moping around for days. "Forgive you for what?"

"Not inviting him to your birthday! Jesus, he can be *so* possessive."

"Oh, good quality in a boyfriend," I said. But what I thought was, *Honestly?* She hadn't invited him? He came to get me at the airport, she made a big deal about us bonding, he sent me flowers, and he didn't get to come? I felt bad for the guy.

She ignored my sarcasm. "You should have heard the awful things he said to me."

I kept my mouth shut. I was kind of on his side at that point, actually. I knew how she could get too. We stared at each other. She must have read my face.

"Well, we were *both* heated," she admitted. "I'm just glad it's over. Honey, that dog. He's a mess. Can't you rinse him out or something before he treks through the house?"

"He's not a dishrag. He's a living being."

"Sand *everywhere*. And God knows what else."

I gave Max love and acceptance with my eyes, since I knew he was listening. "What was up with those men? I mean, it didn't exactly seem like your regular UPS delivery."

"Some of Jake's associates . . ." She waved her hand as if to say, *You don't want to know.*

I probably didn't. Not really. Still. "'Associates'?"

"Oh, people he works with. I've got to say, he's kept some interesting company over the years. Back when he was doing real estate deals in Las Vegas, especially. He wouldn't even *tell* me until we'd known each other awhile. 'You'd have never given me a chance,' he said. People like that scare me, baby."

"People like those guys?"

"No, no. Not *those* guys. They're harmless. They're *delivery-men*. And all that Vegas stuff is behind him anyway. I just mean, sometimes he uses back channels to get things done."

"Oh." I didn't know what "back channels" meant. I understood it to mean slightly illegal but not really. I know, I know—I shrugged it off. It was hard to see this clearly. Lila was *always* dramatic.

"What can I say? I'm in love." Lila shrugged, as if being in love were something she'd accidentally caught, like a food-borne illness.

She was *in* something, all right, but I didn't know it yet.

In trouble.

In danger.

In over her head.

Yeah. That was more like it.

He came over that night. Jake. He drove Lila's Land Rover so we could all fit, and we went out to North Beach. He cut through the Presidio, which he called "the scenic route."

He had music on in the car and the mood was light and it was actually kind of fun. I shoved away anything Lila had said about their fight and *back channels* and *associates*, and even my discomfort on the ride from the airport, because I was trying to get to know him. That night, he became a real person to me. We went to this place called Original Joe's that looked like those old Italian restaurants in the movies, all dim, with red padded leather banquette seats and black-and-white checkered floors and old Italian waiters in tuxedos writing orders on their little pads, bringing big trays of food that they held up high in the air. They seemed to know Jake. They called him Big Jake and Handsome Harry. There was a little . . . I don't know. Fawning, fussing over him, like he was important.

"Big Jake, huh? Sounds like a clichéd Mafia name," I joked. I doubted Mafia guys even really existed anymore. Lila had already ordered a martini and was sitting right up next to him on that banquette seat.

"Aww, you know." He waved his hand, like maybe he was embarrassed.

"I like that name! And I really like this place." I didn't want to say the wrong thing and hurt him again. I was trying to be extra nice to him to make up for our first meeting. I wanted him to see the person I actually was.

"Yeah, it's great, huh?" Jake smiled wide, and then he went on to give this complicated history of how the restaurant was owned by Louis and then Tony and then so-and-so and so-and-so, how no one ever even had the name Joe.

We were all in a good mood. I got this meatball the size of a baseball, so that might have helped. Jake was telling all these funny stories, usually about how he was meeting someone for something and how it all went really wrong, like getting stuck in an elevator, or driving somewhere and getting carjacked. He told us about being a bodyguard in "the old days" too, which was hilarious, but also kind of awesome.

The thing was, I started to like him. I could see why Lila did. When he laughed, you wanted to laugh. I mean, in the candlelight, he was even sort of handsome, with the kind of hooded eyes that made you think of all the intriguing secrets behind them. He seemed like he'd do anything for her too. It was all the helping-with-the-coat and being-super-nice-to-the-daughter stuff that meant he probably wanted to marry her. He paid the check without even looking at the number, and then, when we got up to leave, Lila asked the waiter to take a photo of the three of us. The night was important to her.

On the way home, Jake was driving fast, and Lila was saying, "Slow down, Jake," but I was joking around, saying, "Faster. Faster!"

"You like speed, huh?" he said, and he met my eyes in the rearview mirror. It was dark, and I saw them flash in the passing streetlights.

Actually, I was kind of nervous when he took those curves along the dark 101, but I wanted to please him. I wanted him to like me back. "Yeah, I do," I said.

"We'll go out in my car someday. I'll show you speed. Better yet, I'll let you drive. Practice a little before we get your permit."

"Forget it," Lila said.

"Hey, we can't be like that. She's not a kid. She needs her freedom."

He was looking at me in that rearview mirror, and I kind of wished he'd keep his eyes on the road, but man, it was nice. Him on my side against her. Him noticing and understanding something important about me. And the word "we": It gave me such a good feeling. A family feeling. Like a weight might be lifted. In spite of all the things Lila would say, like *Never rely on a man* and *Always have your own money* and such, the word "we" solved our money problems, those unopened envelopes that said *Final Notice*, the worrisome feeling that we were spending, spending, spending, but not bringing anything in. And *we* meant that *he* could be *her person*, instead of me. He was driving a car at night like fathers do, and Lila was in the passenger seat, and I got to be in back, and suddenly I wanted all of us together, maybe as bad as she did.

"Ah, that sounds like a terrible idea," Lila said.

"Supreme," Jake said.

When we got back home, Lila made both herself and Jake another drink. "Hey!" Jake said to me. "You said you like art, right? Wanna see some art?"

"Sure. Yeah." The weirdness that afternoon with the deliverymen didn't matter. It was over. I *did* want to see some art. I wanted to see what was in those crates.

We all went upstairs. The new arrivals had been moved to the guest room with the others. Lila stirred her drink with the tip of her finger. She stood in the doorway, half in, half out. She was still wearing the yellow dress she'd worn to dinner, and those heels with the butterfly buckles. I'd kicked off my shoes the second we got home. Max was probably making a meal out of them downstairs.

Man, those paintings were really packed carefully. Jake had to use the claw of a hammer to wrench open the outer wood frame. Once that was off, there were layers of plastic wrap, insulating materials, foam, and then, finally, a board and a stretcher. Layers and more layers.

"I don't normally take these out of here, so this is a special treat," he said, shaking his finger my way, indicating he was doing it for me. I could see why he didn't take them out—packing those paintings up again would take forever. "Get that end," he said. To me, not to Lila. She had those nails she wouldn't want to wreck.

We unwrapped and unrolled and edged, edged, edged it out. Finally it was free.

It was a large drawing in a white glass frame. A crazy, frantic image.

"You like?"

It took me a minute to work out what it was. And then I knew, because the clearest things in the piece were the big, round breasts.

"Well, pretty obvious it's a woman."

I knelt to look at the signature. It was hard to read for sure, but I thought it said *de Kooning*. Of course I knew that name. Cora and I had taken every art elective we could. Art History, Masters of Art, Art and Society. "Wait. Really? Is this really by him?"

"Heh. What do *you* think?"

I tilted my head. The woman's expression was flat except for large, dark eyes. "I think it's real. Is it real?"

Jake squatted on his haunches next to me. He stared into my eyes. He maybe stared a little too long. He lowered his voice, like it was just us in there. "You gotta trust your gut," he said.

My stomach flipped with those words and with that long look. I had this flashing thought—I hope I hadn't been, I don't know, *too* nice. Actually, it wasn't even a thought, just a flash. Stupid. "My gut says real."

"Sketches for his *Woman* series," Jake said. "Graphite on paper."

"Wow," I breathed.

"All right," Lila said. "Are we done here?"

"Let's open the others," I said. It was incredible, all the important art that might be there.

But when Lila was done, everyone was done. "Let's get outta here," Jake said, and stood.

"Where did you get these?" I asked.

"Someone selling her collection," he said, and that was it. He shut the door.

The woman in the drawing, though—she looked haunted.

Lila and Jake took their drinks downstairs, but I went to my room. I opened the laptop I had at Lila's, and I looked up those drawings. They were the sketches de Kooning had done for the paintings in his celebrated *Woman* series, all right. I wanted to take a picture of it to send to Cora, because she'd love this.

But I didn't. There was no clear reason why I shouldn't show Cora. *Trust your gut*, Jake had told me, and so I kept my mouth shut.

That night, I read. I learned how, at first, de Kooning painted really feminine and ladylike images of women. Later, he made them more angry and almost violent looking, garish, with fang teeth and globelike eyes. I mean, pretty clearly he was conflicted about them. I studied the images on the screen. Man, the breasts were front and center, but the actual person-woman seemed absent. Gone, or never there in the first place. Sometimes, he drew them with his eyes closed, portraying only what was in his imagination. Often, he'd start with the mouth. He'd cut a woman's lips from a cigarette ad in a magazine and then paste them on a canvas and paint around them. He didn't know why he did this, he said.

I kept thinking about that. How the mouth was such a problem for him.

That night, I could hear Jake and Lila talking and laughing, and then I heard them come upstairs. I heard Lila's door shut with a playful bang.

Shit. It made me uncomfortable, knowing what they were doing in there.

It was late. It was dark. I didn't even know where to go, but I had to get out of that house.

I put on my shorts and my tank top and grabbed a pair of flip-flops. I stepped quietly down the stairs, plugging my ears when I went past Lila's room. I turned off the alarm. I shushed Max, slipped out the front door.

The night smelled like salt water and eucalyptus. I walked

next door like my mind had a secret plan that I didn't even know about. I climbed over construction stuff—piles of lumber, big fat rolls of insulation. I stepped carefully because there were nails and other junk on the ground, shards of the old structure brought down. I wondered what that particular spot of earth had experienced over all the centuries, even before the former mansion was built. I read once that California had ten thousand earthquakes a year, even if they weren't big ones. *Ten thousand.*

I stepped up into the timber-bones of the house. A neighbor's dog began to bark. I hoped he wasn't telling on me. I tried to imagine what each room might be, but there was stuff to step over and around—stacks of wood and tubs of who-knows-what.

I walked on beams, balancing carefully. Under the crescent moon, I wove around the two-by-fours of the skeleton.

I spotted evidence of the workers—a crumpled burger wrapper, a pair of leather work gloves. I picked up the gloves and slipped my hands inside. I wondered if they belonged to him, the guy who watched me. I raised them to my nose. I inhaled the smell of leather and sawdust and sweat. It was a man smell. And then I yanked them off and tossed them to the floor.

There was the outline of a staircase. No rails, just steps. I went up. They led to the open platform floor of the second story. I stepped to the edge and sat down. My legs dangled. From there you could see the sea, the lights, the bridge. It was high up. High enough where you have crazy thoughts about falling or leaping.

I looked out, and when I saw all of it stretched in front of me—the lights, a city, things happening—I felt this huge ache of want. I was filled with it, want for everything that might be coming. It was hunger and a yearning, to desire and be desired, to be large and seen and known, things I hadn't yet been, even though I'd been walking around in the world all this time.

Next door, I could see our patio. Our house was dark. A wisp of fog trailed along the beach like a tendril of cigarette smoke. Goose bumps trickled up my arms. I should have brought a sweatshirt.

I thought of those work gloves. The hands in them. I thought of those hands on me, and I hated it, and I was scared. I thought of those hands on me, and I liked it, and I wasn't.

With no walls and in that darkness, it was too high up there, that's for sure.

CHAPTER SEVENTEEN

Exhibit 31: Woman III, IV, V, VI, graphite on paper,
attributed to Willem de Kooning

"I'm sorry if it seems like I'm using you," I said to Max
after the driver stopped at Lands End and we got out.

He wagged and smiled. He didn't seem to mind.

"You don't think I'm being boy crazy, do you?" If I were, I'd
have to be it in secret. Boy crazy was bad. It was trashy, messy,
desperate. Guys thought so; girls thought so even more. You
should have heard Meredith and her mother talk about girls
like Quinn Jones, boy crazy since the sixth grade.

Max was a nonjudgmental dog, so he yanked me toward
the beach. It didn't matter to him either way, and he was
probably right. Boys were never girl crazy. They could want
and be hungry, and no one judged them for it. Girls were supposed to live the same way we were supposed to eat—politely,

saying no to all the great food, nibbling on celery instead.

I took my sandals off, and just like that, I spotted him in the distance. That boy. He was right—if you went to Baker or Lands End, you were going to see him. Of course, this was especially true if you, um, planned to go to Lands End at exactly the same time and on exactly the same day of the week as when you saw him last. I mean, it was pretty clear by then that any exciting, life-changing *IT* was not going to be delivered to my front door.

He sat on one of the big rocks near the Cliff House. His head was bent down, his dark curls falling forward. I started giggling nervously. A bad beginning. "I know. Stop it, right?" I said to Max. His brown eyes told me not to be such an idiot.

I'd never just walked up to a guy like that. With actual intent. It was always his idea, and I kind of went along. But there was just something about this guy *I* liked. He felt familiar, yet not. Like a new book by your favorite author.

I almost chickened out, because he was concentrating and maybe I shouldn't interrupt. But then Max recognized him too, and pulled hard. We were still a ways off when Nicco looked up. "Hey, I thought it was you!" I shouted. More like, *I planned to try and see you*, but whatever.

And then, shit. It was awful, because he clearly didn't have a clue who I was. I'd gone and made him this big, important person in my head, but he hadn't done the same. I was right in front of him, and he looked confused. Then he saw Max and remembered. "Oh, yeah. Hi! Big Max, Beautiful Guy."

"I'm Sydney. I don't think I told you my name."

"Right. Nice to meet you. Officially. I'm Nicco."

There was some awkward smiling and a few eons of me kicking myself and wishing I could vanish. Then, thank God, words. "You on your break again?"

He was wearing those same black pants and white shirt, even though the sun was beginning to beat down. His black dress shoes were off, and his socks, too, stuffed inside of them. His feet were sandy. God, even his feet were cute, which is next to impossible.

"Nah. Off early. They had a big corporate brunch."

"Are you an artist?" I gestured to his notebook.

He laughed. "Uh, I can maybe draw one of those square houses with a triangle roof? No, it's just . . ." He waved his hand to say *whatever.* He scruffed Max on the neck, which made Max sit totally still so he'd never stop.

"Poetry? 'Dear Diary'?" I pretended to guess. I was trying to be funny, but, ugh, it sort of sounded like I was making fun of him. He looked a little struck. My insides collapsed with humiliation. Okay, making the first move could *suck.*

I opened my mouth to apologize, but then Max flopped down and rolled onto his back and showed off his glorious boy parts. God! Could it get any worse? "Oh, man," I said. "Oversharing."

Nicco handled this way more maturely than I did. "You big goof," he said, and scratched Max's tummy. "No to the poetry. Well . . . sorta poetry . . ." He peeked up at me like, *What the hell, I'm going to risk it.* "Hard to explain, but I just write down stuff I see. So I don't forget. Like today, at that brunch, this old man was holding hands with this old woman. Then he raised them up and kissed hers. You know, so fucking tender. Things you'd forget in ten minutes otherwise."

Picture my heart cracking in two.

"Like that toddler with sandy knees?" I pointed to this little guy wearing bright-red swim trunks and a draggy diaper.

"Exactly. Yeah." He smiled. "I'm gonna write that down." He did. He showed it to me. *Toddler with sandy knees (Sydney).*

Now I smiled.

He bent his head to write something else. Then he turned the notebook around so I could read it.

Sydney turning her heart necklace around in her fingers, nervous.

I was doomed.

I was *seen.*

CHAPTER EIGHTEEN

Exhibit 32: Sworn statement of Eli Mallory, Forensic
Authenticator, Museum of Modern Art

We talked. We covered the basics. Him: Nicco Ricci,
seventeen, four credits shy of graduating early from George
Washington High. Recently moved from home and now living with a friend above a Cambodian restaurant on Balboa
Street, north of Golden Gate Park. His two moms were
nearby on Cabrillo. They supported the idea of his indepen-
dence (they supported pretty much every idea of his, he said,
down to crayon wall art when he was three) and ran a gift shop
of Tibetan wares, featuring meditation cushions, prayer flags,
and singing bowls.

Me: there on summer break to stay with my mother, since I
went to school in Seattle.

No real details. I didn't want to be *that* seen. Not yet. I was already doing the high math calculations you do when you might like someone, because what would he think of the sixteen-million-dollar house? What would he think when he learned about *Lila*?

"Since you're pretty new around here, have you seen the labyrinth?" he asked.

"I tried to find it once, but no luck." The labyrinth was a stone maze, built in a secret spot at the edge of the sea.

"Yeah, it's hard unless you know where it is. I could show you, if you want. I'm not in the best clothes for it, but it's great."

More high math. Did *he* want to, or was he just being nice? Would I seem too eager, going to some secret spot with a stranger? *Was* I too eager, going to some secret spot with a stranger? Mostly, I was just really lonely. The past week, Jake had barely left and Lila was happier, but still. At home with my friends, I was a part of things, and here I was just *apart*.

"Sure. That'd be awesome, if you're okay with it."

The trail was unmarked, which was why I couldn't find it before. The route basically hugged the side of a cliff, and it was kind of scary, especially with Max pulling, because he wasn't great on the leash. There was a steep set of stairs at the end of the trail, leading down. When we got to the bottom, we walked straight through some trees and then maneuvered up a mountain of rocks.

And then, there it was. If you haven't seen it . . . well, I thought it was going to be near the shore, but I was wrong. It's way high up, set at the very edge of the bluff, a maze of concentric circles.

"Oh, man," I said. It was almost an exhale, because *wow*.

Nicco turned and beamed. He was holding his shoes, and the notebook was tucked inside one of them. "Right?"

"That's amazing."

It seemed mystical, ancient. We walked the rings, starting at the outermost one and working our way in. We were quiet. Max was too, as if even he knew he should show respect. People had left things in the center—treasures, like shells, and sea glass, the feather of a gull. It was peaceful there, like the labyrinth had risen naturally from the earth. We made our way back out of it and then sat on a rock nearby and watched other visitors arrive, doing what we just did. I gave Max some water and shared mine with Nicco.

"It's been destroyed a few times by assholes," Nicco said, handing my bottle back to me. "But he always comes back to fix it."

"He?"

"The artist, Eduardo Aguilera. He made it as a shrine to peace, love, and enlightenment. He's lit it with candles a few times. On winter solstice or something, I think."

"Man, there's a lot in this city that's been rebuilt after being wrecked," I said. "By fire, earthquakes, assholes . . ."

"Yeah, I guess you're right."

We watched a seagull pick its way among the rocks. And then we watched two young guys circle the rings and kiss when they reached the center.

"A middle kiss," I said. Nicco took the notebook out of his shoe and wrote this down.

He showed me the notebook. *Middle kiss*, it said.

"I better get back," Nicco said. "I help the moms in the store on Wednesdays. Rent money."

"I totally lost track of time."

I was glad Max yanked me up those stairs like a sled dog, because it was a hard climb. I felt bad for Nicco in those hot clothes. By then, his pants were rolled up to his knees, and his shirt was unbuttoned, sleeves up as far as they could go, but still.

We reached the beach finally, and my mind spun. Would I see him again? Should I ask? But you were supposed to play this game, right? Where you act like you're not that interested? Where you manipulate the guy into liking you by being someone you're not?

"Hey, let's swap numbers," Nicco said. What a relief.

"Great. For sure. I'd really like that. Today was fun." He typed his number into my phone, and I typed mine into his. I wondered if he had, like, thousands of girls' numbers in there, since he was so sweet and adorable. Oh, I was in trouble already. It was going to be hard work, pretending not to be vulnerable.

"Have you ever been inside Camera Obscura?"

I squinched my face to say I wasn't sure.

"That weird little building behind the restaurant?"

"No. I always wondered what that was."

"Next time. We need a clear day, though, so you can see all the way out to Seal Rocks."

Next time.

"I'm late," he said, and jogged toward the parking lot. I watched him get into a VW van, the old kind with the big, round front and friendly headlights. He waved. I waved. Max looked up at me.

"I know," I told him. "Don't even say it."

CHAPTER NINETEEN

Exhibit 33: Sworn statement of Detective Reese Craig,
1 of 2

The house was empty when I got home. I didn't know where Lila was, but I was glad no one was there. I wanted some time alone. I was happy, and the afternoon with Nicco belonged only to me. I wanted to cup my hands around it in my own mind, unwrap it again and again, like a secret present.

Suddenly, too, I felt really, really interested in my appearance. I mean, like, I needed new clothes and to work out and to become a more beautiful and amusing person, pronto. I should maybe lift weights and buy a new bra, since my old favorite was kind of limp. I wanted to do all of that immediately, but I also wanted to just stay still and replay every second of the last few hours.

I went upstairs and changed into my two-piece, got a towel, my book, and a big glass of ice water with a wedge of lime. I laid my towel out on one of the chaises on the patio.

It was so warm that I could smell the delicious sun, plus the sea. Max found a shady spot just inside the house. I tried to read, but ha. It was the kind of reading where you look at the same sentence again and again and it makes absolutely no sense, because you're thinking about dark curls and the way he said *so fucking tender*. The way it made me want all of his so-fucking-tender heart and his so-fucking-tender hands. I was in trouble, because this was nothing like Samuel Crane. Nothing. I'd jumped universes. I looked at my phone on the outdoor table beside me. I wondered if I should text first or wait, and for how long.

Don't be available, Lila had always said. *Make him chase you. Be the prize he has to earn.*

I couldn't blame just Lila for that advice, though, could I? She was only living in the world that was ours. I'd seen it already, how beautiful and disinterested girls were the most popular. You weren't supposed to want or show your want. You were supposed to look sexy without actually being sexy. Be the ice queen with the tight blond ponytail who they wanted to touch but never would.

Sometimes, a cold, disinterested guy like Reed Shaw or Ellis Jackson would also be popular. But so was Ben Avery, that senior guy who pulled girls down on his lap and hugged them from behind and pushed whatever girl he liked up against his locker to shove his tongue down her throat. So was Jason Varide, who took half the girls in our eighth-grade class down to his parents' basement. Guys could be anything they wanted—disinterested, interested, polite, assaulting. No one complained about Ben Avery, because he was Ben Avery. But if a girl ever acted like that, even the other girls would be disgusted.

You were supposed to dangle the candy without giving the candy. I knew that. Everyone did. But what if you *wanted* to give the candy? What if *everything* looked like candy to some people, even a certain T-shirt or a skirt? What about when you thought you'd better hand over the candy to some bully? What about when guys stole the candy, grabbed what was yours right out of your hands? Sometimes a guy could steal the candy and you'd be blamed for not keeping it safe enough.

No wonder even texting was a minefield. I felt suddenly anxious. Every possible choice seemed wrong. Agatha just walking on the beach, being who she was so openly—she was a fearless queen from some fuck-you time in the future. Why were you always told to just *be yourself* when so much else said the opposite?

Right then, my phone buzzed and danced a little circle around the table.

Kid just stuck a piece of Red Willow incense up his nose. Weeping emoji. Thanks for a great afternoon.

You shouldn't text back for at least a half hour, Cora's sister told us once.

I typed, Poor kid. Everything is going to taste Red Willow now! Laughing emoji. GREAT afternoon. Smiling emoji.

Too many emojis, probably. Excessive use of caps.

Screw it.

I pressed send.

I wanted . . . I really just wanted to be *real*.

On the sprawling patio of 716 Sea Cliff, perched above China Beach, I spread the lotion all over my body. Legs, shoulders. As much of my back as I could get. I lay on my stomach on the chaise. I rested my cheek on my arms. I remembered sitting on that second-story platform that night, how you could see our house from there. I got the creeps, thinking he was maybe watching me right then, that man working next door.

Then again, so what? Everyone had a body, and here was mine. The sun felt so good. Dread? What dread? I was happy. I was hopeful. Not for something in particular, just the pure meaning of the word—full of hope.

Max trotted out. He sat down and stared at me.

"Now?" I said.

He stared harder.

"Right when I just got comfy?"

Stare.

Ugh! I got up. The house was still empty. It was strange that Lila wasn't home yet. It was maybe four or four thirty, and there was no note, nothing. I could have called to check on her, but I was glad to be alone. For once, I didn't mind being by myself in that big, empty house.

I let Max out into the walled front garden. I was going to have to go out there and pick up his poop, because no one else had been doing it. No wonder Lila left most of my upbringing to Edwina.

The wall was maybe four feet high or so. I'm not good with heights and distances. The point is, I could see over it. And as I stood there waiting for Max to finish, I saw this car parked across the street. A man was sitting in it. He wore a shirt and a tie, sunglasses, and he looked my way when I spotted him, and sure, he could've just been some real estate guy or something, but it didn't seem like it. He was just sitting there, like he had all the time in the world.

I got a bad feeling. Really bad. Dread, doom, anxiety— all of it. *He's watching our house*, I thought. I had no reason to think it. I mean, when you live in an expensive neighborhood, you always have reason to think it, but I didn't have any particular evidence for it.

And then a truck turned the corner onto our street. It looked like the one that had delivered the paintings a few days before. But it turned a fast circle then. Back the way it came, and in a screaming hurry. Just, *veeroom*, getting the hell out of there.

The man in the parked car started his engine. He looked calm, but then he hit the accelerator, and it was like some chase scene in a movie where lots of cars blow up. It was one of those times when something big and terrible is actually happening, but it seems too dramatic to believe. You blame your own imagination because the truth would be too crazy.

"I'm nuts," I told Max. He tilted his head as if this were quite possible. "I mean, *look*." Aside from the commotion next door, and the arrival of a Molly Maid van heading to one of the neighbors' houses, the street was quiet now.

Max trotted into the kitchen for some water and a cool spot on the marble floor. I felt distracted, but I went back outside. I lay on the chaise again, tried to return to where I was. I forced myself to think about Nicco and his dark curls and his notebook and his olive skin in that white shirt.

And then I heard someone. Max wasn't barking, so maybe Lila was home. It wasn't Lila, though. It was Jake, on the phone. This startled me. He was around all the time lately, even if he still supposedly lived in one of his other houses nearby. But—how long had he been there? All that time, I'd thought I was alone. I suddenly felt weird, since I hadn't been. Did he see me with my straps all undone? I mean, I hadn't exactly been careful.

Jake paced. He strode through the White Room and back again. His voice was intense. On his second trip, he saw me looking at him. A few minutes later, he appeared.

I sat up. I felt a little exposed, you know, there in my bikini. I saw that it had shifted, showing my swimsuit lines, the caramel tan of my skin against white, a dark-light line of what had been revealed and not. I wanted to cover up with the towel, but I didn't want him to think I was uncomfortable with him when I was uncomfortable with him.

"Hey, Syd."

"You're home," I said.

"Yeah. I had some work to do. I didn't want to bother you out here."

The intensity was gone from his voice. He seemed like an entirely different person from the one on the phone, hunched and pacing.

"Oh. Well, thanks. Do you know where Lila is?"

"Probably shopping, huh? She shops a lot, doesn't she? How you doing? It must be kinda lonely here on your own."

At least *someone* had noticed. "A little, but I'm okay. I'm fine."

"Good."

There was an awkward silence. Why did I need to fill it? I wanted him to like me. I wanted to be a team player, you know? He was part of our lives now. "Actually, I saw the labyrinth today, at Lands End." My voice was cheerful, even though what I felt was self-conscious.

"Can you believe I've lived here all these years and have never seen it? Did you feel all woo-woo spiritual?"

"Filled with inner pizza, I mean peace," I joked.

He laughed. "I need me some of that. Man. Get me some of that right now, huh?"

"Exactly."

"Are you watching the sun out here? You're getting a little burned." He gestured to my shoulders and then made a V with his fingers, indicating the space between my breasts. I looked down, and it was true—I'd gotten red.

"Well, hey, you two." Lila dropped her bags on the patio. I hadn't even seen her come in.

"Hey, babe," Jake said.

Now I wrapped my towel around myself. I felt embarrassed, with both of them standing there dressed. Guilty. Her face was all stony and hard, like she'd caught me doing something wrong.

"I didn't hear you drive up." Jake's hands were in the pockets of his shorts, all casual.

"Clearly," she said.

That night, Lila was sweetness and light to me, while she bossed Jake around like he was a servant. To him, it was, *Order some takeout, would you? Why are you calling that place? You know China Harbor has the egg rolls I like! How long are they going to take? Call them back and make it a rush order.* To me, it was, *Are you going to bed, Syd-Syd? Put some good lotion on after being in the sun today, okay, baby? Let me give you some of mine.* It was all *us girls.* Her and me. *Sweet dreams. Love you.*

Lila could do this. Shove one person out; bring one person in. Separate, like her own cattle drive, where a certain cow stays and the other is turned toward the slaughterhouse. I saw her do it with boyfriends, and friends, and even with her agent, Lee, and her manager, Sean James. When I was little, she'd pull me onto her lap whenever Papa Chesterton was displeased with her. When my father was nice to me, she wasn't. When *he* wasn't nice, she was. Maybe I was just starting to notice things because I was getting older.

Sweet dreams.

Not exactly.

I tossed in my bed. I kept thinking about that car out front. Those tires screeching around the corner. I didn't ask Jake about it. I didn't ask Lila. Jake had said to trust my gut, and my gut said, *Don't.*

Lila and Jake's shouting woke me up. Lila's room was directly below mine. I swear, the house shook.

How dare you tell me to get out! Jake yelled. *Have you forgotten where you are? Who are you, some big important star? What a fucking joke.*

I will destroy you! Lila's voice was ablaze.

Oh my God. I hunched down in my bed. It was a warm night, but I pulled all the covers up over me. I plugged my ears. I started to hum a made-up song to drown out the sound.

I could still hear, though.

You bitch!

This wasn't the Jake who'd joked with me that afternoon, or the one who was friendly with the waiters at the restaurant, or the one who bent over backward to pull out Lila's chair or get her coat or bring her coffee. This wasn't the father-Jake who sent little pink roses and who wanted to teach me to drive. Or the one who was around lately, putting food in the refrigerator and fixing Lila a drink.

He was shouting so loud, his voice was getting hoarse. I

kept my ears plugged, and I rocked a little in my bed. I felt sick and scared, but I was also pissed. I mean, I felt betrayed. By both of them, but especially him. I'd tried to be *nice*. I'd believed in *we*, and now look. I'd believed in the pink rose guy. I'd given him my hope and now he'd wrecked it, same as my father had again and again.

There was a bam, a crash. Something hit something else and shattered. A glass against a wall, maybe. I started to get seriously frightened, and maybe Lila was too, because her voice turned pleading. I could tell she was crying.

Oh, it was awful. I couldn't stand it.

And then I remembered: *Big Jake*. The former bodyguard. Mr. Las Vegas with the scary associates. We'd laughed that night at the restaurant, but it suddenly felt like the wrong kind of nickname. She'd tried to tell me too, hadn't she? What kind of man he was, and who he did business with, and how she "loved" him anyway?

I reached for my phone, tucked it beneath my covers. I wondered if I should call someone. Edwina, or the police. Lila's friend Louise. Someone. I needed to protect her, only I didn't know how.

The fighting died down.

I heard creaking in the hallway. My door opened. I lay very, very still. I didn't dare peek. I hoped it was just Max, fleeing the fight. If it was, I'd soon feel his big body leaping up onto the bed.

But it wasn't him.

"Baby?" Lila whispered. "Syd-Syd? Are you awake?"

I lay without moving, barely breathing. It was the second time I'd ignored her like this. I waited for what seemed like forever. Finally she left.

In that city where fire burned things to the ground and earthquakes cracked streets right down the middle and ass-holes ruined art meant to bring peace, I hid like a crouched animal. I wanted to go home. I started to cry quietly into my pillow, because I wanted that so bad. My chest felt caved in, and I sobbed without making a sound. This was the night the ghost had tried to warn me about, I thought. I didn't know that it was nothing compared to what was coming.

After a while, I heard murmurs above me. Softer voices. Making up, probably. I worried about Max all alone down there. I hoped he wasn't scared. Dogs are so sensitive.

I tried to sleep, replacing the bad images in my mind with good ones. I played a different story. I walked the circle of the labyrinth with Nicco. I sat on the rock and watched those two young guys. *Middle kiss,* I said, and Nicco wrote it down.

I set all of that into my own notebook, in my head.

It's still there, even if he isn't.

CHAPTER TWENTY

*Exhibit 34: Photo of Lila Shore and Sydney Reilly, w/
Edwina Short, Acapulco, Mexico, undated
Exhibit 35: Sworn statement of Edwina Short, 1 of 2*

Lila was up early the next morning. As I told you
already, she never got up early. She was dressed in a navy skirt
and a white silk blouse, her sunglasses on her head.

"Are you almost ready, baby? The car will be here soon."

"Ready for what?"

"Oh, come on, Syd-Syd. Don't tell me. Are you even packed?
We can't miss the plane!"

"Plane? What are you talking about?" I was in my pajama
shirt, pouring a bowl of cereal.

"LA for the car commercial? You're kidding me! How could
you forget?"

"You never told me!"

"Of course I told you. I didn't tell you?"

"No! You didn't tell me."

"Four days in LA! I'm working for two, and we're staying the weekend. Edwina's meeting us. I can't believe I didn't tell you. This is what happens when your mind is completely overloaded."

I swear, I was her handbag, or her shoes, or her toaster. You didn't need to tell your toaster when you were about to need toast. You didn't require its permission. You just pushed the lever and expected it to work.

"*God*, Lila."

"What's with the tone? I'm sorry, all right? Now hurry up!"

She didn't mention the night before, so I didn't either. But I could see that her eyes looked puffy and tired.

"Do I have to?" I groaned. "I could stay here. It's just four days."

"Not an option. I can't believe you're acting like this! Girl time!" She snapped her fingers on both hands, to indicate fun, fun, fun.

"What about Max?" I looked down at him, sitting at my feet.

"Jake will be here. Jesus! Get a move on already."

"Baby, don't slouch in the chair like that," Lila said as we waited in the private lounge of the airport. "People are staring." People: two men in expensive suits tapping urgently on their phones. A woman in tight black pants with her arms dripping gold bangles, a man with his gray hair pulled back in a ponytail. "What has gotten into you? You're so teenagery lately. Did you sleep okay last night?"

There was a beat between us, but I could tell she was trying to see if I'd heard anything. If I knew about that fight.

"Yeah, fine," I said.

"Maybe go grab us some coffee." She waved her hand toward the machine, which sat alongside a table of snacks.

I brought her back a cardboard cup with cream and sugar, just how she liked it.

"Smile, Syd. Don't look so *sullen*."

Smile. This was what she always said to me. Smile, smile, smile. I sometimes felt like that doll she put on the bed, with her staring eyes and upturned mouth.

When I sat beside her again, I noticed it. An orange ring around the cuff of her blouse. Makeup. I reached over and flicked up her sleeve. Makeup, all along her arm.

She yanked her arm back. "Stop!"

"Lila, what the heck?" There was only one reason I could think of that she'd be wearing cover-up there.

"Quit it," she said.

"Is that a *bruise*?"

"I banged into the dresser. In the dark. It's fine."

"I heard you guys last night." I stared at her hard.

"Couples fight, baby. Every couple fights. Jesus, at least he's not as bad as *your father*."

Oh, yeah? "What's that, then?" I flicked her sleeve.

"It was the *dresser*, Syd. Stop it. I *told* you. Get that look off your face. People can *see*."

I tried to believe her. I wanted to. Maybe it had been the dresser. But I'll tell you one thing: When someone gives you a bruise—it *always* means a clock is ticking.

The car service drove us straight to the Walt Disney Concert Hall downtown, where Lila would be filming that afternoon. I stared out the window. Scenery passed, fast and confused, like the events of the last few days. The buzzing of my phone startled me.

Clear enough to see Seal Rocks. You in?

Nicco! Oh, happiness. But also, oh, crushing disappointment.

I hoped he wouldn't think I was avoiding him. Would he even believe that I just got on a plane without knowing I was leaving? Who did that? He'd think I was playing games, maybe. Ugh! High math calculations again.

So sorry. My mother went on a business trip and I had to go. Ugh! Back on Mon. Look. I snapped a fast photo of a palm tree and sent it.

Bummer, he texted back.

Giant bummer, I answered.

Beside me, Lila glanced up from her phone. She lifted her chin and leaned my way. I swear, she was trying to look at my screen. I started texting madly to hide Nicco's message, sending the palm tree photo to Meredith and Hoodean and Cora. Look where I am now! LA life, haha!

Be famous for us, Meredith texted right back.

"Who was that?" Lila asked.

"Just Meredith."

"No, before that. The first one."

I swear, she was psychic. Every time I had a secret thought, she'd know it, though Cora said the same thing about her mother.

"Meredith."

"A boy?" She elbowed me teasingly.

"Lila, *stop.*" God! Maybe I was acting teenagery because every move she made was driving me insane.

After all those years of being so desperate for her to spend time with me, now I just wished she'd give me some *space.*

"Okay. I'm sorry." Her face turned sad. She looked out the window. Her hands were folded in her lap, the orange ring of that makeup on her cuff. Those hands had glimmered with shiny, expensive jewelry, and they'd been in movies and photographs. But they'd been through a lot, too. I felt bad.

"Yes, all right. A boy," I admitted, and regretted it instantly.

If you've never been there, the Walt Disney Concert Hall is this bold, modern building, silver and geometric. The crew wanted to film at the golden hour, that time just before sunset when the light is all yellow and magical. Even though it was still afternoon, Lila went right into the trailer for hair and makeup, which took forever. Then they moved out to the front of the building, where the street was blocked off. There was scaffolding and lights, and the camera dolly, and the long tracks it would roll on. Lots of people milled around, and the four luxury cars were lined up.

The cars were supposed to drive past Lila, who'd be waiting at the curb in her plunging white dress. Her job was to ignore the first three entirely, but then the tuxedoed guy in the Buick would slowly slide past, catching her eye. She'd look at him and the car approvingly, and then he'd stop and open the door for her, and she'd slip in. The idea was, if you had a car like that, you'd get a woman like her. Her boobs were all spilling out, so I guess you'd get those, especially.

There was a lot of fawning over Lila, making sure she stayed perfect, which was something I remembered from when I was little, how you weren't supposed to touch her if you were on a set, or even if she was going out and had just gotten dressed and had her makeup done. We waited around a long time, and she and I just sat there and talked phony to each other until Lila somehow managed to cut her ankle with the clasp of her shoe, and it sent everyone scurrying. The medic came over, even though there was, like, one drop of blood. I think they were worrying more about the dress and a lawsuit, honestly, but it livened things up for a few minutes.

I watched the first take of Lila looking bored until the Buick passed. The golden light and that silver building made it seem like an important, enchanted evening. Afterward they had to set up everything all over again. Lila started flirting with the actor in the tux, straightening his tie, standing all close to him.

I was done watching. I got up and started wandering around. I was irritated. I felt angry and weirdly anxious again. I know, I know. Poor girl, on a set in LA on a beautiful night.

A thirty-second commercial can take hours, *days*. People stood outside the barriers, watching. It started to come back to me, how boring this all could get, how, like football, more time was spent lining up and getting ready than actually playing.

I remembered a lot of stuff from before I went away to school—film sets, and learning to swim in that pool of the Santa Monica house by the beach; the birthday party when Edwina took me and most of my second-grade class to the movies; how grown up I felt that time my father took me to dinner and ordered me a Shirley Temple. But the farthest-back thing I could recall was a night at the height of Lila's fame, when I was about two. We were coming out of a hotel. There were so many people outside that the manager suggested we take the back exit. Edwina lifted me into her arms. We walked down a corridor and through a kitchen. The minute the door was pushed open, there were shouts and flashes and people shoving. A crowd surrounded us. I felt hands on me. I saw Lila disappear into a limo.

I started to cry. My grandmother and I were shoved into a second car. I lost a shoe. I didn't know where my mother had gone. "Wave to the people," my grandmother said. But I didn't want to. I started to sob. My mother had disappeared.

That was my first memory. The way I'd lost her.

* * *

DEB CALETTI

That evening, at the Walt Disney Concert Hall, there were only a handful of interested people watching from behind the barriers. Probably tourists, because the people who lived in the city saw that kind of thing all the time. Still, I was inside, and they were out. I felt important but lonely.

My phone buzzed, and I got all excited, and my heart dropped, but it was only Hoodean, responding to my LA life text.

Loser, he'd written.

It had been only six or so hours since Nicco's last text, but it didn't matter. I thought for sure I'd wrecked things and he was gone for good.

But I hadn't, and he wasn't. Lila and I were in the car again, heading to the Beverly Hilton, when my phone buzzed.

Look! Nicco texted. It was a cypress, in response to my photo of the palm. Tree for tree. It was the best cypress I'd ever seen in my life.

When we stopped at a light, I took a blurry photo of the first thing I saw out the now-dark window—a lit-up ARCO station. Look!

Look! A photo of a microwave oven, in his apartment, maybe. Look! My turn. A nail salon. Look! A box of Totino's pizza rolls on his counter. Look! His kitchen faucet. Me: a revolving cheeseburger outside a restaurant, glowing in the night. His eyebrows, my sandals. It was . . . I don't know. Strange, because the photos made me feel very close to him. Wonderful strange. God, I couldn't wait to see him again.

"What's with all the texting?" Lila asked. She was back in

140

her regular clothes, but she still had her makeup on, a bandage on her ankle.

"Nothing," I said.

"The booooy," she said, singsongy. "Tell me all about him."

I ignored her.

"What's his name?"

I was the CIA agent with state secrets.

She moped. She stared out the window as the lights of the city flashed across her face in the darkness.

When we got to the hotel, Edwina had already checked us into our suite. She'd ordered dinner. This was supposed to be a vacation for her, on Buick's dime, but she was back in her old job of taking care of us.

"Gran!" I said, and ran to her as if I hadn't seen her in a million years. It was kind of bratty, because I hadn't given Lila a greeting like that.

"What happened to your foot?" Edwina folded her arms and scowled at Lila's bandage.

Lila dropped her purse on one of the padded chairs. "They gave me a shoe with a razor blade for a buckle. I am in such pain right now. And what the hell. You never told me that our baby grew up."

She sounded mad about it. Like it was something I'd gone and done without her permission.

CHAPTER TWENTY-ONE

Exhibit 36: Sworn statement of Edwina Short, 2 of 2

I got out of going back to the Buick set by saying I had a migraine. I feel bad about this now, because I was kind of being a shit that whole trip, but Lila understood migraines because she had migraines all the time. I don't think I've ever really had one. Edwina said, *Let her rest, and I'll bring her by later.*

We sat around in the suite, watching Edwina's favorite morning shows in luxury. The suite had a living room and three bedrooms, thanks to Buick. Then we went out for a late breakfast at the Griddle Cafe and ate until we were about to bust.

Look! I texted. Pancakes.

Look! The guy who washed dishes at the Cliff House restaurant, flashing me a peace sign.

* * *

"Everything okay at the house?" Edwina asked. She crumpled up her napkin and tossed it onto her plate before pushing it away. She must have seen Lila's bruise, because she stared across the table like she meant business. I licked a bit of sticky syrup from my finger.

Telling her the truth felt like tattling, but she was supposed to be looking out for me. Edwina was the one person who always did. And I was probably the one person who loved and cared for Edwina. I mean, look at the history: Her husband, Hal, ditched her and Lila. Her own father had done the same thing. She was pretty much raised by *her* grandmother after that. And *she'd* been the baby in the arms of the beautiful Ella, escaping a violent man during the 1906 earthquake.

And now, a lot of the time, Lila treated Edwina like a servant.

Then again, it was Edwina who'd brought Lila to LA when she was fourteen to get her into acting. She pushed her into it so they could make money to survive. Lila wasn't at that particular coffee shop by accident. If you thought about it, Lila had sort of been a toaster to Edwina and Hal, too—useful, an object, discarded when it stopped being shiny. The women in my family have probably felt like that doll with the blank eyes and the smile for years and years and years—beautiful, voiceless, occasionally played with, tossed wherever their owner put them. Being an object was something that got handed down, same as that doll had.

"They fight." I didn't tell Edwina about the paintings, or

the man parked outside our house. I didn't tell her how bad the fighting was.

Loyalty was confusing when there was always a triangle.

Blame was confusing when stories went so far back, you couldn't see where they started.

Edwina and I didn't meet Lila later like we said we would. I could tell she was hurt, but we didn't want to go. We sat around watching TV in our hotel robes and then hung out by the pool, me in my bikini, Edwina in her white shorts and flowered shirt and Rite Aid sandals. We picked up Lila when filming was over. We went to dinner. Then we went back to the suite and ordered all these room service desserts. It felt like the old days, since Buick was paying. I didn't feel guilty or worried about the cheesecake and the torte and the lemon pie.

It was fun. Lila was kind of leaving *me* out then, buddying up with Edwina, teasing her about the old days, when Edwina would sit up and wait for Lila to come home after a date, even though Lila was thirty-three and already had a kid.

An object, an owned thing. A napkin. A magazine. A knife. A toaster.

A kid.

Me.

The next day, we went out for breakfast again, the three of us this time. Edwina had brought along the latest *Inside Entertainment* magazine. She just loved all that stuff, which is probably why she pushed Lila in that direction in the first place. Plus money, of course. But while we waited for our food, Edwina folded the magazine to a particular page and pushed it across the table to Lila.

"Look. Look who it is. Did you see this? Asshole."

"I saw." Lila spread the thinnest layer of jam on a piece of toast. "Karma. Finally getting what he deserves."

It was Rex Clancy, the director. Accused of sexual misconduct by dozens of female actors. I'd heard Rex Clancy's name in our houses for years. He was important. He'd given Lila her first role, in *The Girl Is Gone*. She'd also worked with him on *The Winding Road* before *Nefarious* and *The Grange*, that historical drama that no one saw. Rex Clancy, well, you know. He's got, like, four chins and is the gross kind of guy with unidentifiable food in his beard.

"What? What'd he do? Did he do something to you?" It was shocking news, but I wanted to know stuff that summer. All stuff. I wasn't the child with tender little flower-petal ears anymore.

"More than something, and he wasn't the only one, as we're well aware," Lila said, and met Edwina's eyes. Important stories passed between them. Really important.

"Did you ever tell anyone?"

Lila made that scoffing sound in the back of her throat, meaning she knew things I could never imagine.

"No, I didn't *tell* anyone. For the same reason no one else did." Lila waved the magazine. "Safety in numbers. It had to take, what . . ." She read the magazine. "*Two dozen* women before anyone would risk it. That man was in charge of my bank account, and my career. My whole *life*. *He* sat in the big chair. *He* signed the checks."

"He was a sex maniac," Edwina said. She looked like an old lady when she said it. Her eyes got all narrow, and her face wrinkled up like she'd eaten something sour.

"Oh, stop! It's not about sex! It's about *power*, and that's all. Who has it, who doesn't, who can just *take* whatever they want. Assholes with big egos, that's who. I'm over this conversation," Lila said. And then she tossed the magazine onto her dirty plate, where it sat on the smear of yellow from her eggs and the toast crusts, and the napkin with her lipstick marks on it.

That afternoon, the three of us went shopping. Edwina was usually all judgy and careful about excess spending, but she was having a blast. She was wearing her polyester pants and blouse, and those shoes with the thick bottoms that didn't hurt her feet, and she was like a girl on her birthday in those boutiques. Well, she was beautiful once, too. I saw the photos of her wedding to Hal, which were in an album she kept hidden in a drawer.

Lila bought herself a purse and some earrings and two scarves, and she bought Edwina the same purse, plus this satiny dress that you could tell Edwina wanted so bad but would probably never wear. Lila bought a pair of sandals in gold for her and white for me. We all got these necklaces with our initials on them.

She used a debit card. No credit this time. I would never admit how much she spent. I won't say the number. It was probably a good chunk of the Buick money. I didn't know how we could spend like that, but apparently we could.

When Lila was in the dressing room trying on this peach silk sheath, Edwina and I waited next to a table of jewelry and accessories.

"What did Lila mean when she said Rex Clancy wasn't the only one?" I asked. I couldn't get it out of my mind—that look they'd shared.

It wasn't the time or place. The saleswoman hovered nearby. A woman with a dog in her purse reached for a bracelet.

"A neighbor man. When she was twelve," Edwina whispered. "He told her not to tell. We moved after that."

Lila came out of that dressing room with the shimmering peach sheath over her arm. The relaxing music played in the store. Edwina had gone on to look at a table of scarves, as if these were the sorts of things that just happened to everyone in one way or another. My stomach ached. I felt sick. I had thought, you know, that one day you weren't in the world where grown men wanted you and then you were, but this wasn't really true. Grown men had always been there, in our world.

The next day, before our evening flight home, Lila had a car take us to Disneyland. I know it's hard to imagine. Edwina in her Lane Bryant shorts and her sun hat, and Lila in that tight yellow sundress with her big sunglasses, and me, walking between them like a little kid. Lila had gotten some special pass that allowed us to get to the front of the line. We hurried around. They kept saying, "The baby needs to go on the pirate ride! The baby can't miss the haunted house!" And we'd all get on, except for any halfway wild ones, when Edwina and Lila would wait, Lila sipping her iced coffee and autographing stuff like mouse-ear hats and park maps and whatever women had in their purses. A lot of people recognized her that day. Some tried to be respectful and only snuck glances, and others barged right up to ask for photos, but most fell somewhere in the middle, pretending to take a picture of the Dumbo ride while trying to get her in the background.

When I told Meredith about it all later on the phone, she said, *Weird, Syd.* Her voice sounded full of . . . horror. I thought she'd say, *How awesome* or *Lucky you.* I think it was the *baby* stuff that freaked her out. It was one of the many things that were so normal to me that I couldn't see how abnormal they were to anyone else. Meredith—well, it was funny, because a lot of people actually do have those perfect families like the ones you see on TV, but a lot of people don't.

And that day, I'm not sure I really minded all the *baby* stuff. I mean, there'd been that bad fight with Jake, and the way she'd cried that night, and the orange makeup on her arm, and the disturbing news about Rex Clancy and the neighbor. At

Disneyland, she held my hand, and she and Edwina were both shoving me this way and that, having fun like kids without a care in the world, and people were remembering to shower Lila with love.

It was like I was giving her something that made her really happy.

When Lila and I got home that night, it was clear that something had changed at the Sea Cliff house. Max greeted us as usual, but it was dark downstairs. The big doors were open, though. Out on the patio, there was a towel on the chaise longue, and Jake's shoes were tossed on the White Room floor. A warm wind blew in, ruffling the pages of a magazine. It was eerie.

"Jake?" Lila called.

In the kitchen, that stack of bills had disappeared. Jake's sweatshirt hung over the back of a chair. Jake himself was up in the media room. He had his cocktail next to him, and he was watching a movie. It was a hot night, and he was wearing only a pair of shorts. His shirt was off. He was stretched out, his legs up on the ottoman.

"Hey, girls," he said. He didn't get up. Lila went and kissed him hello. She kissed him like the air had cleared between them. *You bitch!* he'd screamed, and there'd been a bruise on her arm, but she'd forgiven him, which meant I was supposed to forgive him too. There was this strange moment when I just stood there, and I knew I had to greet him, so I gave him a hug, a quick hug, and my hands were on the bare skin of his back. He smelled like sun lotion and sweat and alcohol.

The thing that had changed was that Jake had moved in. Permanently.

There would be the three of us now. A triangle.

CHAPTER TWENTY-TWO

Exhibit 37: Photo of Female Torso, *by Kazimir Malevich*
Exhibit 38: Photo of Jacqueline, *by Pablo Picasso*

Do you know another great thing about Nicco? He wasn't a social media person. You couldn't just look him up and find out everything about him. Or rather, look him up and see some perfect version of him. He worked a lot too, to pay rent and living expenses, and so when I got back, I couldn't see him for a few days. We talked on the phone and passed photos back and forth, and that's how I got to experience his regular life. There was his cereal box (Chex) and pieces of his bedroom (a stack of books, a messy bed, a pile of laundry). There was a meal he and his roommate were having (pizza in a box) and his morning stubble (sigh). I tried to keep our house out of the images. I still hadn't told him about Lila. I sent a lot of pictures of Max, who wouldn't let me out of his sight since we got back.

The night before I finally got to see Nicco, Jake was in the guest bedroom again. Another crate had arrived while we were gone. Why he opened some of the crates and not others—no clue. But he had his hammer out, and a screwdriver, and he was working to dismantle the outer wood frame.

Maybe I was in a good mood because I was going to see Nicco the next day. Or maybe it was because Lila, noticing my coldness to Jake after their fight, had grabbed my elbow on the stairwell, right under that huge picture of her, and spit the word, *Please*. But I went in there. I told myself that there might be something great to show Cora. I'd just had a long talk on the phone with her, about how she'd met a guy she really liked at a softball game, how Meredith was being all critical, but even more, how she'd decided to start a blog about important female artists no one had really heard of. Cora was always doing something amazing like that.

"Hey," I said.

"Hiya," Jake said.

I plopped on the floor. Max sat his big, hot self right next to me. "Man, I wish you'd just open *all* of these."

"Yeah?" He stopped what he was doing and looked at me.

"Yeah."

"You like 'em, huh?"

"Who wouldn't? They're so cool." I felt a sick little twist inside when I said it. A guilty twist. I mean, they *were* cool, but I could hear my own voice, kissing up, acting all admiring, trying to get his approval. I didn't know why. I still don't entirely understand it. If I'm being honest, I wasn't there just because of Lila and Cora. Why do we still crave the approval of people who make us feel bad and uneasy and who are cruel? No idea. But I needed it. I wanted it.

He grinned. He tilted his head and lifted one eyebrow and examined me as if he were a judge at an art show. He gave me that look again, as if I were really something. He chuckled, almost like a proud dad. And it was kind of great. It made me feel really good. It helped push that bruise and that fight into the past. My own father gushed and fussed over me when I saw him once a year, but he didn't know me. He was a different sort of ghost. His absence was even louder than Lila's presence. But this was a real guy who lived with us. Looking at me. Seeing me, right there in that room. He might not be perfect, but at least he was *there*.

"Well, I can't open them all, or else I gotta pack them all."

"Why would you have to pack them? Are they going somewhere?"

"I can't keep all these. I'm a broker."

"You mean you're getting broker and broker buying so many?"

He cracked up. "Something like that."

"Come oooon," I whined. "Hurry up and get it out. I want to seeee."

"All right, all right," he said. "You could help, you know, instead of sitting there on your ass."

It took maybe a half hour to free it from the box. Wrapping was everywhere. The painting was beautiful but strange. Bold, colorful stripes, a figure with just a red oval for a head, but no face. "I really like the colors. But . . . weird. No face."

"*Female Torso*, Kazimir Malevich. Oil on wood."

"I don't get why they're all women. All these paintings."

He ignored me. He was gathering up the layers and layers of mess we'd just unwrapped.

"One more!"

"I told you, no way. I'm gonna have to get professionals to come package it up to ship. Plus, the best ones are hanging right here in the house. What about the one in the dining room? Did you take a good look at that?"

"Not really."

"For God's sake. There's your prizewinner."

"What is it?"

He smiled, pleased. He paused for dramatic effect. "*Jacqueline*. Pablo Picasso."

"No way."

I was stunned. Honestly, my mouth fell open.

"Yup."

"And it's real?"

"Yeah. It's not so crazy. He made, like, ten thousand pieces of art."

"Who was Jacqueline?"

"His wife. Last one he had before he died."

"Oh."

"All I know is, she was twenty-six and he was seventy-two."

"Gross."

"Supposedly, he drew a dove on her house with chalk and then gave her a rose every day for six months until she'd go out with him."

"Uh-huh, wow, roses would make you forget he was a creepy old guy."

"Yeah, well, she never got over him after he died." He made his fingers into a pistol and shot at his head.

"Oh, God. You're kidding."

"Nope. She was crazy about him."

"Or just plain crazy."

"And, hey, she was ancient compared to another girl of his. Marie-Thérèse Walter. She was seventeen and he was forty-five."

"Whoa." It made my stomach feel sick.

"White Room," he said.

"What? That crying woman with the yellow hair?"

"Girl. *Crying Girl* is the title."

"She's a little old to be a girl."

"Lichtenstein. Enamel on steel."

"No *way*. Really?" He nodded. "Why is she crying?"

"Over a man, probably."

I scrunched my face, but I couldn't argue with that. If you looked at it, I mean. She doesn't look like she's crying over a missed promotion at work.

"Old Roy Boy." Jake chuckled. And then he winked at me,

as if we were both in on a secret. "Lichtenstein *loved* women."

The wink, Picasso's young girls, the way he said "Lichtenstein *loved* women"—for a split second, I felt like we had turned down some unexpected road. And then Lila pushed the door open. She had to shove it a little, from all the wrapping. She wore her short green satin robe, with her hair loose to her shoulders. "What are you guys doing?"

"Look," I said. I pointed to the painting.

"Faceless. Super," she said. "Just a body, huh?"

She was right, but I could hear her tone. It meant, *Uh-oh, watch out.*

"You feeling better, honey?" Jake asked.

"It'd be nice if someone offered to get me a cup of tea or something."

"I'll make you a cup of tea," Jake said.

"My throat is killing me. And, Syd, baby, you really need to get some *friends.*"

Wow. It came out of nowhere, that cruel little bomb. It felt like a slap.

"God, Lila."

"What?"

"That's so mean."

"I'm just saying, it's not good to be always hanging out here with the adults."

"My friends are at *home*, because I'm *here.*"

"Come on now, girls . . . ," Jake said.

"I don't know *what* has gotten into you since Christmas."

Even without her makeup, she looked beautiful. She supposedly didn't feel well, she was "coming down with something," but her eyes were still so blue and her features so perfect. It didn't matter, though. I saw ugliness. I saw her urge to inflict pain on other people, on *me*.

"You are *such* a bitch." It came out before I had a chance to think. I'd never talked to her like that before. Never. And now it was like I'd removed a cork from a bottle where a serpent had been curled up and waiting. The room filled with a horrible energy, and she roared and then lunged at me.

I ran. I ran out of the room and down the stairs. She was behind me. I felt her grab at my hair. I fled out of the open White Room doors and across the patio. I darted down the 104 steps into the darkness of China Beach.

The tide was in. There was only the slightest strip of shoreline. You had to be careful out there. You could get caught on a bed of rocks and find you had nowhere to go. I stood on the sand in my T-shirt and shorts, my heart pounding with anger and fear and adrenaline. I could hear voices up at the house, traveling down. The surf rolled out, a *crickle-crickle* of water against pebbles, and then it came back in with a *boom*, rolled across my bare feet, sprayed seawater against my cheeks. My feet sank deeper into the sand with each wave.

Before, I'd wanted only to be close to Lila. To have her attention and her love. But now I felt misunderstood, and weirdly, wrongly accused. And, too, I felt something burning that had only sparked before. Hate. It curled up inside me and rose, the way a flame does when a match is struck.

Hate is dangerous. Hate makes you feel like doing dangerous things. Vengeful things. Things that would get her back. I'd wade out in the waves, or walk on the high beams of the house next door, or fling myself at that construction worker and let him do whatever he wanted. I'd slap her, or dig my nails into her skin. I'd strike a real match, or leave and never return. The possibilities seemed endless.

"Syd? Syd-Syd?" she called.

Great.

Lila never came down to the beach. And now here she was, struggling down those steps, her hand against the wall for support. She couldn't see well in the dark. This was one of her things. Something about the rods and cones and the particular shape of her eyes.

"Baby? Come on. Let's not do this."

I wanted to run away, but there was nowhere to go. I stood where I was and folded my arms. I watched the moonlight dance along the lifted tips of the waves.

She stood next to me in that green robe. We were about the same height now, I realized. She wore these satin slippers, and they were sinking into the sand and were likely ruined.

"Syd, *please.*"

I didn't say anything. She started to cry.

God.

The waves *crickle-crickled* across the pebbles. And then, *boom. Crash.*

I sighed. The thing was . . . even when she was raging, she seemed like she was four years old. A little girl. I felt sorry for her. My anger slid away, leaving a slime trail of guilt. There were lots of little girls who weren't little anymore. Daddy's girls, lost girls, harmed and lonely girls. *Crying Girl.*

"Okay," I said.

"Okay?"

"Yeah."

"Do you still love me?"

"Of course."

Neither of us said we were sorry.

The point is—it was complicated. The point is—it was confusing.

The point is—it was getting intense, very intense, at the house above China Beach.

I think of her standing there on the sand, crying like that. And I think of her words in that restaurant, about power. But men and women both—we learn about power and powerlessness from our mothers and fathers first, right? And they learn from their mothers and fathers, and so on and so on?

Fix *that* shit.

CHAPTER TWENTY-THREE

Exhibit 39: Photo of Crying Girl, *by Roy Lichtenstein*

Do you know those View-Masters that you played with as a kid? That's what the Camera Obscura building looks like. A big white View-Master, with a little pointed tower on the top, and the words GIANT CAMERA painted on the side. The building sits at the edge of a cliff, with the sea spread out below. Everything that summer sat at the edge of a cliff. The Cliff House, the labyrinth, Camera Obscura, our house. Lila. The summer itself. Me.

Nicco and I walked inside. God, it was just so good to see him. He was starting to feel known to me, after all those photos. "Okay, so how does this work again?" I asked.

"The light comes through the top and then hits a big lens? Reflects the image down on that flat part right there?" Nicco said.

"Meaning, you have no idea."

"Something science." We giggled.

When the door shut behind us, it was totally dark in there. Then we really started to laugh nervously. Our shoulders bumped.

"Man, I'm blinded."

But then my eyes adjusted and I saw the incredible lit-up image on the large circular surface in the center of the room. The image curved as if we were looking through an enormous fishbowl. It spun slowly, so that we could see Ocean Beach and then the sea and then Seal Rocks, with all the seals lying around, fat and lazy. Next came the highway and then Ocean Beach again. The light that came through the pinhole was dim, so it all had the feel of a vintage photograph, even though it was astonishingly clear.

The camera operator explained how it worked, but I wasn't really paying attention. After Nicco picked up my hand in the dark, that was all I could think about.

Back outside, Max jumped on us with joy, as if he'd been worried we might disappear into that strange building and never return.

I untied Max, held his leash. "Magic," I said.

"Right?" Nicco said.

It was. The spinning image, the seals on the rocks, Nicco's hand and mine, the joyful dog. All of it was magic. Things were getting more and more unsettling at 716 Sea Cliff Drive as the house and the people in it sank deeper and deeper into a dark crevasse, but I was happy right then. All the rest of it disappeared when we were together.

Nicco and I got fish-and-chips. We sat at an outdoor table and grinned ridiculously across it at each other. Our knees touched underneath.

He was wearing tan board shorts and a green T-shirt, and it made me realize how brown his eyes were. Really brown. Brown like a deep pool that might go on and on. I liked his wrists, too. I never knew I could like wrists. But, my God, I liked wrists. A lot. And his hands. I kept looking at them. I imagined those hands doing things—turning a steering wheel, holding a pen, touching me. I wanted their weight and strength. I'd never wanted before. Not really. Not like that. With Samuel Crane, it was more about what the kissing made me feel than what he made me feel. I never felt some raging attraction. Maybe I never even felt attraction. I always thought Samuel looked a little geeky when he got his hair cut.

The want—it was distracting, honestly. It made it hard to focus. Maybe that's what desire is—utter distraction.

We ate the fish-and-chips and talked about how Nicco was graduating early and how he wanted to go to college and then get his master's so he could teach literature. Literature held all the small moments he tried to put in his notebook, he said. I told him how I'd started seeing the moments too. Like this woman who pulled up alongside us in a parking lot when we were in LA. Her car was a million years old, and it was so beat up that the door wouldn't open. She was trying everything, but it had finally had enough, locking her out so it could die in peace.

He laughed. And then he told me about his moms' old cars—the Blue Pony, the Dark Devil. They always named their cars, and the cars were always breaking down in awful places.

He told this story like we understood each other about old and broken cars. I needed to tell him about Lila. I'd avoided it for too long already. In some ways, we lived in very different worlds, and I needed to say so before things got awkward.

"*That* Lila Shore?" he asked.

"That Lila Shore. I'm sorry I didn't say anything before. It's just . . ."

"Wow." He even pushed his chair back a little. Away from me, I thought.

"It's okay." I didn't know what was okay. I didn't know what else to say.

"I live in a crappy apartment. My family's idea of fancy is Thai takeout."

"*She* used to live in a crappy apartment. Most of the time, I live in a dorm room that's so small and messy, I can barely walk across the floor." It wasn't exactly true. I'm a pretty tidy person. There was maybe, you know, that usual pile of laundry and a few term papers.

"Sea Cliff Drive, huh?"

"She rents it from Jake. Her, uh, boyfriend."

"You don't like him?"

"Why do you say that?"

He pointed to his eyebrows, the scrunchable part between them. He was always so observant. Unnervingly observant. The sort of observant that kind people often are.

"I'm *trying* to like him. I sort of like him. I mean, he lives with us. I'm expecting to see a ring on her finger any day."

"Still, man, that kind of life. I can't even imagine it."

"*This* kind of life is what I like best. Right here," I said, and gave a fry to Max.

It sounded like a lie, even though it wasn't. I worried I'd wrecked something by telling him. I was always worrying I would wreck something by revealing who I was.

But maybe I hadn't.

"You ready to get out of here?" he asked. "I saved the best for last."

"Can't wait."

The best was the off-leash part of Ocean Beach, which I didn't even know existed.

"Now he can run and run," Nicco said.

"Oh, man! I love when dogs get to go as fast as they can."

And so we unclipped Max and he took off. He ran like a galloping horse that was part rocket ship. I thought we might never see him again. He zoomed toward the water and swerved in. When a couple of dogs came speeding down the beach, a big one and a small one, he got out and wrestled with them. They growled and snarled and played, turning figure eights.

He swam and ran some more. He tried to eat some gross seaweed thing. He was having the time of his life.

When it was time to go, I called him, but he wouldn't come, same as a toddler at the playground. But then Nicco whistled, and Max came right to him.

"That is so wrong!" I said.

Max shook his big, wet self all over us.

"Yikes!" I squealed, but Nicco didn't mind.

"I could give you a ride home," Nicco said.

"This big, wet, stinky thing in your car?"

"I think you smell just fine," he said, and I punched his arm.

Nicco slid open the van door, and Max hopped in. We brushed sand off our legs and feet. Up front, I got comfy in the passenger seat, which was covered in a beach towel with a palm tree on it. I looked for more clues about him. There was a fat, laughing Buddha sitting in the open ashtray. His gold arms were raised, and it made it look like he was on a thrilling roller-coaster ride.

"The air conditioner's busted, so we've got to roll down the windows."

I watched his hands on the window knob, and on the steering wheel, and on the radio dial, because that's the only music the van had. The song sounded far away, like it was coming from a distant solar system. Everything rattled, and Max was panting in my ear. It was hard to talk, so we didn't.

I just felt it. Summer, your perfect idea of summer, the

warm car, the wind coming through the windows, a happy dog, your sandals sitting on the floor beside your bare feet, a VW van that knew about summer, since it had seen so many. Nicco, pushing his hair out of his eyes when the light turned red. Whatever *IT* was, well, I felt the pieces of it right then, swirling around me like fireflies.

When we went through the pillars of the neighborhood, he turned the radio off. I saw the street through his eyes—how everything was so boring and quiet and well manicured, how it looked as unreal as a film set.

"Oh, man. I feel like they might arrest me here for driving this piece of shit."

He didn't know what went on behind closed doors, our doors. I hadn't told him that part yet.

"The orange one," I said, and he pulled up to 716 Sea Cliff.

"Wow."

"Want to come in?"

"Uhh." He waved his hand over himself, indicating his day-at-the-beach-with-wet-dog self. "Maybe next time?"

Next time. Those were beginning to be my very favorite words.

"There's this all-ages live music venue in South of Market. Wanna go?" he asked.

"That'd be great."

"I'm off Saturday night."

"Sure."

Good people didn't make you guess. There weren't shit

games. He got out, and so did I. He opened the door for Max, who jumped out too. The three of us stood there, looking at each other. I wanted him to kiss me, bad. I don't know why he didn't do it. I don't know why I didn't do it myself. The first kiss, the first *I love you*—you waited until they were bestowed upon you, even if that kiss was sitting right there between both of us, and belonged to both of us.

Next door, all that sawing or drilling or whatever was making the noise—it stopped. The sudden quiet caught Nicco's attention. He looked over that way. I did too. The guy, that man—he was staring at us, watching. Out of the corner of my eye, I also saw the blinds shift in our upstairs window. I didn't know whether Lila or Jake was spying, but it seemed like everyone was watching me. I felt that way the whole summer.

"They're building a mansion over there," Nicco said.

"I guess."

"Giant House," Nicco said.

"Giant House," I repeated. It was a joke from earlier that day, after GIANT CAMERA on the Camera Obscura building. As if every building should declare what it was. Small Café. Medium Coffee Shop.

"See you?" He gave my fingers a little shake.

"See you." I smiled.

"Bye, buddy," he said to Max. I liked that so much. Some people forget to say good-bye to dogs. Nicco was such a great guy. There are lots and lots of great guys, and you shouldn't forget that.

He drove off, and I watched him leave. The man next door made sure I saw him looking. He folded his arms and stood there a long time. Then he put both hands in the air, palms up, and shrugged, like, *Hey, I can't help myself.*

Whatever. I didn't even care. *Watch until your eyeballs fall out*, I thought. There was nothing to see.

And that's what kept driving me crazy. The nothing part. The no kiss. No kiss, no kiss, no kiss!

Desire—it was a force too.

Inside, Max ran toward the kitchen because Jake was there.

"Hey!" I called.

"Hey!" he said.

I didn't see any signs of Lila, either downstairs or up. I went into my room. I felt dirty and sticky from sand and salt water. I stripped out of my gritty beach clothes and ran the water in the tub. I poured in some bubble bath.

No kiss, no kiss, no kiss!

I dropped into the water. It felt clean and hot and wonderful. I imagined telling Meredith all this, about Nicco. I kept thinking how Meredith would probably say, *Slow down.* How slowing down did not sound good, but how *slow* and *down* did.

CHAPTER TWENTY-FOUR

Exhibit 40: Evidence bag containing alprazolam (Xanax), zolpidem (Ambien), oxycodone (OxyContin)

The water slurped down the drain. The sound seemed to travel through all the old pipes in the house. I got out of the bath. Wearing shoes made of bath bubbles, I got a nice white towel from the cupboard and dried off. I wrapped the towel around myself. I felt that good kind of tired that makes you really hungry. I combed my hair back.

When I stepped out of the bathroom, Jake was coming up the stairs. He was wearing workout clothes, heading to the exercise room next to mine.

"Oh!" I said. I felt caught there in my towel. So often, he made me feel caught.

"Hey. You coming with us to dinner tonight? I gotta make the reservation."

"No thanks. I think I'll just stay in."

"No problem. Whatever works for you."

I didn't exactly want to stand there like that and have a conversation, but I didn't want to be rude, either.

"I'll just order Chinese or something."

"Sure."

When I got to my room, I shut the door and I locked it. I didn't lock it because Jake had done anything wrong. I locked it because it was there again, that *I think I'm uncomfortable/I'm kind of uncomfortable/Am I uncomfortable?* feeling. It was hard to even know what it was or wasn't. I could hear him in the room next to mine, grunting with exertion as he lifted the weights, then clanged them down again. I just wanted the distance of the lock.

But when Lila arrived home, she came upstairs. I had my music playing. I didn't hear her. She rattled my doorknob. Honestly, I might have locked it to keep *her* out too.

"Syd? Open up."

"Just a sec!"

She pounded. "Syd! Now!"

I poked my head out. "Hey."

"What are you doing in there?" she said.

"Nothing."

"Why is your door locked? You never lock your door."

"Privacy."

She narrowed her eyes. "Is everything all right, baby?" she asked.

"Yeah, fine."

"Are you sure?"

"Yeah."

"We're going out for dinner. Want to come? We're going to RTB." Which meant more food like abalone blah-blah and shaved mushroom whatever. Food for the bored. Food for people who'll pay big bucks for some piece of fish the size of your thumb.

"Nah, I'll just stay here. I had a big lunch."

"All right. Put whatever you want on the card if you decide to eat."

The problems with the card had magically disappeared. I wondered if Jake was the magician. She didn't protest me not coming either. She probably hoped I'd say no.

The locked door, though. It maybe said something to her that it shouldn't have. Then again, that thing that happened when she was twelve—maybe that's what kept speaking and speaking.

I ordered Chinese. I talked to Meredith on the phone while I waited for it to arrive. She told me stuff I already knew, that Cora met a guy at a softball game. That Meredith saw them kissing that same night. She thought Cora was acting stupid and reckless. I didn't tell her I was on Cora's side. I didn't tell her about Nicco.

When the food arrived, I took it to the patio over the ocean. It was still warm out, but it wouldn't be for long. The sun was setting. The sky blazed orange and pink, unreal, looking full of rage or beauty. I fed Max chow mein noodles and some barbecued pork. He had to keep going inside for drinks of water. I forgot how Chinese food makes you thirsty.

I took a picture of him and texted it to Nicco. Big dog. He sent me one back, a photo of his foot. Bigfoot. I felt a hundred smiling emojis but sent only one. Even his feet were cute. I know, I know—I said it before, but it was astonishing. No one's feet are cute. He was so cute that all of him was cute.

I liked it better out there than in the house, where the quiet had an eeriness that reminded me of the ghost whispers. What if someone was on one of the other floors and I didn't even know? How could I tell? The thought was unsettling. Even with the darkness falling, even with the black sea stretching to forever, and the *crickle-crickle* of the waves rolling out across the pebbles, and the crash of them coming in, it felt safer outside than in that house with all its years of history. It was built in 1925. The grand Victorian Cliff House mansion had long since burned down by then, but the Sutro Baths were still operating, with their multiple pools and trapezes. I could feel the way 716 Sea Cliff held decades of emotions and memories. Like its walls had soaked up nearly a hundred years of tears and joy and tension and regrets and longings. The whole city felt that way. Old and tragic, but still standing.

It was starting to get cold, and I rubbed my arms against the chill. The lights of the bridge twinkled on. I wondered how many people driving across it right then were falling in love. I wondered if I might be.

Max came outside and looked at me with those eyes.

"All that water. And now you have to pee. What was I thinking?"

Outside, the street was dark, but not so dark that I couldn't see it. A car, parked across the street. *That* car.

I froze. The same man, I was pretty sure, sat inside. He was tapping stuff on his phone, which was a lit-up rectangle in the night. It scared me. I actually felt afraid.

I did that thing we're so good at—I talked myself out of the alarm that was creeping up my neck. Maybe the neighbors were having domestic problems, and this was some private investigator. Maybe the guy just liked our street as a place to hang out. Maybe—

Shit! He saw me. I saw him see me.

"Hurry up, Max!" He could take a long time, too long, deciding which bush.

I rushed the dog back inside. I shut the back doors. I went around making sure all the windows were locked. I didn't know what to do. I couldn't play a movie in the theater room, because I needed to listen, and it was too hard to hear anything in there. It was silly to be afraid, I told myself. Sea Cliff was one of the safest neighborhoods in the city.

I climbed the staircase. Max raced ahead and then waited

beside me on the landing, where I stopped. I faced that image of Lila. I stared her down.

"What are you doing?" I asked her.

I tried to watch a movie on my laptop with the sound way down. It was too hard to concentrate, though. It got really late, but I couldn't sleep. I was anxious. I kept peeking out the window until, finally, the car was gone.

I didn't want to get woken up by the sound of sex or fighting, either.

I don't know why I'm telling you this part. It maybe just speaks to the general direction that things seemed to be going at home. Down, down, down.

I headed to Lila's bathroom and found her sleeping pills. I'd never taken one before, so I bit it in half. I went downstairs and unpopped the cork in the wine bottle on the counter. I took a swig straight from it. I'd forgotten how disgusting wine was, but whatever.

I took both of those things—the half pill, the wine—because I wanted to sleep like the dead.

CHAPTER TWENTY-FIVE

Exhibit 41: Surveillance images, 716 Sea Cliff Drive

I loved Max, but God! Early the next morning, when he went out to pee, he saw that the gate was open, and he went for it.

I took off after that stupid dog. He wasn't exactly well trained, if you couldn't tell that already. He wanted to be good, but if you handed him an invitation to be bad, he wasn't going to say no.

Of course, he flew right past the house next door, so I had to too. The men were already there—they always started early, too early for that kind of noise, if you ask me.

Max was a blur as he headed toward the entrance to Baker Beach. If he reached those stairs before I did, he'd have a million ways to be gone.

"Max! Max!" I yelled.

God, he was speeding like a galloping horse, all hunched down low, his haunches pumping. He was almost to those stairs.

And that's when I heard a whistle behind me. That shrill, sharp whistle people make using two fingers in their mouth, a whistle I could never master even though Hoodean tried to teach me once.

I looked over my shoulder as I ran. But that guy was catching up to me. Of course it was him, and he was trying to help, but fuck him, assuming that he could step in and handle this better than I could. And then something happened that made me even madder. Max stopped in his tracks. He came to a screeching halt, like some part of his stupid, infuriating brain *knew* that whistle. That guy assumed he could handle the situation better than I could, and he *did* handle it better, and it was infuriating. I mean, thanks a lot, Max.

By that time, the man had passed me, caught up to that turd dog Max, and had him strongly by the collar. He led him to me. The worst part was, I had tossed on only my tank top and shorts to let him out, and I felt really embarrassed and awkward there with no bra. I had to lean down to get that stupid dog while having one arm crossed over my chest, and honestly, my boobs were probably in full view with the loose neckline of my top.

"Thanks," I said.

"No problem. I'm around a lot of dogs."

Yeah, I bet he was.

I snuck a look at him. Up close, he was younger than I thought. Maybe late twenties. Younger, but still old. Older. Too much older. Handsome. Handsome if he were maybe some guy on TV and not a real one who watched me all the time. Handsome could make you forget for a second all the stuff you learned about strangers. He had bright, playful eyes. Man whiskers. Big shoulders. Really big. Strong, tan arms, from working construction. Jeans, T-shirt. This is another construction-man cliché, but he looked like the kind of guy who would knock back a few beers with the bros, or have sports parties out of the back of his truck—I forget what those are called.

Our hands brushed as I took Max. Skin slid against skin. "There you go. Have a good day, princess."

The word "princess" skittered up my back like an insect. Whether that guy was handsome or not, old or young, I wanted to smack that word, and him for using it. That word always felt small and bad and dehumanizing. My father called his girlfriends princess. He called *me* princess. As if all females, even his daughter, were indistinguishable from each other.

Of course, I didn't smack him, or do anything close to it. He was twice my size, older, and he, you know, had a *car* and a *job* and *muscles* and stuff, and I was just me, a girl in her tank top and bare feet. I couldn't even speak. The only thing I could do was smile that smile that really isn't a smile, the tight-lipped one, the one that says, *I'm barely tolerating you*, but says it nicely so he won't get pissed off.

He was supposed to read my smile, so why didn't he?

Because he thought he was supposed to pursue? Because he could do whatever he wanted? Because he didn't take me at my word? Okay, I wasn't using actual words, because *maybe they weren't the best idea.* I would never forget how Cora tried for months to get creepy Lance Sweeney to leave her alone, until she finally told him straight out to go away. Then he called her a cunt and got all aggressive, and she had to avoid him for weeks until he moved on to Hailey Xavier, like a game of asshole hot potato.

I walked down the sidewalk, hunched over as I held Max by the collar, holding my shirt against myself to cover my boobs.

"Hey!" the guy called.

I could pretend like I didn't hear him, but he was right behind me. He'd just helped me with my dog. I was going to have to keep seeing him every day until that house was done. I turned.

"My name's Shane."

I should have used some useless little weapon, like a fake name, but I didn't. I don't know why I felt I owed him. I don't know why I always gave things I didn't want to give.

"Sydney."

"See you, Sydney."

When I got back in the house, I was so angry with myself. I'd given over my name. I wanted to pinch my own arms. I wanted to scratch out my eyes. I was so mad that I took it out on Max.

"Goddamn you!" I glared at him.

But then his eyes looked so remorseful that I felt bad.

"What am I going to do with you," I said.

I was surprised to find Lila in the kitchen. "You're up early."

"I need coffee! How do you work this?" Lila looked at the new machine Jake had bought like it was a set of complicated instructions to build a bomb. Honestly, she had her own production company, she was capable, but sometimes she acted like she was a toddler when she was around someone who might do stuff for her.

"Put the thingy in the compartment and push the button."

"Wow. Easy, tiger. You don't have to snap."

"I just chased Max halfway down the block, so good morning. And I stayed up half the night because there was a creepy car parked out in front of our house."

"A creepy car." She sounded doubtful.

"I've seen it there before."

"Baby, you've watched too many of my movies."

"Thanks for taking me seriously."

She waved her hand at me. "Syd-Syd. Really. It's the safest street in the city."

"Okay, okay. Fine. It was just a stupid car. Being alone in this house freaks me out."

"Well, your day is about to improve. We're having lunch with Riley today." Riley was Lila's partner in her production company, Lilac Films. "Come with! I think he has some good news. One, he made a special trip just to tell me. Two, his voice gave him away."

"What news?"

"Eek! I don't want to jinx it."

I don't remember the name of the place. I suppose it doesn't matter. Jackson Square neighborhood, brick building. Starts with a *C*. Upscale Italian. Fancy wood-fired pizza.

Everything about Riley was crisp and efficient—his clothes, his haircut, the way he spoke. Crisp and efficient pretty much means you're terrified everything is going to fall apart at any second. His eyes searched for the waiter, and then he ordered the most expensive bottle of wine. It seemed kind of early to drink, but it was clear that this was a celebration.

As we waited for the wine, Lila politely looked at all of the cute photos of Marco Alexander, Riley and Jessica's toddler, but you could tell she was impatient to get on with it. As soon as Riley put his phone away, she said, "Well?"

"Green light."

Lila shrieked. It caused a few people to look our way and then look again because maybe that *was* Lila Shore. San Francisco wasn't a big city for celebrities, which is what Lila said she wanted but probably didn't really want.

"I wasn't going to say anything before," she said to me.

"You know how superstitious I am. It was in committee, but we had to wait for it to be gaveled by the president *and* the CEO."

"What, what, what?" I asked. She'd been pissing me off lately, sure, but it was great to see her so excited.

"Warner. A project I've been wanting to do for a long time." She paused a beat for suspense. "A contemporary remake of *Peyton Place*."

She waited for my response. I had no idea what *Peyton Place* was, but I did know that a studio had just agreed to give them a bunch of money to make a film. This was a huge deal, something that was nearly impossible even with a big star attached, let alone sort of a falling star like Lila.

"That's amazing."

"Three women in a small town. Sexual frustration! Steamy undercurrents! God, it's wonderful. We want it to be stylish, rich, all coastal beauty and beautiful people. I'll play the mother of the teenage girl, but she's not a mother-mother. Not a frumpy middle-aged mother. She's the most attractive woman in town. Just repressed. Blond bombshell. Mothers of teenage daughters don't have to look *dowdy*."

"Who are you kidding? You'd never play frumpy and middle-aged," Riley said. "And wait. A little something to help you celebrate." He reached under the table. He handed her a box of chocolates and a bottle of champagne with a ribbon around its neck. Lila loved presents.

"Aw!" She air-kissed him twice and then was on to business. "I want you to scout out Sea Ranch. New Hampshire of the West Coast! Well, small town by the sea. Charming as hell. The main street is perfect. They'll hate us, but we can handle it."

This is what I meant about the Lila who handled things, the Lila who would never be with a guy who pushed her around. And yet, there was that makeup on her arm that day. How were you supposed to understand it? Well, God, 90 percent of history wasn't *understandable*—it was just shit people did to each other.

In the car, Lila gave my cheek a great big kiss. "Things are looking up, baby."

"Wow, Lila."

"There's no guarantee, you know, what will happen. But it's the best news we've had in a while."

"I'm really happy for you."

"For *us*."

"For us."

She took my hand and kissed it. What I felt most was a huge swell of pride for her. Edwina grew up poor, and Lila grew up poor. She changed all that. Men like my father, like Papa Chesterton, like Rex Clancy—they helped her, but they were also obstacles she had to overcome.

"I've got to tell Edwina." In spite of their rocky relationship, she always wanted my grandmother to be among the first to hear any news. Lila called her before we even left the parking lot.

"I'll play the mother of the teenage girl, but she's not a frumpy middle-aged mother. Mothers of teenage daughters don't have to look dowdy," Lila said again.

She kept repeating that part.

CHAPTER TWENTY-SIX

Exhibit 42: Maker's Mark bourbon bottle containing
60 of 750 ml

Everyone was buoyant. Everyone—Lila, Jake, me, and even Max, who sensed the energy in the room and was going with it, speeding around and skidding, snitching kitchen towels and running off.

We ate take-out Indian food. Jake popped open Riley's bottle of champagne. There seemed to be a little sparring and smoothing between Jake and Lila, as if there'd been a disagreement. I couldn't figure it out at first, but then I did. Jake wanted to be a producer on the project, but she said no. He was still kind of pissed about it, but she was joking and kissing and tickling him, all the stuff you do with a guy who gets angry.

We were putting the dishes away when Jake said, "You

know what we should do tonight? For good luck! We oughta watch it."

"What?" I asked.

"*'What?'* I can't believe you just said that!" Jake threw his arms up in disbelief.

I suddenly knew what he meant. *Nefarious*. The film that made her so famous. The one where she plays a murderous seductress. "Nooooo," I pleaded.

"That's not going to boost my confidence," Lila said. "It's only going to make me feel old." But she smiled a little. You could tell she wanted to.

"Aw, come on," Jake said. He put his meaty hands on her hips.

"Ugh. For the absolutely *last* time, then," she said.

I couldn't do it, even if it was supposed to be some part of the celebration we were having. I didn't want to sit there being the third wheel, plus a hundred other reasons.

In my room, I got a text from Nicco. I was surprised because he wasn't supposed to use his phone at work. Tomorrow night, it said. I sent one back: Tomorrow night . . . I let the dot-dot-dot say the stuff I didn't: how much I missed him. How badly I wanted to see him. And then I FaceTimed Meredith.

She was supposed to be coming to see me in about four weeks, but right then, she was getting ready to go on a camping trip with her family. They did stuff like that, camping trips, with aunts and uncles and cousins, fishing and boating and being together. It was like witnessing life on an alien planet, but a really nice planet.

She was in the kitchen, and there were big coolers on the counter, ready to be filled the next morning with stuff like the potato salad Ellen was making in the background. Meredith was trying to look at me and I was trying to look at her, which meant we weren't looking in the camera and could see only each other's eyelids.

"Smell that?" Meredith said. "Brownies."

"You're so mean. Chocolate cruel is the worst cruel."

"Bo said he's going to teach me to water-ski, and that I'm going to get up if it kills him." Bo was her older cousin, who she worshipped. "Don't laugh."

"I'm not laughing! You can totally do it." On crew, Meredith was one of the bow pair, a position where you had to be technically perfect, and she was. But Meredith always made fun of herself in small ways, as if she weren't a good athlete, or weren't smart enough for all the AP classes she was already taking. She was *really* athletic and *hugely* smart, but she did those little subtractions to make other people comfortable.

"He said I should go off the dock at first, which sounds terrifying. Hey, my mom's already worrying about getting to the airport on time when I come see you."

"Never mind!" Ellen shouted from the back.

"She bought a box of travel-size hand sanitizer at Costco."

"Hey, you won't have to buy more until you're eighty."

"She thinks I'm going to fall off one of those cliffs you sent pictures of."

"No way," I said. "Tell her I'll guard you with my life."

"I hear you, Sydney, and I appreciate it!" Ellen yelled in the background.

Meredith told me that Hoodean broke his wrist playing beach volleyball, and then Ellen reminded Meredith about the brownies. Meredith said, "Oh, shit," and then Ellen told her not to say "Oh, shit," and then Meredith had to say, "You just said it yourself," which resulted in some playful shoving. It was like the mother-daughter dream life that maybe 10 percent of the population really had but that you always saw on TV.

"Syd, I better go. I still have to pack for tomorrow."

We said good-bye. I didn't tell her about Nicco or the paintings or the car parked in front of the house. I didn't tell her about the construction guy or Lila's new film deal or about trying to be friendly with Jake even though he sometimes made me feel weird. I didn't tell her that every night when I shut my eyes, I could still feel the anxiety and the icy breath of those ghost whispers. What would she think if she knew?

When I hung up, my chest ached. Hiding makes you so lonely. My throat got tight, and tears welled up, and one dropped off my nose, but I hate to cry, so I forced myself to stop.

Lately, I felt like the part of the cliff that had broken off from the large, solid land. Separate. Sliding, and maybe the waters would be deliciously cold, but wow, they were deep and far down. I'd never really been part of large, solid land, but still.

Max abandoned me to trot downstairs, because we smelled popcorn. He loved popcorn. He could catch it in his mouth if you aimed well. I was double lonely then. Full-on 9-1-1 lonely. I wanted the Mom-and-me moment Meredith was having. I wanted the dad loading the camping cooler into the back of the car. I followed Max to the media room.

"Popcorn!" I yelled to warn Jake and Lila that I was coming so I didn't catch them doing anything I didn't want to see.

Too late. Jake's hand was up the hem of Lila's robe. He moved it quickly when I came in. A half-empty glass of brown liquid and ice sat next to the bowl of popcorn.

"Baby!" Lila said. "Sit down. Come watch."

I looked at the enormous screen. A younger Lila/Alexa was getting ready in the tiny bathroom of her apartment. Putting on lipstick, pulling up stockings. Wiggling into a skirt with nothing underneath. In a minute, she'd be driving over to Brandon Searing/Leo Garfield's house, where she'd climb that ladder in his library.

"We're almost at the best part," Jake said.

What was I thinking? Loneliness was way better than that. *Way.* Stick me out on an ice floe for a hundred years. "Never mind," I said.

"Baby! Where're you going? You can stay! Come back."

"Never mind!" I yelled.

"Push pause, would you?" Lila said to Jake. "Syd-Syd!" she called.

"Leave me *alone*." I was halfway up the stairs, but I could still hear it.

"Leave her alone," Jake said.

Jesus, that house. You could hear everything. Including Lila and Jake going at it that night. Having sex, not fighting. Ugh! I don't even want to think about it. I mean, come on! I just wanted out of there. I felt like I was in one of Lila's movies, the trapped daughter of a seductress mother. This was another premonition, only I didn't know it yet.

I pulled on the shorts and tank top that I'd worn that morning, plus a hoodie. It would be cold out there in the dark, up high without any walls for shelter.

No one was parked outside that night. The street was empty, except for a neighbor's cat, who scurried off to hide under a car when he saw me. It was creepy. Shivery, eerie. But, strangely, I wanted that right then—the nervous thrill you feel in the pit of your stomach. Danger could seem like an answer to loneliness and boredom and restlessness. It could maybe fill hungers that didn't have names.

Every day, new fragments had been added to the house next door. More skeleton bones; additional rooms growing skyward. The streetlamp cast freaky shadows in there. I walked around in the empty spaces. Here was the living room; here was the kitchen; this was a guest room, probably. On the third floor, up that staircase with no rails, I sat at the edge of what was likely the master bedroom. I hung my legs over, a story higher than last time.

That view was killer. Oh, shit—pardon the word. But the point is, I looked at all of the twinkly lights. I pulled my sweatshirt over my arms against the cold and the darkness. And I wanted *IT, IT, IT* again—everything, the safety of those rooms, the danger of that exposed height. Like Lila, I wanted to feel protected, but also like Lila, I wanted danger, too. I wanted that as I stood with my toes at the edge of that high-up place and let the sea air swallow me. I wanted to feel alive. To *be* dangerous. To do dangerous things. Couldn't I have that?

I sat down. I stared at the moon.

And it sucked, you know. I was angry.

Because only a guy like Shane, with his physical power, knew he could have both. I didn't have arms like his, and arms like that could be used against me, so I had to be careful. I couldn't be dangerous whenever I wanted. I would never feel as safe as Shane, or Jake, or even my father likely did. And I understood it then, why we sometimes pick guys like that—to have a set of ruthless arms, even if they aren't our own.

Sometimes, it seems like your whole world is made for someone else.

CHAPTER TWENTY-SEVEN

Exhibit 43: Photo of master bedroom from doorway,
716 Sea Cliff Drive

"So who is this boy?" Lila asked.

"Just a boy. Don't make a big deal about it."

They were about to meet. Nicco was picking me up to take me to that all-ages music club, Slim's, in South of Market. He'd gotten us tickets to see Armor Class Zero, a new band I'd never heard of. "Who is this boy?" didn't mean his name, which she already knew. It meant, *Tell me everything about him before he hits the buzzer for the gate.*

She had her full makeup on, with her hair loose, and she wore a white tank top, with fitted jeans and a big belt. Bare feet. You know, famous-person casual. Of course, she looked stunning. Her voice was bright, like she was already getting into character. We were in the kitchen and she was fussing, straightening the coffee maker, wiping a smudge on the counter with her fingertip, as if these were the things a regular mother did.

I know all of this sounds like I'm being critical. I *am* being critical, but of course I'm saying this now. *After.* Right then, I was just anxious. I wanted her to like Nicco, but I also wanted him to like her. I felt worried and protective of her. I wanted him to see all of the good, loving parts she had.

The gate buzzed and Max lost his mind. I let Nicco in. It was funny to see him in my house. Two parts of my life were smashing together, and it looked wrong. But there he was, with his sweet face and tousled hair. Wearing jeans and a white T-shirt, an outfit very similar to Lila's, whereas I was in an orange sundress. When Max realized who was there, he went crazy. He bumped against Nicco, and wound through his legs, and tried to jump up with his big body. Two parts of *Max's* life were smashing together.

And then Lila breezed in. Clichéd word, but really, she moved like wind past a curtain.

"Nicco! Is that right? Do I have that right?" She held out her hand.

He held out his, and Lila gave her famous two-handed shake, swallowing his hand in hers. "Yeah. That's right. Great to meet you, Ms. Shore."

"Lila! Call me Lila! And look at us." She lined herself up next to him. "Twins."

"I guess so." He smiled but kept one hand on Max, scruffing his neck. Nicco's eyes jetted around the White Room and out at the view. "Wow. Beautiful."

"Hey, I'm old enough to be your mother," Lila said, and then she laughed her twinkly laugh at her own joke. "So, you're going to Slim's?"

"Yeah."

"Who're you seeing?"

"Armor Class Zero?" He sounded unsure.

"Oh, yeah!" Lila said, like she was remembering an old favorite. Lila rarely listened to music, let alone a punk band that had just started playing together, like, a year ago.

"You've heard of them?"

"'Barbarian.' Crazy guitar riff after the second bridge."

"You do know them," he said, and she winked.

She looped her arm around me then. Sometimes she tried to act like we were sisters, but we weren't sisters.

"We better get going," I said. I inched away. Zipped my bag so my phone wouldn't fall out.

"Have a great time! Have her back by . . . well, you guys are old enough to decide."

There was more awkward hand shaking. Outside, Nicco said, "Oh, man. I just froze."

"It's okay," I said. "You did great."

But he didn't do great. That sounds awful, but I'm trying to describe how it was. He didn't do great because he didn't do all the stuff he should have. He should have said he was honored to meet her, or that he loved her work, or something.

He should have laughed at her joke and made one back. I felt a slide of worry. She wouldn't like him. I should have told him the rules. I should have told him how to *be*.

Then again, maybe he knew the rules. Maybe he knew them and had broken them anyway. Maybe he'd just acted the way he always did.

When we got in the car, the awkwardness came with us. It sat there as he started the van and pulled away from the curb. As we drove down our block, the Lamborghini rounded the corner.

"Whoa," Nicco said. "I'm pretending I see those all the time."

"That's Jake."

"*That's* Jake? Should we stop?"

"No. You can meet him another time."

But he saw me. Jake did. He caught my eyes. I saw it in two seconds: bewilderment, concern. Curiosity. Eyes, eyes, eyes.

"No biggie. My moms drive those. Leslie, blue. Amy, red."

I looked over at him. I'd lost track of the conversation.

"Leslie, shit-brown Honda. Amy, one-hundred-thousand-mile Hyundai that runs on twenty bucks of gas money at a time."

He took my hand, and he was Nicco again. It was us. The us at the labyrinth and Camera Obscura, the us in our photos. It occurred to me that if he'd broken those rules, he might break others. He might, oh God, *disagree* with Lila. He might say what he really meant. He might be entirely himself. The thought gave me a sick pit in my stomach. It would be bad then. The clash would be awful.

But the thought gave me something else, too. A thrill. A quiet, underground tremor of hope. He might be entirely himself, and it would be good then. The clash would be magnificent.

At Slim's, the line stretched to the corner. Night was falling and there was that excited energy of anticipation. Little clumps of friends were pushing each other and laughing. The smell of weed wafted past.

It was already crowded by the time Nicco and I got in there. A few people sat at a couple of tables by the stage, but aside from them, everyone stood, all packed in. The opening band started. I forget their name. They seemed to play forever. We edged our way to the bar. Nicco got us a couple of Cokes. I was surprised he didn't have a fake ID or something. It seemed like everyone there was drinking, even people our age. Maybe they'd snuck it in.

Nicco was reading my mind, because when he handed the cup to me, he said, "This okay?"

"Oh, yeah," I said. "Of course." I was glad. I mean, I'd just turned sixteen. My group of friends didn't drink a lot, not yet, or maybe never. Meredith hated that kind of thing. Hoodean thought his brother already had a problem with it.

"I don't know," Nicco said, leaning in so I could hear him with all that noise. "My moms are always . . ." He mimed inhaling a joint. "Hazy. It bugs me. I don't want to miss the—"

"Dragon belt buckle." I pointed.

"Twin haircuts of love." He nodded toward the two girls with the same short hair moussed high up, holding hands. "I want to be *here*."

I hooked my fingers in his belt loop and gave it a shake. "I want to be here, too." We met eyes. It happened. That crazy electric thing. Even with that smooshing crowd of people, we held our gaze, and damn it, *that* would have been the time for him to kiss me.

We edged through the crowd to get closer to the stage. The place was really packed. Someone grabbed my butt, but when I looked around, I couldn't tell who. It was like a party for ass grabbers. A free-for-all. Hey, you're welcome, because yeah, an actual body could be treated like a dish of candy.

Finally, the opening band stopped and gathered their stuff, and Armor Class Zero came out one by one. The crowd whooped and yelled and whistled. I didn't know what to expect, but I liked it. It was fun punk, not angry punk, and Nicco settled in behind me and we danced until we were sweaty, and occasionally he'd bend and say something in my ear, and his breath was hot, and it made me shiver.

They played "Barbarian," and yeah, it was the song everyone knew, but it wasn't the best song.

The bass player struck a few opening chords of another piece the crowd recognized. There were a few catcalls of "Yeah!" The flashing lights slowed. The room seemed to settle. Nicco put his arms around me from behind. I loved that. I loved it so much.

And then they played this song, "Divine Spell." Slow. Smoky.

God. Even in that room, which was growing almost unbearably hot and steamy, the song did what music can do, what the energy of a concert can do, and I turned to face Nicco and we danced close. And, Jesus, we still didn't kiss, but things were charged between us. The energy was.

It stayed that way, the energy. The crackle of electricity. Different tremors underground, but definitely felt. Strong enough to rumble, to tell you that something much larger was coming.

We got out into the night air. It was so cool after that steamy room, it was almost like diving into a pool.

"Let's go," he said, and we ran. We wanted to get out of that parking lot before it got jammed.

We reached his van. Suddenly we weren't in a hurry anymore. We were up against that van. He put his hands on either side of my face and leaned in and kissed me hard. It got hot fast. Oh, wow. Our hands . . . all over, and the door handle dug into my back and I couldn't care less. This was nothing like Samuel Crane. *Nothing.*

Nicco felt it too. He pulled away. "Whoa," he said.

We got in the car. It was still there, that heat. He put his hand on my leg as he drove, and God, even that.

When we got back to the Sea Cliff house, Nicco pulled up in front. He kept the engine running. We said good night, but he was being careful. It was like we both held a burning torch just a few inches away from what was there between us.

I was glad that no one was awake when I got in. I was stricken.

So that's what desire was.

No wonder it caused such trouble.

CHAPTER TWENTY-EIGHT

Exhibit 44: Photo of master bedroom, bed, 716 Sea Cliff Drive

The next morning, I got a text.

You, it said.

You, I texted back.

Nicco was working at his moms' shop that day, and at the restaurant that night. I wouldn't see him. Damn, you know, he worked *a lot*. I felt a yearning, an empty, endless cave, but a nice cave that could lead to another, enchanted land. It was a delicious not-having. All of me felt awake. A giant barrier to how the world worked had been rolled away, and now I saw past it, and I understood so much more, like all those words in the songs, and maybe even why people did stupid things for love. Or crazy things for love. You didn't feel just hungry, but *hungryhungryhungry*.

A worry gnawed at me, though. I had kissed back so hard, and my hands had been free all over him, and this wasn't the game you were supposed to play. Not if you were a good girl, not if you wanted love, too. There were two choices, to be the sexy girl or the good girl, and there didn't seem to be an option to be both. You had to choose your camp, and if you chose good, you'd better hide your desire, because desire said you were lying about your goodness. I hadn't hidden it very well.

My hunger was seeping through the cracks of the secret vault, because *wow*. No one else had felt *this*. This exact thing with this exact person. Our chemical reaction seemed too particular and powerful to be regular. The formula felt epic.

Lila and Jake were sleeping in. It was Sunday. Two Sundays ago, Jake had actually made French toast. He had all that fancy cooking stuff. I liked it so much, that smell in the house. It was a family smell. It sounds stupid, but French toast was another thing that made me forget that bruise on Lila's arm. Regular, daily stuff can pile up on a terrible thing so you can pretend you never saw it.

On that morning, though, after the concert, Jake wasn't up, opening kitchen drawers and cracking eggs. Their bedroom door was shut. I ate some cereal. All of the little oat circles kept saying Nicco's name, and showing Nicco's face, and Nicco's hands and mouth. Then, so did the milk carton, and all of those glossy white cabinets, and the ticking White Room clock.

After the night with Nicco, I wanted the whole world, *all* of life, more than ever. I wanted to eat it like it was a giant sandwich. I wanted to go outside and stick myself into the middle of the city and wrap it around me. I decided to get on my bike and explore, maybe go all the way over to where North Beach connected to Chinatown, where City Lights Bookstore was. Five miles on some serious hills, big deal. That morning, I could conquer anything.

"I wish you could ride a bike," I told Max. "You could come." He looked sorry about that too. "I'll make it up to you, okay, boy?"

I leaned down. I kissed his soft dog head. "I love you," I told him. He said it back with his eyes. He always said it, like, a hundred times a day.

I mapped my route and filled my water bottle. And on my way out the door, I did something I should have done long before. I dumped R. W. Wright in the trash.

How had I never really noticed that every day was a new day? What a fabulous, amazing idea that was, whoever decided it. I wheeled my bike out of the garage.

And then I stopped. I stopped cold.

There was that car again. It was definitely the same car.

And Jake was there too. *Outside.* He wasn't asleep next to Lila after all. No, he was up, and he was in this white spa robe, the kind Papa Chesterton used to have. His hairy legs stuck out underneath. He looked like he'd just woken up. He was leaning in the driver's-side window of that vehicle. I couldn't hear what they were saying, but I could hear the tenor of their voices. And the conversation was heated. He was out on our street, not dressed, arguing, and this was a street, understand, where you just didn't go out in your robe and show your short temper, the uglier sides of yourself.

His voice got louder. An actual shout. "You'll hear from my lawyer, asshole!" He flipped a middle finger.

Something was very wrong. Something was off kilter, and it was bad. And I knew it because his feet were bare, and his chest hair was spilling out of his hurriedly tied robe, and because the venetian blinds parted on the neighbor's house and someone peeked out.

You just didn't do stuff like that. Not on that street, where there was order and beauty. Not where even a leaf on the ground was a sign that things were out of control.

I pedaled away fast, so Jake would only see my back retreating. This was supposed to be a happy and brave excursion, but God, what just happened? I tried to steer my thoughts back to the blue sky, my hands gripping the handlebars, the big world, yet all I could see was Jake yelling in his robe. I rode down Lake Street and into fancy Presidio Heights, quiet, tree lined, mansion filled—well, you know.

And then—what was I thinking?—I had to ride up Nob Hill. But it got so steep that I had to get off and walk. I huffed. *You'll hear from my lawyer, asshole!* my mind repeated again and again. I didn't know who exactly was in that car, but it was very clear that Jake was in serious trouble, and that the man was a threat to him and us.

I was approaching Chinatown. I could tell by the red Chinese lettering on the signs, and by the markets, and the red lanterns on the lampposts. I got glimpses of San Francisco Bay. I was almost there. And then, wow, things got really busy. Traffic, the streets going this way and that, the big triangle of the Transamerica building. I shoved Jake out of my mind; I forced him away, because, you know, look around—I'd gotten my own self right to the center of things. I was proud about that, and it was exciting out there. Lombard, the crookedest street in the world, was to the north, and beyond that, Ghirardelli Square and Alcatraz. And more and more and more. I'd been hanging out at the beach, yet there was all this stuff, too.

And then there it was. The big orange-and-black building on the corner. One of the most important bookstores ever. I was seriously thrilled, because I knew it had been the gathering place for all of those beat poets and writers in the fifties. The street in the back is even called Jack Kerouac Alley. Meredith loved that stuff, so I started taking pictures like mad and texting her, and she was texting back. In the windows, they had all these signs, like STAND UP TO POWER and THERE IS NO PROGRESS WITHOUT STRUGGLE and COURAGE IS THE TRIUMPH OVER FEAR. I felt like, *Yes, yes, yes!* And when I went in, I was overcome by all those spines and words, because it seemed like I'd entered one of the only places where you *could* actually find true power.

It was hard not to buy everything, but the ride was hard enough without a heavy pack. I limited myself to two books, even though I went up and down every aisle. I was about to head to the cashier when something caught my eye. A familiar pouf of white, a sun hat tied around a neck.

Agatha.

Agatha! Agatha, Agatha, Agatha! It was so awesome. I was so happy to see her. I almost said, "Hey!" except I remembered that she didn't know me. It was funny to see her with clothes on. She wore little jeans and an orange T-shirt with a half-risen sun on it. I forgot she'd have to wear clothes at places other than Baker.

She was sort of my lucky person. She had things to tell me, I was sure. So I watched her for a minute. She was in the travel section. She pulled out a book. I crept closer so I could spy on the title. *Destination: Oregon Coast.* She briefly held it to her chest and then went to pay for it.

It made me so happy. God, I felt great. In spite of Jake and that car, I felt *so great*. Look at all the beautiful coincidences and adventures and . . . and . . . *and* that life had!

Since I'd just broken up with R. W. Wright, I got an Elena Ferrante novel with rough-cut pages, and that ancient and superthick *The Agony and the Ecstasy* book that Cora kept talking about. I tucked my treasures into my pack.

Back on the street, I decided to walk my bike for a bit, until I got out of that busy intersection of Broadway and Columbus.

I was passing this funny, old-time motor inn, thinking about how it was such a weird place to have a motel, when a man called out.

"Miss! Miss!" he yelled. It was urgent, and my first thought was that he was warning me. Like maybe I'd dropped my wallet, or was walking where I shouldn't. I was trying to take it all in, this middle-aged white guy in front of me wearing track pants and a T-shirt, when, boom, there it was. His penis, over his waistband, looking more like a mollusk dangling out of its shell than anything else.

"Ew, ick," I said.

I wasn't trying to be brave or bold. The words just popped out. I mean, I'd seen plenty of dicks at Baker Beach, and this one was pretty stomach turning. Kind of like when a fast-food ad shows some new disgusting creation, and you're just . . . *Uh, no. Gross.*

When I really realized what was happening, though, what was actually happening, I got scared. I hurried away. I got on my bike and rode. I was speeding, but then all of a sudden, my legs were wobbly. My stomach rose to my throat with nausea, and I pedaled a couple of blocks but then I didn't want to ride anymore. My eyes darted around, nervous. I was seriously creeped out. I worried other men would spring out at any moment, saying, *Miss! Miss!*

It took something from me. I know that's what that asshole probably wanted, but it worked. It forcefully grabbed my joy and slammed it down. All the good feelings I was just having about the world and my place in it—they were snuffed out like a lit match under a boot heel. Flame extinguished, made dirty, kicked to the nearest curb. A few years ago, I could put vinegar and baking soda together and make a papier-mâché volcano explode, but I didn't feel so powerful now.

I tried to talk myself out of what I felt. I was okay. Nothing had happened, really. Nothing terrible. Every dude has one, big deal. I was fine.

I wasn't, though.

I dialed. "Lila?"

"Baby! What's wrong? You're crying! Are you okay?"

"Can you come get me?"

CHAPTER TWENTY-NINE

Exhibit 45: Photo of master bedroom, floor, facing
north, 716 Sea Cliff Drive

Lila sent Jake. He was driving her Land Rover because my bike wouldn't fit in his car. He got out and manhandled the bike into the back. I took my helmet off, and it looked kind of sad down on the floor, because it had failed to protect me.

"Hey, thanks," I said. He wasn't the yelling, raging man from that morning. He was calm and in control, wearing fashionable jeans and a crisp, bright polo shirt. His cologne wafted over, a little too strong, as he settled into the driver's seat. It almost seemed like I'd imagined it, him in his robe out on the street. "Where's Lila?"

"She hates driving in this part of the city. I was up anyway. What happened? Some flasher?"

"Yeah."

"You can't let that stuff get to you, you know?"

I didn't say anything. He was there to help me. But my distrust of him was sliding back, and it pissed me off, too, what he said. *He* didn't have to let that stuff get to him, because it would never happen to him.

"Hey. Look at this day, huh? Blue sky. Summer in California!" He looked over at me. He was trying. "This isn't the Lam, for sure. But I bet I can still make this baby go fast." Jake hit the accelerator and we sped up, the engine revving. A biker looked over his shoulder and glared. We were going to end up in that Acura's back seat.

"Jake!"

He chuckled. Slowed. "I thought you liked speed."

"I do."

"You do?" He hit the accelerator again. The light turned red just as we crossed.

"Maybe not now. And not when you're about to kill us!" I gripped my armrest.

"All right, all right," he said.

He turned on the stereo for a minute and then turned it off. "Speakers are worthless."

We sat in awkward silence for a while, and then he finally said, "I saw you in that piece-of-shit van last night. Who was that? You got a new boyfriend?"

"Not exactly."

"What exactly?"

"Just . . . Nicco. A boy I met."

"What do you know about him? Do you know who his friends are? You gotta know who his friends are."

I remembered what Lila had said about the people Jake used to do business with. His *associates*. And after that morning, it seemed like we *all* should know who his *enemies* were.

"Said from personal experience, huh?" I lifted my eyebrows in accusation.

He gave me a funny look and then drummed his fingers on the steering wheel.

"I saw *you*, too. By that car this morning. Who was *that*?"

"What?"

"This morning. You were arguing with some guy. I've seen him parked out there before. I mean, *why*? You were *yelling*."

Jake waved his hand. "Forget about it. It's nothing. Business. One of my guys. You don't need to worry about it. I got it handled."

I folded my arms, stared out the window.

"Right? You hear me?"

I kept my mouth shut. It seemed like there were a lot of things I was supposed to overlook or forget.

He drove around the city, assertive and confident. He rolled down his window and stuck his elbow out. He sped through the yellow lights. He spoke like everything he said was fact. He was the one who knew the ultimate truth about Lila's speakers. And I'm embarrassed to admit it, especially now, but he was big, and intimidating, and powerful, too. He had it *handled*.

And all of those things together made him feel . . . God, I'm sorry to say this: *safe*.

But intimidation and power could be used against you as much as for you. And the biggest dangers can start right under your own roof. They spread and stretch like fire, like the multiplying cells of DNA.

Like the generations. Like history.

That evening, Lila lit a bunch of candles outside, and the doors to the White Room were flung open. The outdoor table was set. She was really trying. We all were. Trying hard to be regular, whatever that was. Artisanal pizzas were warming in the oven. Little glasses of red wine were poured, three of them— one for me, as well. She wanted to be the cool, progressive mom, but I wasn't sure I liked wine. And I kind of preferred the nerdy mom, like Ellen, who didn't even let you drink diet soda, let alone alcohol.

Jake was there too, wearing one of those expensive Hawaiian shirts guys over forty wear. He thought he saw a blue whale. He could have, but maybe he didn't. He kept saying they migrated that time of year, and we were making fun of him, but he might have been right. He kept *insisting* he was right, ticked off that we'd doubt him.

"Come on, girls! Let's have a look!" He had the binoculars. He was heading down the stairs to the beach. I followed, but Lila protested. "My shoes!" She had her platform sandals on. "I hate getting all messy!"

Down there on the sand, Jake and I handed the binoculars back and forth. He had his shoes off, feet in the water. Nothing. It was maybe a log. Or a sea lion. "We lost him," he said finally.

"Bummer," I said.

My own dad—the last time I saw him was at his house the year before. He kept saying I should come for a visit, so I finally did. He had a new girlfriend. She was young and walked around in her bikini, and it wouldn't last. He liked women as if he wanted all of them. He'd flirt with baristas and department store clerks, girls on his staff, women on street corners. The first day I was there, he was all bright and interested, asking me questions, taking me out to restaurants, introducing me to people he knew. But by the third day, his eyes would stray when I talked to him. He wasn't listening to anything I was saying. He went out with the girlfriend on the fourth night, even though I was leaving in the morning. I felt like the Christmas toy you asked for, were all excited to get, but that was actually kind of boring.

A shot of water hit me in the cheek. It was Jake, squirting me, doing that cool trick with both hands cupped together.

"Hey!" I protested. Then, "I always wanted to know how to do that."

"Like this." He showed me. "Try it."

I did. I managed a little burble.

"You gotta practice." He laughed. "Aw, shit. I sounded just like my old man right then."

"Did he teach you how to do that?"

"Yeah, like, when I was seven. He was an asshole otherwise."

"Too bad."

"The ladies loved him, even though he was a mean motherfucker."

Lila leaned over the edge of the wall. "Guys! Guys!" she yelled. "Guys, come on!"

At least, that's what I thought she was saying. All I could hear was *Eyes, eyes, eyes.*

"We've *got* to talk about the boy!" Lila said. The sun was setting. The candles flickered, and there was all that ocean and orange sky, the Golden Gate Bridge glittering and majestic in the distance. It was really beautiful. We had so much.

"Noooo," I said.

"He was so nervous! He was a deer in the headlights!"

"Well, Lila . . . ," Jake said. He refilled their glasses. Drank from his. "What do you expect?"

"Confidence. A firm handshake."

My stomach twisted. I felt protective of Nicco, but there was an awful knot of shame, too.

"You gotta see who his friends are," Jake said again.

Lila sipped her drink. "I'm sure Syd can take care of herself."

Jake laughed a little *heh-heh-heh*. I'd heard that laugh before. He used it when Lila tried to order the wine when we went out to dinner once. But my father used it too, when his girl-friend said something about the stock market, and heck, even Meredith's dad used it whenever Ellen talked sports. It was a superior laugh, meant to imply that no words were even needed to convey how silly you were.

"She's right. I can," I said.

"I wouldn't let that one date until she was twenty-one. At *least*." He waggled his finger in my direction.

"Oh really." Lila's voice had an edge.

"Look at her! I know how boys are."

"You certainly are protective."

Just like that, the evening took an abrupt turn.

"Damn right I am," Jake said.

"Wow, even *her father* isn't *that* involved in her love life."

"Gee, thanks a lot," I said. But no one heard me, because right then, Lila and I both reached for our glasses at the same time, and I knocked mine over. It fell against the plate of breadsticks with a crash, soaking them. The glass was full, and the red liquid gushed, rapidly covering the table.

"Shit," Lila said. "Shit!"

"I'm sorry!" I said.

Lila pushed her chair back in anger and went inside. As Jake mopped up the mess with a stack of napkins, I saw the muscle in his cheek twitch, in that place where anger sits and simmers. I pressed a kitchen towel to the tablecloth. Our hands bumped. His big, thick knuckles met mine. He caught my eyes. He held them again, same as he did before.

"Hey," he said. And then he shrugged. I didn't know what that meant, but I knew what it felt like. Us together, her not there at all.

Flame on paper, catching on kindling. Before you know it, the house is on fire, and then the block, and then the city, and you are running outside, holding only your wedding photo.

That night, Nicco called after work. I didn't tell him about any of this, how tense our house was. I didn't tell him about Jake and that guy in the car, or about the huge fight Lila and Jake had after the wineglass spilled. You should have heard how loud they were. I'm sure the neighbors did.

I didn't tell him about the flasher, either. It felt shameful, to be the one that man chose. I worried it said something about me. Like I had an invisible marking that meant I would invite things other people wouldn't invite.

I didn't want to tell Nicco about all the ways things were broken. The way *I* was. My real self wasn't shiny and perfect and fascinating and whole. Even my own dad was only interested in me for two days max.

I was afraid to be seen. But I really, really wanted to be seen. More than anything.

CHAPTER THIRTY

Exhibit 46: Sworn statements of William and Eva Rand, 128 Sea Cliff Drive
Exhibit 47: Sworn statement of Priscilla Ruby, 129 Sea Cliff Drive

But Nicco let himself be seen. It was always a risk, to show yourself, one that some people were more willing to take. Or more *able* to take, probably because it hadn't sucked so bad when they tried it before.

By this time, Nicco and I were talking on the phone several times a day, meeting whenever we could at the beach or some food place or for ten minutes in his car. We'd take whatever we could get, you know, just to see each other. And then, God, there'd be the twisted clothes and the frustration of public places and gearshifts and all that kissing.

Finally, though, we were going to his apartment for the

first time. Before we did, we had to stop by his moms' house on Cabrillo. Leslie, his mom-mom, the one who gave birth to him (his words), had something to give him. The something was a vegetarian casserole and corn muffins. His moms lived in a Victorian house that they shared with a single guy who rented the basement apartment. We pulled up in Nicco's van, and then he looked at me and shrugged, like, *It is what it is.*

"Stop," I said.

"Okay, come on, then."

We took the steps up to the front door. In the entry, there was an old piano that now held several potted plants. In the corner, a huge, flat-leafed palm wound its way up another set of stairs and to the ceiling.

"Hey!" Nicco shouted.

"In the kitchen!" Leslie shouted back.

I was nervous. This was Nicco's mom. One of them. And you could tell she and he were close, by the way he talked about her. Upstairs, Leslie was crimping foil over a large baking dish. The windows of the small kitchen were open, and I could hear the neighbors playing Latin music. Framed vintage fruit crate labels hung on one wall, and a long row of salt and pepper shakers in various forms—chefs, dogs, smiling tomatoes, cowboy hats—lined the windowsill. Leslie wore a breezy sundress, which covered her solid frame. Her short hair was a lawn of gray, spiky grass. She took my hand in her warm one. Her eyes were as kind as Nicco's. "You must be Sydney," she said.

I was happy she knew about me. "It's great to meet you," I said.

"Likewise. Definitely." She looped her arm around Nicco's waist. "This kid. This one." She kissed his cheek.

"We're only here for a minute," he said.

"No worries. Next time, you can stay longer and we'll talk more."

She hugged us both, and Nicco took the food and thanked his mom. In spite of our differences, I saw the similarities Nicco and I had too—no siblings, no father, more than enough mother. On the way out, I spotted other pieces of his life in this house where he'd grown up. A cushy sofa and a jammed bookcase with a bong sitting on one of the shelves. A wood coffee table that was stacked with magazines.

"Small house," he said.

"Big hearts," I said back.

"You know that casserole was just an excuse to meet you, right?"

"I figured."

"It could feed ten people on a yoga retreat."

In the van, Nicco started the engine. I was nervous, but I wanted to get there. "How far to your place?" I asked. The Buddha smiled at me.

"Not far." Nicco reached over and took my hand. And then it happened again, as it always did when his fingers laced in mine—the sudden energy, the want. I moved my other hand up his arm. He let go, set his hand on my leg, and stroked my skin. Then he gripped my leg hard before he took his hand back.

"Oh, man," he said.

"I know."

"There's too much space between us."

"For sure."

A red light. He leaned way over, kissed me hard. It was easy to get lost in that. The car behind us honked. Who knew how long the light had been green.

"You've made me lucky," he said, because he found a parking spot right in front of the Cambodian restaurant. Across the street, there was a Russian bakery and a Russian bookstore, and I spotted an Irish bar and a sushi place. Four countries of cuisine on one block—what more could you want?

He punched a code to open the door next to the restaurant, which led to a staircase. We hurried up. Another door, another lock. It opened to a small room with a futon and two old leather chairs, and a kitchen with a pot in the sink.

"Vince never does his dishes," Nicco said, but I couldn't care less. I just covered his mouth with a kiss, and his hands were on me, and we were back-back-backing up to his room until we landed on a bed. A whole, huge, luxurious bed. Luxurious, meaning there was space and privacy, not that it was fancy. It had been made in a hurry—green sheets, a duvet flattened by the years, a woven blue blanket on top. The smell of the restaurant was in the room—something frying, something fishy, plus smoky wood barbecue. None of that mattered. When I opened my eyes, I saw Nicco above me, as well as a huge, beautifully patterned tapestry, from his moms' store probably, a deep blue and red with little gold threads and shiny discs.

We kissed for a long time, too long, until it turned into hands, mouths, fingers, up, over, in—a fevered *hurry*. I wanted more, more, more. Our T-shirts were off, shorts half undone. His skin felt so good against mine. But then he rolled off of me. Sat up.

"Wait, wait," he said.

"It's okay," I said. I didn't think I wanted to wait. I was nervous, yeah. This was a huge leap from Samuel Crane, but I wanted to know what sex was, and I wanted to know with Nicco. *I* wanted to choose this. My body seemed to belong to everyone else. It might *never* be mine, when beliefs about it went back eons.

Me, my choice. If this would change me, I wanted to be changed. This was part of *IT.* Not the whole thing, but a big piece, and I knew that for sure from the way my heart pounded like a fist on a door. I held his wrist, pulled him back toward me.

But Nicco stayed where he was. He was trying to slow things down. I was embarrassed. I sat up. I held my shirt to my bare chest. I didn't understand what was happening. I'd thought he was making sure I wanted to do what we were about to do, but that's not why he'd pulled away. Was I being too aggressive or something? Did he think I was *that kind of a girl*, so now he was turned off? Was he crazy? Was he from another planet? I mean, supposedly every guy wanted sex, and was ready for sex at any second, right? Do you see how complicated this all was? Because girls could have misconceptions about guys, too.

"Syd," he said. His voice was hoarse. He shook his head. *"What?"*

I wanted to cry. Maybe I was a little mad. I didn't know what this meant, because I'd never been in this place before. I was wondering if I was doing stuff wrong. And Nicco *had* been in that place before. He'd had sex with a girlfriend before me, Anna. When I thought of her and him, I was sure I was doing stuff wrong.

"Don't look so sad! I just don't want to rush this, you know?"

He sat there with his pants undone and his arm around my bare shoulders. I felt stupid like that. Humiliated. I put my shirt back on. "God, don't misunderstand. I want you. I want you so bad. But I want some time in this part. The getting-to-know-each-other part. If we have sex . . . it'll change every-thing."

Okay, okay, I understood, I guess, even if I was embarrassed and ashamed and suddenly worried about what he thought of me, though Nicco was never like that, not ever. But the thing was, it had already changed. From the moment we kissed out-side after that concert, when we stumbled into this whole, I don't know, *landscape* of desire, nothing had been the same. How were we supposed to pretend it wasn't there? We felt it when we were in his car and at the beach and just eating some sandwich at a café. When we were at his apartment, we felt it. When we were sitting on a blanket at Golden Gate Park, we felt it. This force, this power between us. Something deep and necessary and urgent.

When he drove me home that day, there it was again. Even though he'd tried to slow it down earlier, it was there. Good luck getting rid of it. Good luck ever getting that out of your head. I was glad. I liked it. It felt huge and powerful, and I wanted him to *know* it wasn't going anywhere, as if he didn't already. People said this changed over time, that you felt less desire the longer you were with each other. This seemed impossible. How could it change over time? It felt like a heat that would only build upon itself, more likely to blaze out of control than burn out.

CHAPTER THIRTY-ONE

Exhibit 48: Sworn statement of Leslie C. Ricci

When I went home, I found something awful. Not at first. At first, I went upstairs. My mind had gone all irrational and self-pitying, you know, thinking maybe I'd never be good enough for a man to really want me. I mean, sure, the Shanes of the world might like my boobs, my ass, the candy in the dish, but what about the whole, real girl and the men who mattered? In my frustration and confusion, I took off my shoes and dropped my purse on the bed. My lip gloss fell out and rolled underneath, and I was mad at everything, so I just thought, *Good. Stay there.* The lip gloss out of my reach seemed like the way my life was going in general.

Before we left Nicco's apartment, he'd changed into the familiar black pants and white shirt. I watched him do up the buttons and zip up the zipper, which was the wrong direction of things, I thought. A failure, for sure.

I didn't know what I wanted to do with the whole night ahead. No one was home, so I had no idea what the dinner plan was. I didn't really want to be around anyone anyway.

And then I realized: It was quiet. In my stupid fog, I hadn't noticed that Max didn't come to greet me. He hadn't even barked, as he always did when a car drove up. And Jake never took him anywhere. Max was pretty much another thing that Jake had acquired, like his car, like that art, like his various properties. Like Lila.

This was an emergency. Suddenly, I had no doubt.

"Max?" I yelled. "Come here, boy!"

I ran downstairs. What if he'd gotten out somehow? Maybe Lila had left a door open.

"Max! Come on, bud!"

I dashed around, searching the rooms. And then, oh God, I saw him. He was in the kitchen. Under the table. He looked at me with those eyes that meant he was obviously not okay, eyes that said something had gone really wrong. I looked around. In the kitchen, I found that box of chocolates that Riley had given Lila that day in the restaurant. The box was open. The lid was flung off and partly chewed, and little brown paper cups were scattered on the floor. The chocolate was gone. There was also a coffee cup nearby, knocked on its side. Max loved coffee. You had to be very careful where you put your cup, because you'd come back to find him slurping like a hurried businessman late for work.

"Oh, no. No." I didn't know much about dogs, but I knew chocolate could be lethal. Chocolate and coffee—man, it was like finding the rock star with a pile of empty syringes.

I tried to call Lila. My hands shook from panic. No answer. I tried to call Nicco, but he must have had the ringer off already, since Mary, his boss, had a no-phones policy.

Alarm raced through me, but I didn't know what to do. How could they have let this happen? I found the pet poison control line. How much did he weigh? No idea. A lot. How much chocolate had he eaten, and what kind? No idea, no idea. "Bring him in to see a vet," they said.

"I'm sorry, buddy. Hang in there, Max boy." What was the matter with these people? How could they be so careless with living beings? I tried Lila again. Nothing. Then I called Jake's cell number, written on that pad by the phone. When he answered, I told him everything in a rush.

"Can't come now, Syd. I'm right in the middle of something important."

"*This* is important. I can't get to his vet! I don't even know who his vet *is*! I don't know where to go or what to do! *Please*, Jake."

"Give me an hour."

"They said to bring him in *now*! Not an hour from now. *Now* now. He could *die*. Jake, we need you! *I* need you."

"Shit! Shit, fine! I'll be right there."

I urged Max up. I wished I could lift him in my arms, but no way. I yanked and pulled and got him outside. I didn't want to waste another minute. I had no idea how long he'd been there like that, sick on the floor. The very second Jake drove up, we'd take off.

I was standing outside with him, bent over, frantic, you know, when I heard it. A shrill whistle. Shrill enough that I turned my head. And there was Shane, out by the truck. It was the end of the day, and they were packing up. He gave me the okay sign with his thumb and forefinger. He shook it, as if to say the view, my ass in the air, was mighty fine.

Fury shot through me. I was so angry. God, I was pissed. I mean, look, there I was, obviously in distress with an animal in distress. How could you miss what was going on? How could you miss the fear, the pain we were both in? But hey, what did that matter? What did my pain have to do with anything? Why even bother to notice it? My body was a billboard to remark on. My body was someone else's entertainment, a story that had nothing to do with me at all. I was a painting. *Girl*, oil on canvas.

I wish I could tell you I got in his face or went over and kicked him hard in the nuts. You'd be all, *Way to go!* if I had. You'd see me as heroic. Instead, I fumed. What should I have done? I was a girl and he was a man. Being heroic like that is dangerous. Sometimes it's just plain stupid. Don't blame me for not speaking up. Blame him for me not speaking up.

It didn't take long for Jake to get there. But it was long enough for it to dawn on me as I waited that we'd never get

Max into that stupid Lamborghini. I didn't have to worry, though, because Jake thought of that too. He drove up in a van. Not a van like Nicco's, but this big moving truck. Like the one that came to our house before, but larger.

"Vet's open till seven thirty," Jake said as he got out. He lifted Max right up in his arms and placed him on the front seat. I got in next to him.

"Where'd you get this truck?" I asked. I mean, I was *glad* a van had appeared out of nowhere, but then again, *a van had appeared out of nowhere.* It smelled like cigarettes inside the cab. Gross. There was a baseball cap on the floor, and a crushed can of Red Bull.

Jake just shook his head. He was in no mood to talk. He looked pissed. Maybe pissed at *me*, like I had something to do with leaving Max alone with a box of chocolates, when Max was his dog, and it was Lila who'd left them out with her coffee.

"Damn dog," he said. *"Fuck."*

At the vet, they made Max throw up. They checked his heart, which was normal. Poor guy, he looked miserable. Like the day had really gone wrong. First, it was awesome, being alone in the house, finding your favorite coffee, a bunch of delightful treats, and then, boom, here you were in your most hated place, being forced to puke. But he perked up after that. He wagged. It turned out that there hadn't been a lot of chocolates left, so he hadn't eaten that many, but we didn't know that until later.

We all got back into the truck. It was a quarter to eight by then. I know, because Jake looked at his phone and said, "Shit! It's a quarter to eight!" It seemed later. Clouds had rolled in, fog too, and it was dark already. He was driving fast. He was taking the corners hard enough that poor Max slid on the seat.

It was making me nervous. I was getting a terrible feeling.

"Where are we going?" I asked. Because even though the city was still mostly unfamiliar to me, I knew we weren't going home. It was taking way longer. Everything looked a little industrial. I had no idea where we even were.

"I need to make a stop."

"What kind of a stop? I'm starving. We should get Max home. He's been through a lot, you know?" And so had I. I just wanted to put Max on my bed and get into my pajama shirt so we could rest.

"A work stop. Nonnegotiable."

"Work? At night? It's going to get dark any minute."

And then, at a stoplight, he looked over at me. Really looked, long enough that the light turned green. "What's that?"

"What?"

"Right there."

He put his fingertip on my neck.

Oh, great. Oh, no. Shit! We hadn't moved from that stoplight, because we were in some empty part of the city, and no one was around.

"Jesus." His voice was full of disgust. "Is that a fucking

monkey bite? Have you and that kid been fooling around?"

Shame washed through me. I'd never heard that expression before, but I knew what must be on my neck. Those words sounded dirty and vile. Animal-like and filthy.

"No." I put my hand over the mark. It wasn't his business anyway. It might have been someone's business, but not his.

"Shit," he said. "*Goddamn* it." He shook his head, furious, like he didn't know what to do with me. He floored it through the light, now red.

I rode in embarrassed silence. The humiliation sat like the dense, dank fog. We were clearly near one of the piers now. I know, I know—there are lots of piers in that city. Maybe it was near Pier 70? I'd tell you if I knew, but I don't. I think I saw a sign for 70, but I can't remember for sure. We were in a shipyard of some kind. I could see big cranes, too, the ones that take the containers off ocean transports. But we were driving around to the back part of a brick building. A warehouse, or at least that's what I thought it was, with a chain-link fence all around.

It was hard to see because Jake backed the end of the truck up near the building. In the side mirror, though, I saw the orange glowing tips of cigarettes in the setting sun. Three guys were waiting on the stairwell that led to the door. There were a few Styrofoam containers between them, as if they'd decided to have some food while they waited for Jake. I saw the Lamborghini parked there too.

"Stay here." Jake yanked the brake. The headlights illuminated the fence and an abandoned lot, which was overgrown with grass and weeds. He flipped off the lights. He hopped out. The door clanged shut. Max and I looked at each other.

"No idea," I said to him. I tried to make my voice calm, because he'd just been through something awful, but I didn't feel calm. I mean, what the heck were we doing there? It was off. Way, *way* off. I was uneasy. I was disgusted with Jake and disgusted with myself about the mark on my neck. I tried to call Lila again but only got her singsongy message, which made me want to throw my phone out the freaking window. I mean, how could she let this happen? What kind of mother was she?

And then things got worse. The three guys got to their feet, and I couldn't see anything. It had gotten dark, and I could see a little halo of light appear, as if maybe a door had opened in that building.

There was a terrible clatter, so loud and jarring that Max tried to scurry to his feet even though we were in the cab of the truck and that was impossible. He started to growl at the sudden sound, and I held his collar. I whispered reassuring things into his velvet ear. The back of the truck was rolling up. I couldn't see this from the cab, but I could hear it. I could feel the rumble. In the side mirror, I caught a glimpse of—what are those low things with wheels called? Dollies.

A dolly. I saw a huge dolly, and the three men were pushing it. It took all of them to move it, because there was this enormous thing wrapped in plastic on it. I couldn't tell what it was. It looked like a big body. A huge dead body. Too huge to be human, though.

I couldn't see anything, but I could sense the effort, you know, of them moving that thing up the ramp. I heard them call muffled directions to each other, swearing. It was a cool summer night with those clouds, but I cranked my window a little. I wasn't sure I wanted to hear, but I thought I'd better listen anyway.

And then there was a tremendous thunk. Jake said, "You fucking idiot! Be careful." One of the other guys said, "You dumb fuck." And then another said, "What do you expect? This thing weighs a million tons. Jesus."

The rolling sound came again. And then finally, the truck door opened. Only, it wasn't Jake. It was one of the guys. I don't know how to describe him—he just looked like a guy. Like a younger version of Jake, stocky, but with brown hair. Jake came around to my window. "Jimmy'll drive you back. See you at home." And then to Jimmy: "Don't get into an accident or anything, fuck."

Jake was gone. I was in this truck with a strange man and Max. I probably felt a little like Max did, where the day had at first seemed so awesome and then had turned into something awful. I didn't want to be in that small space with that guy with no way out. The man reeked of cigarettes and whatever garlic thing he had for dinner. Max sniffed his pant legs.

"Sick dog, huh?" he said.

"Yeah."

He reversed the truck and then pulled forward. He drove slowly and carefully around the building.

"What's back there?" I asked.

He looked over at me and then *really* looked, as if seeing me for the first time. And then he grinned. "A beautiful naked woman," he said, and laughed. "Made of stone."

I turned away, stared out into the foggy night. I didn't respond, but I flushed. I sat against the door, as far from him as possible. When we were on the road, he looked over at me again, and the corner of his mouth rose in a smirk. He could see that I was afraid, and he found it amusing. He wouldn't be afraid in a car like that, or in an elevator, or a parking garage. He never would be.

"You want music? We can turn on some music."

"No, that's okay. I'm fine."

"Nice, relaxing music?" He lifted his eyebrows in an invitation.

"I said I'm fine."

"Ooo-kay," he said. "Just trying to be friendly."

He didn't say another word, just drove with the corner of his lip raised in that little smile. The little smug smile that held the information, the power, the knowledge of what was or wasn't going to happen. When we finally got home, I hurried out of there and so did Max.

"Thanks for the ride," I said, and hated myself for it.

It was what you were supposed to do. Have manners. Be polite. Be grateful for whatever messed-up thing they gave you.

CHAPTER THIRTY-TWO

Exhibit 49: Photo of scratched and chewed inner garage
door, 716 Sea Cliff Drive
Exhibit 50: Dog tags

We had a huge fight, Lila and I, when I got inside. I was so mad at her, I could barely speak. I put a bowl of water for Max in my room. His bed was already in there, but I would keep my eye on him like the vet said to. One of us had to be a responsible adult around there.

"Baby?" Lila shouted up the stairs. And why did I always have to go to her, huh, whenever she shouted?

"Come lay down, bud," I said to Max.

"Baaa-by! Come here and tell me what happened. I got your message."

I sat on my bed and folded my arms and wondered what

I was doing in that place. I wanted to go home. To my real home. Where things were nice and good. I'd stay in that empty dorm if they let me. I'd stay with no heat or food, whatever. I had a brief, pointless fantasy of putting Max in a dog crate on a plane to Seattle. I patted the bed, and Max hopped up.

"Get your hair all over if you want," I said to him. "You're the only respectable person in this place."

"Baby!" Lila thumped on the door. "Open up! I'm talking to you! It's late. Aren't you hungry or anything?"

No answer, plus I wasn't. That whole strange, scary night had made my hunger vanish.

"Are you *mad*?"

I rolled my eyes at Max. I'm sure he would have rolled his eyes back if he could.

"Syd-Syd, open up this minute, or I'm going to go downstairs and get a hammer and bash my way in." Max's ear twitched. The pounding on the door was upsetting him, so I got up and flung it open. I didn't even want to see her face. God, beauty could be ugly.

"What?" she said. "Why are you so mad?" Really, I was clenching my teeth, and my hands were fists at my sides.

"You *left* your *chocolates* right on the *table*."

"How was I supposed to know he'd get up there?"

"You're supposed to think about these things. You're supposed to think about other people's *safety*."

"Well, he's okay, by the look of it."

"He could have *died*. And then I had to ride home alone with your boyfriend's creepy *associate*. After they did God knows what with some giant *statue*."

"What are you talking about? I thought you were at the vet."

"We *were* at the vet. And then we were at some scary warehouse with a bunch of guys and they were moving some giant statue or something. In the dark? When no one's around? Come on, Lila. Open your *eyes*." This made it sound like I knew what was going on, but I didn't.

"What statue?"

"*I* don't know! How am *I* supposed to know? *You're* supposed to know!"

Well, I know now. The beautiful naked woman was that statue the *Aphrodite of Knidos*. The missing Aphrodite, from, what, the fourth century B.C.? Marble goddess of beauty, preparing for the bath that would restore her purity. And don't ask, because you can ask and ask a million times, but I don't know what happened to it after that.

"He doesn't tell me *everything* that goes on in his business!"

"Well, did he tell you why he was screaming at some guy in that car I keep seeing?"

"A car out front?"

"Yes, a car out front. I told you before! Something's going on. Something bad. Obviously *illegal*. People don't move art around in the dark."

"He's a broker! Clients sell and clients buy! Stuff moves around. People meet other people. Baby, stop *yelling*."

Lila's eyes filled with tears. She tried to touch me, but I stepped back.

"Where *were* you?"

"We met with Evan! Then Evan and I drove out to Sea Ranch. I was working!" Evan was Evan Dunne, the director she and Riley wanted for *Peyton Place*. The director everyone wanted for everything, after he did *Endless Kingdom*.

"With your phone off?"

"I couldn't have *interruptions*. *Evan Dunne?* Come on! He's perfect! He *gets* it. He *understands* Constance, how she's gorgeous and only *seems* repressed—"

"Stop it! Stop. It!" I had my fists in my hair. I was in the worst sort of hall of mirrors, where you never see your own reflection, where you begin to doubt whether you're there at all. "I am here! I am here and all these things are happening. . . ."

I started to cry in frustration. Poor Max, he had his chin on his paws. It was the worst kind of day, where you just plain give up on it. Where it seems the bad stuff will keep coming and coming until the sun rises again.

I stared out the window at the sea. Or where the sea would be if it were visible in the darkness. It was ridiculous to feel so miserable and so alone in a house like that, where people had everything. I put my arms around myself. Tears rolled down my cheeks.

And then I heard a sound. Oh, I'd heard it before, the wounded-animal cry, but I'd never been the one to cause it. When I turned around, I saw Lila on the bed, her face in her hands.

"Lila."

She refused to look up.

"Lila, look at me." She lifted her head, and I saw her stricken face. It was like, I don't know, she was a child again, like that night on the beach. A child who'd done wrong. She looked innocent and beautiful, and, shit, I remembered that she wanted things too. *She* wanted to be seen, because she kept trying and trying for that and it never happened. In spite of her face so large up there on theater screens, she was *never* seen. In spite of her face and her body in magazines and on TV, she wasn't. I was the only one who saw her, really. And because I did, I felt, you know, that it was my job to take care of her. I felt responsible for her. She was *my* baby, not the other way around, as much as I wished that weren't true.

"I'm sorry," I said. Of course, *I'm sorry* means a lot of things. Sometimes it just means *Never mind*.

She was sobbing, though.

"Lila, it's all right."

I knelt beside the bed. I put my arms around her. I felt bad and guilty. I wasn't sure what she might do in this sort of state. I mean, there were all those pill bottles. I shouldn't have been so hard on her.

"I'm doing the best I *can*," she cried.

That night, after Jake finally came home, I heard their voices. More fighting. *The Summer of Fighting*, that's what *this* film should have been named. *Dark Summer. Endless Summer. Frightening Summer.* I put my pillow over my head. Visions of

the day spun in a disturbing mix. Nicco and the fire between us. Jake, with his finger touching the mark on my neck. That statue.

Maybe it *was* Jake's. Or maybe it *was* stolen. I was confused about what belonged to who, who was allowed to take what, what was mine and mine alone. And it gave me the creeps, the way Jake was guarding my own body. Hovering over my "purity" and virginity like those dads who threaten the guy who comes to date their daughter, their prize, the prize they'll one day hand over to the man they approve of. The whole virgin thing was seriously messed up—how could you be revered *and* sacrificed to the gods? Why was virginity always *taken* or *lost* instead of just given? Why were you *de*filed and *de*flowered, as if your cleanliness and true beauty were gone forever? And what was so dangerous about me having sex, compared to a guy? Lila was right—even *my father* didn't protect my purity, but then again, he didn't protect me at all. He'd fled the scene, leaving me to hold things that were way too heavy for me. Like a mother, one made of fragile marble.

And then—even through the pillow—I heard it. Those words, yelled: *all day alone with Evan Dunne.*

That was what they were fighting about? Jealousy? Not stolen art or irresponsible mothers? Jake was jealous. The "jealous type." Which means: *You're mine, and I'll decide when I share.* The jealous type is a toddler. The jealous type is an insecure baby, apologies to babies.

The jealous type is dangerous when someone touches his stuff.

She was an object to everyone, and I was an object to them, and we were *Woman I* and *Woman II* and *Jacqueline* and the *Aphrodite of Knidos*, and that charcoal study Jake showed me a few days before, *Nude in a Black Armchair.* I mean, *Nude in a Black Armchair.* God, she didn't even get to be *Woman.* Just *Nude.* Breasts and body, stolen, gazed upon, owned, going back to the fourth century B.C. Images with dangerous, pasted-on mouths. *Here is my face, assholes,* I wanted to shout down through the generations. *Here is my* voice.

Let's just say it was a bad time, a very bad time, for Meredith to come visit.

CHAPTER THIRTY-THREE

*Exhibit 51: Sworn statement of James (Jimmy)
Columbo*

"A car? Like, a limo car?"

It was so good to see Meredith. But it was weird, too. It had been only eight weeks, but so much had happened. Nicco felt like a fracture in the earth after a quake, the before on one side, the after on the other. Those legs in the boat before I left, the ones with the knobby knees and the child bruises, they were long and tan and wanted to be wrapped around Nicco, and I had covered the mark on my neck with a dab of concealer. When Meredith got off the plane, it was like seeing your old friend from middle school. That happy familiarity, but the distance, too. You were the same person you were then, but definitely not the same person.

"Yes but no. More like a town car. Lila didn't want to wel-

come you here with some cab." Lila would never get up that early to meet Meredith herself was more the truth.

"Cool." It sounded casual, but she didn't look casual. Meredith's eyes were all excited.

I could tell Meredith liked it, the way the driver opened the door for her and took her luggage and asked if the temperature in the car was okay. She opened the bottle of water that was offered and drank. She'd been talking, talking, about Cora and how she'd gotten boy crazy, or really, Bryce crazy, because Bryce was the guy Cora had met at the softball game. And then about Hoodean, and how he had broken his wrist at Shilshole when he was trying to spike the volleyball, showing off for Sarah, which pissed Meredith off. I'd never noticed it before, but maybe she liked Hoodean, who'd always seemed like a brother to me.

She stopped talking, though, as we got out of the airport area and into the city. I felt kind of shy with her. Her neck was craned, and she kept looking at me to see if I was seeing the same things she was. It was fun, though, to take in where you live through the eyes of someone who'd never seen it.

And when we drove through the pillars into Sea Cliff, I saw her taking it all in even more. She actually grabbed my arm, like this was a new thing happening to both of us.

"Whoa," she said. "This is really nice. I mean *really*."

Meredith had met Lila only one other time, when Lila came to my ninth-grade graduation. Just one time, even after all the years we'd known each other. Lila didn't usually fly out to see me; I flew to her. And that day on the lawn of Academy of Arts and Sciences, Lila was in full Lila mode, dressed entirely in ivory with only a green silk scarf as color. Big sunglasses. Vibrations coming off her, you know, of importance. Very un-Seattle. It was like bringing the Hope Diamond into Zales. Even if she just sat there, she'd be utterly large and shining.

Ellen and Paul, Meredith's parents, were there too, of course. They all shook hands and stood in an awkward circle. Edwina and Ellen gave us these bouquets wrapped in cellophane that they'd gotten at the grocery store, but Lila set a lei of orchids around my neck. There was talk about how proud everyone was, but then the conversation stalled, and Lila took my elbow and said we had to be going.

Now, Meredith was coming to our house, and I hoped we wouldn't have a repeat of the uncomfortable Nicco and Lila meeting. It was a Saturday morning, and no one was working at the construction site next door. It was quiet over there—no hammers pounding, no saws screaming and then going silent. It wasn't quiet at our place, though. Max had heard the unfamiliar car, and when we opened the front gate, he went crazy.

"Yikes," Meredith said.

"It's okay. He always does that. Don't be afraid. He also barks at the neighbor's recycling bins." I was rolling Meredith's little roller bag up the walk, and she had her other bag slung over her shoulder. "Max!" I called. "It's me!"

"I'm nervous," Meredith said.

"He's really a sweetheart."

"No, I mean your mom. I don't usually hang out with movie stars."

She never did that kind of thing at home. She never got all weird about Lila. At Academy, I was myself, and none of my friends ever even mentioned her. At least, not the famous parts. She was my annoying mother who called when it was inconvenient and kept me on the phone when I wanted to get off. I thought they'd forgotten about the rest, but maybe they never really had. Of course, this was different, Meredith coming to stay in our house. Lila would be real to her, not a story I told.

Max jumped on Meredith with excitement, and he was all we could deal with at first. And then he calmed down, and Meredith set her bag on the floor and looked at the White Room in astonishment.

"Holy shit," she whispered. Meredith hardly ever swore. She walked straight to the windows. The view pulled you in like that. "This is incredible. The bridge is *right there*."

It was a strange combination, feeling self-conscious but wanting to show off, too. I opened the doors to the back patio and walked out so she'd follow. The fog had already lifted, and the ocean was also showing off. Seeing it through Meredith's eyes—it looked magnificent.

"Down there, that's China Beach. Anytime you want to go down there, feel free."

"Look at those stairs. That is so cool. Like a maze." She moved her hand back and forth, indicating the switchbacks. "Wow."

"Sometimes the fog is here all day and it's not as awesome. It gets depressing."

"I can't imagine being depressed here. You're never going to want to come home."

"The tide is really low right now. We could walk all the way to Baker Beach, which you usually can't do. Want to go?"

"Sure."

"I'll show you to your room and stuff."

"Okay. But where's your mom? It's like we're all alone in this huge place."

I wanted to say, *Welcome to my life*, because that's how I always felt. Instead, I just said, "Sleeping? She doesn't like to wake up before noon, at the earliest."

"Whoa. That's so late! My mom did that, like, once in her life, when she took a pain pill after her dental surgery."

We bump-rolled Meredith's bag up the stairs as Max sped ahead. Meredith stopped at the landing and looked up at that huge poster of Lila in *Nefarious*.

"Nice to see your mother's crotch every time you go up and down," I said, and we both cracked up. It felt like the old Meredith and me.

But then Meredith said, "We watched it once."

"You did? You never said."

"My dad got all embarrassed at that part. He left the room to find us some sodas."

I lived in two different worlds. And right then, I felt like a visitor in both of them.

*　*　*

"Your room. Your bathroom. Wi-Fi password: 'Nefarious.' Is this okay?"

"Okay? I've never even seen a house like this before, let alone stayed in one."

We left Max at home until Meredith could get more used to him. He scared her a little. Meredith and I raced each other down the orange stucco stairwell to the beach, wearing our bathing suits, me carrying the beach bag. It was colder than it looked, and I could see goose bumps rise up along Meredith's arms.

"Want my sweatshirt?" I asked.

"I'm good!"

"I usually find a big rock to lay behind so I can sunbathe out of the wind."

We walked the stretch of shoreline to Baker, where I promised Meredith that she'd get the best photos. She stopped along the way to look at the starfish and anemones, which you could see because of the low tide. At Baker, we rolled out our towels, and she told me more about Cora and Bryce, how Bryce's family had this boat docked at Shilshole, and how they'd go there alone. Meredith was shocked at this. Cora was going to *get into trouble*. Cora was *going too far*. I wondered if Bryce was going to get into trouble. I wondered if he was going too far. I hoped the concealer on my neck wasn't too obvious in the sun. I tried to tell her about Nicco, how he was more than just a casual friend. We were supposed to all go out together on Monday night. I guess I wanted to warn her. I would have gone to an empty boat with him in two seconds.

"Nicco's bringing his friend Carlos."

Meredith made a face.

"Don't look like that. He sounds really nice. It seemed better than it just being the three of us."

Then we dropped the subject. We replayed the shocking ending of *The Night Dweller*, and I pretended I still loved R. W. Wright. We laughed about the time Ivy Reese caught a crab during a race and flew out of the boat. *Caught a crab*— when you put the oar in the water at the wrong time, which can shoot you up and out like a cannonball. We talked about how we should do something big next year to celebrate our seventeenth birthdays, like run a half marathon or do a polar plunge.

The sun was shining, and kids were playing on the beach, and my best friend was sitting next to me on a towel, so there was no real reason for the feeling I had as we were talking about crossing finish lines and dashing into icy cold waters. It was the strongest feeling, empty and deep as a newly dug grave, and dark as one too. The ghost—she stood beside that grave and shook her head. All of the stuff we were talking about doing next year—none of that was going to happen. None of it. The feeling passed over me, a cloud over the sun, and then the sun was out again.

We were laughing about something, I don't even remember what, and Meredith was drinking sparkling water out of the bottle and I was putting lotion on my legs, when this guy came up to ask us for directions to Golden Gate Park. He was maybe, I don't know, thirty, with that kind of straight haircut that makes you look like a newsman. Blue shorts, shirt off, to make sure we saw that he worked out. By the way he was looking at us, I knew he didn't really care about Golden Gate Park.

"No idea," I said.

"You tourists, too?"

"No idea," I said again. Meredith crossed her legs and folded her arms over her chest.

"Wow. Wouldn't kill you to be friendly," he said, before turning away and walking off, pissed.

"Ew." Meredith grimaced. And then, "Oh, God! Don't look!"

Which of course made me look. It was just old Chet in his Dodgers cap, strolling down the beach in all his glory. As the summer had gone on, he'd been getting tanner and tanner. He was brown as a handful of . . . well, I was going to say *nuts*.

"That's just Chet," I said.

"You *know* him?"

"Well, not know-know. Familiar with. He's here all the time. He's harmless."

"You said you saw nudists, but wow." Her face was beet red.

"I tried to take pictures once to send to you guys."

"Syd," she said. She sounded like Ellen.

It was pretty clear that only *I* had gone from my regular legs in the boat that day to these legs now, stretched before me, legs that made a guy stop and look, legs that belonged to someone who wanted things. Only I had moved from the place where you're separate from the bigger world, to the place where you aren't.

"Let's go back," Meredith said.

But there was really no going back, was there?

CHAPTER THIRTY-FOUR

Exhibit 52: Photo of the Aphrodite of Knidos, *fourth century* B.C.

When Meredith and I climbed our stairs again and reached the top, there she was, Lila, sitting at the table on the patio, wearing her sunglasses and her ivory satin robe with the embroidered sleeves, and eating a bowl of strawberries. Max was lounging in the shady spot under the roof. His tongue was out, and he panted his *huh, huh, huh.*

"Baby!" Lila said when she saw us. "And Meredith! We're so glad you're here. Look at you two beauties!"

"Oh, I look awful," Meredith said, brushing sand off her legs. "And thank you so much for having me. I can't believe I'm here. And, oh my God, you're so beautiful in real life."

Lila stood, drew her into a hug. "What a sweetie you are." This wasn't the regular Meredith, who held that oar with her muscles bulging. This was a less confident Meredith, but it was okay, because she was pushing every Lila button, and Lila was loving it.

"My parents are huge fans." Wrong move, because it would only remind Lila of her age. "And so am I. All of our friends are." Recovery. Meredith for the win.

"Anything you need, you let me know. Our home is your home."

"How about the keys to Jake's car?" I joked.

"All right, baby, you smart-ass. Anything but *that*. He loves that thing more than me."

"Yellow Lamborghini," I said.

"You told me."

God, I was being a show-off. With Meredith there, all my insecurity floodgates had opened, and I was plugging the holes with stuff we didn't even care about at home.

"I made a reservation at Foreign Cinema. Sound good? I thought you girls might enjoy that."

"Great," I said, as though I knew what it was, even though I didn't. Insecurity can make you such an ass.

"I thought it'd be fun for Naomi to join us. She just arrived in town. She's here playing Tink at the Orpheum, but the first show isn't until Friday."

"Naomi Meadows?" I said to Meredith. She'd been in the pilot with Lila, but everyone knew her better from that TV series *New School*.

"Oh, wow." Meredith's eyes went wide. She loved that show.

On the way back to our rooms to shower and clean up, I showed Meredith the painting in the dining room. "This is kinda cool," I said. I pointed to the corner of the painting where his signature was.

Meredith squinted. "No idea."

"Picasso."

"No way."

"Way."

"It can't be *real*."

"It's real. *Jacqueline*. His second wife. She was twenty-six and he was seventy-two."

"That's disgusting."

"He was a ladies' man. I read that he had two wives and, like, six mistresses and hundreds of affairs."

"I don't know where that expression came from, 'ladies' man,'" Meredith said. "They should just be called creeps."

I'd heard that expression so often, I'd never stopped to think about it before. My father was always called a ladies' man. Papa Chesterton, too, and even Jake. But there was no such thing as a men's lady. And Meredith was right, because *ladies' man* made it sound almost polite, when what they really did was go through women like a sick kid goes through Kleenex.

The point of this story, though, about Meredith and the beach and Lila and the painting, is not really about naked Chet, or the rejected, shirtless beach guy, or ladies' men, or even the ways I needed to show off to Meredith how great things were in San Francisco because I was actually miserable there.

The point is those sunglasses. The ones Lila was wearing. Because that evening, as the sun was beginning to set, as we were driving toward the Mission to the restaurant, Lila still had them on. Meredith and I sat together in the back seat, but I noticed anyway, because it had to be hard to see in those, now that the sky was turning golden.

"What's with the glasses, Lila?" I don't think Meredith had even seen Lila's eyes yet.

"Oh! I look horrible! Bruised my silly cheek walking into an open cabinet door. Good thing this place has low lighting."

She lifted her glasses to her head for a moment, and even with the yellow evening light in the rearview mirror, we both could see it, Meredith and me. It was covered in makeup, but there was a dark ring under her eye. I remembered the night before, the fight she had with Jake.

My stomach felt sick. It was the second bruise. The horror trickled in. *Tick, tick, tick* went the clock.

In the car, Meredith looked over at me, and I looked back. *A black eye*, our glance said. Meredith looked out the window after that, pretended to watch the scenery. She looked uneasy. She started picking at her fingernails, the way she did when she was worried.

CHAPTER THIRTY-FIVE

Exhibit 53: Sworn statement of Naomi Meadows

Naomi Meadows was already at the table, and so was her leading man, Gavin Isaacs, who played Captain Hook in their production. Naomi was stylish and stunning, wearing slim jeans with a wide belt and a red silk blouse, and he was a very, very good-looking Captain Hook, with dark eyes and shadowy stubble and shoulder-length dark hair. The kind of good looking that shuts your mouth in nerves. Charisma came off him in waves. He looked familiar, but I couldn't place him. Later, we realized he was one of the bad guys in that series of action movies, *Thriller Road*, one, two, three, etc. Mer and I had seen maybe the first one and that was all.

The restaurant was large and industrial inside, but the outside patio where we sat was romantic, strung with white lights, the tables candlelit and warmed by heat lamps. It was called

Foreign Cinema because a movie played on the wall of a building in front of us. That night, it was *The Princess Bride*. You couldn't really hear it, it was too noisy out there, but the flickering images played above that beautiful patio, charming and dreamlike.

There was a lot of talk about the hip new version of *Peter Pan* they were in—how audiences were different in various cities, a recounting of where the show would go next and next and next. Naomi Meadows, who was a bigger star now than Lila, was still all *Miss Lila* this, and *Miss Lila* that. There was playful, fun reminiscing about the shooting of the pilot years ago. They ordered drinks and appetizers—antipasto, a pear and endive salad, another salad of beets and blood oranges—but we didn't order dinner yet because Jake was supposed to be joining us later, something Lila hadn't mentioned before.

Meredith was acting so shy and nervous that it was making me nervous. Or maybe I was nervous on my own, because people kept staring and whispering and someone came and asked Gavin Isaacs for his autograph, proving that people had watched way, way more of those action movies than I had.

The waiter kept returning to ask if we were ready to order dinner, but we were still waiting for Jake. The appetizer plates were taken. Meredith asked if she could take a photo with all of them, which embarrassed me, but Lila loved it. Gavin Isaacs got his third Mosswood whiskey. Lila was on her third glass of wine. Naomi Meadows ordered another sparkling water with lime. Lila kept looking at her phone. Gavin Isaacs said he was starving, so we all ordered anyway. He was acting like the leader, the way that some guys do, even at a table of women.

In spite of the beautiful plates—the swordfish and Kobe steak and duck breast and sesame seed fried chicken—as well as Naomi's laugh and Gavin Isaacs's joking (probably due to the fourth Mosswood), I could feel the mood slipping. Lila kept saying things like *He must have gotten caught up* and *There must have been an emergency* and *His phone must have died.* Meredith kept looking at the movie screen, and Gavin Isaacs's eyes began to search for the waiter. The waiter brought complimentary desserts, and Gavin Isaacs's face dropped, as if the tray held a stack of pressing paperwork instead of cheesecake drizzled with a pomegranate and cranberry sauce.

If the mood was already slipping, it then took a plunge. Naomi Meadows leaned across the table and set her hand over Lila's. "I hope you're all right," she said. In that loud room, it sounded like, "I HOPE YOU'RE ALL RIGHT."

Lila took her hand back. "I'm fine."

"I mean . . ." Naomi Meadows circled her finger in the direction of Lila's eye.

"I walked into my closet door."

Meredith kicked me under the table. Of course I'd heard it too. How she'd told us *cabinet door* and now said *closet door.* I started to feel anxious. No. I felt *alarmed.*

"I hope you know I'm always here for you," Naomi said. Things turned suddenly too intimate. Gavin Isaacs pushed his chair back and hunted down the waiter. I saw him shove his credit card at the poor guy; he wanted out of there so bad. Lila was smiling, but it was like cracks were forming on her face. Bits of her psyche were showing through.

"And I am always here for *you*," she said.

We rode home in silence, though Meredith kept nudging my foot with her foot. Lila was driving a little too fast. I was sure Meredith had been counting those glasses of wine. Meredith's fingers gripped the edge of the seat. I didn't know what she expected me to do. When we got home, Lila threw her car keys on the kitchen counter. "Fucking bastard," she said.

Meredith and I crept upstairs away from Lila and her anger. Awkwardness sat like a third person between us. It reminded me of when weird Andrew Wilcox would sit with us at lunch.

"Do you want to watch a movie or something?" I said.

"I think I'll just go to bed. I'm really tired," Meredith said.

"Okay. See you in the morning."

I took Max out to pee. On the third floor, the window of the guest room was open. Over the sound of the Max waterfall, I could hear the low murmurs of Meredith's voice on the phone. I wondered who she was talking to. At that hour, it was probably Ellen. As I stood in the garden, I felt the shame of us, the truth of us, my so-called family. In the moonlight, Max trotted around the yard, and I watched the clouds glide through the skeleton bones of the house next door. Finally, it was quiet. Meredith must have hung up.

I took a photo of the sky. Big moon, I texted Nicco. We

hadn't talked all day, with Meredith visiting. I was so lonely for someone who knew me. I'd probably felt that way my whole life.

Big missing, he texted back.

I stared at the guest room window. I wondered what Meredith was thinking up there.

Even in the garden under the moon, I could feel Meredith's worry. In that house, the tension had been ratcheting up and up and up, but I'd been living with it. I'd maybe even gotten used to it, little by little. But there was something about having Meredith there. There was something about seeing *everything* through someone else's eyes, not just a city.

And for the first time, I was anxious because *she* was anxious. I was shocked because she was shocked.

I was scared because she was scared.

CHAPTER THIRTY-SIX

Exhibit 54: Sworn statement of Gavin D. Isaacs

Meredith and I had fun the next day. I was trying hard to erase the night before. I took her to City Lights Bookstore, because I knew she'd love it. I ordered us car service again. I wanted Meredith to have a really good time. No more Creeps of San Francisco.

And it *was* good. After City Lights, the driver dropped us off at Fisherman's Wharf, and we went to the places Lila had taken me to the first time I visited. We went to Ghirardelli Square and bought chocolate. Meredith FaceTimed Hoodean from Lombard Street. We walked all the way to Pier 39 to see the gross, blubbery, stinky sea lions lying around on the docks. I took her to Madame Tussauds wax museum, and she went crazy taking pictures and texting them to her mom and

Hoodean and Cora. We went to Nick's Lighthouse and ate chowder from a bowl of bread.

That night, we ordered dinner on our own and watched a movie in the media room. It was a surprise for Meredith, something I knew she'd like even if I'd come to despise R. W. Wright's sexy, murdered girls—an old movie of one of his earliest books, *The Most Regular Evil.* It was pretty cheesy, really. We made fun of the big hair and the super-high-waisted jeans. There was a lot to make fun of, until it got scary. What was scary in the 1980s was still scary now. A young woman, stalked on a dark street. She was the good girl, though, the heroine. She kept her blouse buttoned all the way up, so she got the knife away from the guy and jabbed it in his throat. I had to hide my eyes, but Meredith was brave.

"I could do it," she said.

"Not me. No way," I said.

"You cringe cutting into a chicken breast." It was true. There was just something too unnerving about knives plunged into skin.

"Sick." I shivered.

"You'd need a baseball bat," Meredith said. "Then you could do it." It was a weird conversation, but not. It was just Meredith and me being Meredith and me. It felt good. I'd made a successful day, all the way through to the end.

But then, right when the guy popped back up and the girl had to keep stabbing, Jake joined us. Meredith had finally met him that afternoon when we got home, but now he plopped himself down in the big, cushy leather chair.

"Hey, ladies," he said.

"Hey, Mr. Antonetti," Meredith said.

"Hey," I said.

The room hummed with discomfort. All I could see when I looked at him was Lila's black eye, and I could feel Meredith thinking about it too. But the awful awkwardness wasn't just about the black eye. It was the way he sat there with his feet up on the footstool with the legs of his shorts open, revealing a dark cavity, his arms hairy and bare in his tank top.

"Watching a movie, huh?"

"*Trying* to," I said. Meredith nudged me with her elbow. She wanted me to be polite, even though she felt the same as I did. I could see it in the way she pulled the blanket up over her pajama top.

"It's nice to see you with *girl*friends for a change," Jake said.

I could feel Meredith's unspoken question in a wrinkle of her nose. I knew her so well. God, I wanted Jake to go away.

But he didn't go away. He just sat there and sat there. In my space. Pressing on me somehow. He watched the movie until the end, until the dead stalker lay on the floor and the camera panned away from the house in a way that almost made you feel sorry for the guy. R. W. Wright's books never end happily. They just keep making you uneasy, all the way until the final page and afterward.

I don't think I even really watched the last part of that film.

I was too distracted with Jake there. Maybe Meredith didn't see that last half hour either, because she got up the very second the credits rolled, as if she was just waiting for her chance to escape.

"I think I'll go to bed now," she said.

Upstairs, I asked Meredith if she wanted to go down to China Beach. It was only ten.

"It's really awesome there at night," I said. "The waves are like silver. The bridge is all lit up. Photo op!"

"It's kind of dark," she said.

"Want to stay up and play Mad Libs or something?" We used to do that with her family during sleepovers at her house.

"That's okay," she said. "I'm really tired."

I couldn't exactly blame her. I wouldn't be able to think of a funny plural noun or a humorous article of clothing anyway. I wouldn't be able to take in the magic of the silver tips of waves or run around on the beach. I couldn't feel free if I didn't feel safe.

When I went out to the garden, the moon was a shade fuller. Max lifted his leg on the very same bush, and I heard the murmur of Meredith's voice on the phone again.

I'd failed. Shit, I was such a failure.

CHAPTER THIRTY-SEVEN

Exhibit 55: Sworn statement of Meredith Jenkins,
1 of 2

I had this great idea for Meredith because of R. W. Wright—a night tour of Alcatraz. R. W. Wright's *Hell House* is set there. I wasn't sure we could get tickets on short notice, but when I mentioned it to Nicco, he said that his mom knew someone in the National Park Service and that he'd see what he could do. Four tickets, Monday night, bam. I thought of all the ways I'd like to thank him, mostly involving my mouth and his mouth, but then I tried to put that out of my mind.

We met Nicco and Carlos at Fog City Diner by the Alcatraz boat dock. Meredith couldn't believe how Lila just gave me her credit card and let me call the car service whenever I wanted. She was used to the Seattle me, who rode my bike or walked everywhere because Edwina made me use my own money for everything, and you couldn't exactly do anything too splurge-worthy with what I made at Jitters during the school year.

They were waiting outside. Nicco was wearing his jeans and a green T-shirt and a blue hoodie, and I remember this so clearly because I was shocked again at how incredibly good looking he was. It'd been only three days, but it was like, *Oh, yeah—you*. Wow. That hair, you know? His eyes.

He brought me close, and I didn't even care what Meredith saw or thought. He smelled so good. I wished we were alone. I wanted his hands on me, and mine on him. Samuel Crane—he had dry lips that he wet with his tongue just before he kissed me. He kept a tube of ChapStick in his pocket. This was atoms and particles, the kind of nuclear fusion that fuels the sun, light molecules bashing together to create energy. And that was before we even touched. That's what sat between us in the empty space. I could feel it there, crackling.

Carlos had been Nicco's best friend since they were kids, same as Meredith and me. He was going to be a senior next year at Nicco's school, George Washington High, and he was a barista at Jive, near the beach. Carlos was a big guy. Tall, wide, and sweet. Super funny. Really nice.

"Greetings, inmates," he said when we first walked up. Meredith laughed. She even blushed, or it might have been her sunburn. I was really glad Carlos came. I was sure he would distract Meredith from all the times Nicco and I had our hands on each other, but I was wrong.

We ate fried fish and onion rings, which was an awesome

beginning to a night, if you ask me. Anything that starts with onion rings generally goes well. Since Carlos and I worked in coffee places, we talked about all the annoying things people did, like ordering overly complicated stuff, and calling espresso "expresso," and getting upset about a drink that wasn't even theirs. "Relax about the 'no whip'! Is your name Marybeth?" Carlos joked. Carlos told us how he'd met Nicco during swimming lessons when they were eight, when Nicco was crying by the fence. Meredith told them about our seventh-grade skit, when she was Alexander Hamilton and I was Aaron Burr and we dueled with swords from Party for Less.

We waited at the dock. The boat going to Alcatraz Island was leaving at seven. We shoved on with everyone else and watched the skyline fall away as the boat got farther from the city. It was freezing out there, and Carlos gave Meredith his hoodie, which she kind of liked, I could tell. The hoodie went down to her knees, and she looked cute in it. She smiled, pleased. He was a good guy, and this was proof. In retrospect, I'm not sure why girls don't have to get cold, but whatever. Nicco put his arms around me. The sky began to turn hues of gold, and then the water did. The rock with the old prison on top grew larger and larger. As we got closer, wisps of fog appeared and started to thicken. It was spooky, to be honest.

I leaned on the ferry railing and looked out as Nicco pressed against my back. I wished everyone would get off that boat except for us, but I was excited to see the place, too. We practically ran up the big hill, same as kids on a field trip. It was creepy and fortresslike, a prison that had housed the most notorious criminals in history—Al Capone, and the Bird-man, and Machine Gun Kelly. In its twenty-nine years as a prison, no one had escaped from there. People had tried, but you couldn't survive those torrid currents and frigid waters.

You can tell I listened to the audio tour.

Or at least, I listened for a little while. I listened until Meredith and Carlos got far enough ahead of us, until they were paying rapt attention to the tiny cells, with their sickening green walls and rusted urinals, leaning in to look at the same time, the earbuds in their ears.

Nicco yanked his, let them drop to his chest.

"I can barely stand it," he said. He brought me to him. His hands moved down my back.

"I know."

"You look so beautiful. I want you so bad."

Oh my God—the word *want*. It just did me in. To be beautiful and wanted—it made you feel *so* powerful and amazing. But those very same things could make you feel powerless and ashamed. No wonder want and desire were confusing. No wonder they seemed like something that should be kept secret.

"Prisoner of love," Nicco murmured, and then he scribbled in the air, like he was writing it down in his notebook.

Prisoner of love.

This is a horrible story, given what happened. Horrible. But the point is, I heard it: *love. Love* made me want him even more. Love was the promise of something bigger than sex. It was proof that I was interesting and worthy for way more than two days. And love supposedly made desire okay, since desire by itself was too dangerous. This was silly, honestly. Love could be so much more dangerous.

The lights went off with a huge *chunk* sound. Suddenly, it was pitch black. I screamed, and Nicco put his arms around me. He'd been on this tour before and knew what to expect. We were in almost total darkness, with only the sick yellow glow from a few of the cells.

We'd fallen behind, so far behind that we were all alone. I could hear the creaks and groans of the old, old building, the pings of pipes or maybe spirits. You could feel what it was like to be alone in there, sitting with your wrongdoings. Festering and tormented from your moment of violent passion or years of doing bad shit to other people. Oh, God, it was creepy. The biggest punishment was making you a lonely, lonely outcast.

Nicco was still thinking about my body and his. His hands were everywhere. I was a little distracted by how scary things were in that place. I felt the presence of those bad men on the thin mattresses, peeing in those rusted urinals. I kissed back anyway.

His tongue was in my mouth, his warm hands up my shirt. A guard appeared down the hall. "Hey," he said. "Hey, come on. Stay with the group." We were two kids causing trouble. We were two teenagers feeling what every person has felt from the beginning of time, only no one wants to admit it.

When we caught up, Meredith was pissed. I could see it in

her face. I'd known her forever, so I understood what that tight closed mouth meant. Maybe it didn't take years of friendship, because Carlos obviously knew what it meant too. He kept trying to make jokes. He was using the last resort of good guys in awkward situations—punching a friend in the arm. Poor Carlos.

We'd been selfish. I felt bad. I wanted to blame my actions on desire, but I wasn't a caveman. I wasn't one of the evil men without a conscience who had been locked away in that place.

We came out into the night air. You'd think it would be a relief, being out of that vacant, haunted building, but it wasn't. It was still so eerie out on that rock. People felt it. Hands slipped into other hands. The fog was so thick, you could barely see out. But you could hear that frigid water crashing and crashing against the rock. It crashed like a bad omen. The fog said that lots of things couldn't be seen. So many things were hidden and obscured until you got up close to them.

We piled onto the boat. It seemed unsafe to ride that stretch back to the city. The water was rough. We sloshed around, and a few people squealed (okay, me) when the nose of the ferry rose and then banged down. You couldn't see two feet in front of you.

The guys went to get hot chocolate for the four of us. I couldn't imagine drinking it, or even how it would stay in the cup. Maybe they just wanted to get away from the tension that sat there between Meredith and me.

"Mer," I said.

She didn't answer. She sat in one of the seats with her arms crossed.

"Mer, come on. What?"

"You just went off. You left me with someone I don't even know."

"I thought you guys were having fun. I thought you might like some time alone."

This was a lie, and she knew it. She gave me that look.

"It seemed like you liked each other," I tried again.

"Uh-huh." I hadn't seen her that mad maybe ever. "Right. Nice try."

"Mer," I pleaded. "I'm sorry."

"You're not the same person here," she said. "You and that guy. You're worse than Cora. You're not even yourself in this place."

But she was wrong. I *was* myself. I was Linda Short's daughter, and Lila Shore's daughter, and I was nice and not, cautious and reckless. I didn't want to be one thing. I wanted to be all things.

CHAPTER THIRTY-EIGHT

Exhibit 56: Sworn statement of Meredith Jenkins,
2 of 2

Nicco offered to take Meredith and me home, but I said
no. He kept giving me those *Is everything all right?* looks. I called
the car service to pick us up. On the drive, Meredith was silent,
her shoulders turned away from me. I saw her reflection in the
window, staring out into the night. There was no excited water
bottle opening or nervous chatter with the driver. She'd gotten
used to all that pretty quickly. It was a quiet, strained car ride.

But at home, things got worse.

Way worse.

All the lights in the house were off. Max didn't even bark
when Meredith and I arrived. Dogs feel the mood of a house.
Dogs use their instincts, and he was lying under the dining

room table, his ears down, *Jacqueline* looking over him with her wide, empty eyes.

It quickly became clear why Max was hiding. Upstairs there was yelling. *Screaming.* It was louder than Jake and Lila's previous fights. It was more vicious.

Protecting us! Like hell! Lila's words dripped sarcasm. I didn't know what this meant. All I could feel was her fury, swirling down the stairs like a cloud of black smoke from a fire, a fire horrible enough to burn the city to the ground. And all I could see was Meredith, my friend whose parents played Mad Libs with her and her sister, standing by me in shock. The outing with Nicco and Carlos didn't even matter anymore. It was a petty squabble that had vanished the second the earthquake rumbled, because who cared anymore?

Meredith looked at me, horrified. I doubt her parents even raised their voices. Ellen might make a snippy remark when Meredith's dad was late to a regatta.

"What do we do?" she asked.

I didn't know. "Let's just go upstairs," I said. The *just* meant I had it handled. That I understood how these things should be managed. Of course I didn't. You can't handle an out-of-control blaze. You can't manage a natural disaster.

We went to my room. Max didn't even budge from under the table. It reminded me of the earthquake drills we had when I was a kid, where you hunched under your desk.

Meredith and I sat on my bed. She looked terrified.

What did you think? Like you didn't know? Jake yelled.

One of your guys? One of your guys! Lila kept repeating this. *Why didn't you tell me? You never told me!*

Back off. Back away, I'm warning you. Jake's voice was menacing. That's such a dramatic word. An R. W. Wright word. But it was the only word for it.

Protecting us, what a joke! A fucking stakeout? Watching us? You're going to fucking prison! What the fuck. This can't be happening!

Lila was furious, but she was crying, too. And I knew what this was about. The car on the street. Jake had told me the same thing when I first asked. *One of my guys.* But now he was telling her the truth. It wasn't one of his guys. It was a detective. Those paintings, that art—it was stolen, I was sure now.

Back away. *Get out of my* face!

I could hear a crash and a scream and then a thud. A push, a fall.

"Sydney," Meredith said. "Jesus! We have to do something. You have to call someone."

"Who?"

"I don't know! Your grandmother. Your father! Nine-one-one! This is *scary.*"

Something shattered. There was the sound of glass breaking. "Sydney!"

"Okay! Okay."

I fished my phone out of my bag. Meredith got up. "I don't want to hear this. This is so awful," she said. She went to her room. She shut the door. I didn't know who to call. Edwina was old and eight hundred miles away.

If his name hadn't been programmed into my phone, I wouldn't have even known how to reach him. Jeff Reilly gave his number out to only a few select people. Lila would be angry and betrayed if I called the ghost man that was *your father*. I remembered the time I went to his house for a few days when I was around ten, when Lila and Trace Williams needed some time alone to *work things out*. He took me shopping. He wasn't sure what to do with me, so he gave me stuff. He bought me a sequined top, which I thought was shiny and beautiful, but we got it in the women's department, and at lunch, he hit on the waitress. Lila was livid when she saw that sequined top. It went missing after that. When I found it shoved in the kitchen garbage can, she wouldn't let me have it back. I started to sob so hard my stomach hurt. I loved that top. Lila said, *A piece of trash belongs in the trash*, but I was the one who felt like garbage.

That afternoon with my father, he'd grinned at me across the table at lunch. *Daddy's little girl, huh?* he said. And I liked that so much. It made me feel really special. That's who he wanted me to be in relation to him. Little, and his. A daddy's little girl, the doll with the adoring eyes he occasionally played with, but only when nothing else seemed more fun.

What was I supposed to do, though? How many options did I have?

His phone rang and rang. *Not available*, his voice on the

message said, which was true in a million ways. *You know what to do*, but I didn't.

I hung up. It was just as well. Lila would never forgive me if he acted like a father. I called Edwina.

"They're fighting," I said. "It's bad."

"It'll blow over." Edwina didn't sound too sure. That fire in the city way back in 1906—it blew over, all right. And over, and over, until the city was consumed.

"She had a *black eye*. Things are breaking. They're *screaming*."

Edwina didn't say anything.

"*Why* is she with him? Why doesn't she *leave*?" I wanted Edwina to *do* something, even if she *was* old and two states away.

Edwina sighed, as if there were things I'd never understand. And she was probably right, but I was beginning to form my own understanding.

It looked like this: no more. No more, no more, no more.

"Mer?" I said through the door.

"What?"

"Can I come in?"

The fighting had calmed down by then.

"Sure."

"I called my grandmother. If they start up again, if we ever feel in the least bit scared, we're supposed to call the police." Edwina never said that. But it seemed like what an adult should say, so this was what I told her.

"Okay."

"I can just stay here with you."

Meredith's arms looped around her knees. She looked so young. She looked the kind of young you could look when you came from a family like hers.

"That's all right," she said. "I'm going to try to go to bed."

"All right. Mer, I'm sorry. I'm really, really sorry."

"It's not your fault," she said, but I could tell she didn't all the way believe it.

When I went back to my room, I felt sick. I'd wanted to show off all the great things we had. But the awful parts were mine too.

CHAPTER THIRTY-NINE

Exhibit 57: Recorded statement of Sydney E. Reilly,
2 of 5

The next morning, I was still half asleep when I heard a tap on the door.

I sat up.

"Syd?" Meredith called. She didn't just knock and then come in, like she would have at Academy. Knocking and waiting was what we did with people we didn't know that well.

When I opened the door, she was standing there with her roller bag. She had her jacket on.

"What are you doing?" She wasn't supposed to go home for three more days.

"My mom got me a flight. The taxi will be here any minute."

"Mer, *why*? Don't *go*."

It was confirmation of my utter failure. She'd seen who I

really was, and now look. She had always loved me, but not anymore.

"Syd. This is not good. None of this feels okay. This is all . . . dangerous."

She was right, of course. It was, it was.

"Syd? Did you hear me? This is *dangerous*. For you, too. My mom said to call her if you want to come with me. She said she'd have a ticket in two seconds."

I briefly imagined it—flying home beside Meredith, staying in their guest room, which also held Ellen's sewing machine and craft bins. There was no way I could leave Lila, though, not now. There was no way I could leave Nicco, either. But even more—it was hard to remember the girl who used to hang out with Meredith and her family, watching movies and making sundaes. That girl was like a town I'd once been to but would never see again. "No, Mer. Everything's fine now. I *promise*."

"You really should come with me."

"I can't do that! We're having our vacation, Mer, *jeez*."

"Okay. I'm going to wait outside."

"Mer, *please*."

I followed her down the stairs. When she opened the door, I could see her taxi already at the curb. That taxi was a sickening sight. If she actually got in it and drove away, it would mean that all of this was real. Serious and real.

"Mer, *come on!*"

"*I don't feel safe*," she said. "Something bad is going to happen. Something *worse*."

The taxi driver hauled Meredith's bag into the trunk and then slammed it shut. She got in the back of the car. She wouldn't look at me.

And, you know, I didn't realize it then, but I do now. In spite of everything we had, in spite of where we lived, and Lila's fame, and beauty, and money, and soaring views, and fancy cars, Meredith had something I didn't. She could use her voice. People had protected her and seen her and listened to her, so she could protect and see and listen to herself.

It was Tuesday morning. As the taxi drove off, Shane and one of the other guys, an older, heavyset man, took some orange cones out of the back of a truck and set them in a large rectangle in front of the property. Later, a big cement truck would come to pour the driveway. But right then, they just dropped the cones in various places, marking territory.

Shane looked at me and then made a gesture involving the finger of one hand and the cupped palm of the other.

"What're you doing?" the other man said. "For God's sake! Don't do that shit."

But Shane only smiled. He *winked* at me, as if we were playing that game together, the one you were supposed to play, where he chases and you say no until you finally give in.

I wasn't playing that game, though. I wanted to claw his eyes out. I wanted to yell and shout in his face. I wanted to put my chest right up against his and scream my outrage. But I could also imagine his voice. *Back away!* All he'd have to do was put one hand against my chest and shove.

* * *

I heard the garage door lift. The Lamborghini roared out. I was glad I didn't see Jake. I didn't want his approval anymore. I just wanted him gone. I was scared of him and scared of those paintings. I wanted to turn their faces to the wall, starting with *Jacqueline* and moving to *Crying Girl* and moving, maybe especially, to that poster of Lila.

I sat at the table in the kitchen, my hands around a cup of coffee, petting Max with my foot. I was still in my pajama shirt and shorts. I don't know how long I sat there. Long. Long enough that Lila woke up and came downstairs, her voice bright.

"What are the plans for the day, girls?" she said.

"Girl." I kept petting Max. I was so angry. I was getting angrier and angrier. Inside, my temperature was going up and up and up. At this rate, a person could, you know, *blow.*

"Where's Meredith?"

"She went home, Lila."

"She went home? Why?"

"Uh, *last night?*"

She was turned away from me, toward the coffeepot. Her shoulders looked guilty. She was guilty of some things, true, but not of others. It occurred to me that sometimes the wrong people carried the biggest burden of a crime, and that the ones who should didn't even bother to give it a glance.

When she faced me again, her eyes were wet. "I'm sorry, baby."

"She didn't feel safe, Lila. And neither do I. Do you hear me?" I said it, same as Meredith. But it lacked Meredith's certainty. It had no authority. Maybe because Lila wasn't protecting me and seeing me and listening to me even right then. She was looking at me and talking to me, but I was that toaster again.

"Jake isn't what he seems."

"You mean violent? Among other things? I saw proof. Your *eye*? We *heard* proof. Something bad is going to happen, Lila. Something really bad."

"I know he seems like this big, powerful guy. But he's a little boy inside. God, Syd-Syd. His childhood was a nightmare. His father used to *beat* him. He's just . . ."

"A bully. A bully with a lot of money."

I shoved my chair back and left the room. And I may not have had actual words for it right then, but I saw it. How men taught their sons how to be, and showed their daughters how much they were worth. How mothers could tell their daughters the truth about objects, if they knew it themselves.

CHAPTER FORTY

Exhibit 58: Recorded statement of Sydney E. Reilly,
    3 of 5

The fog and the fog and the fog! Maybe it was every ghost from 1906 suspended above, hovering. Three thousand people died from falling structures and fire then. All those spirits, and no wonder they never left. Lost souls, so much trauma—every ghost around us and in us shares that particular history.

A few days later, I met Nicco at Ocean Beach after work. It was late. Dark. Up on its rock, the Cliff House glowed with yellow light through the still-clear night, and the water that pooled in the nearby ruins caught the golden shimmers of the moon. I waited. It was cold, and I rubbed my arms against the chill. And then there he was. In his work clothes. His eyes caught the shimmers too.

His arms went around me, and mine went around him. He smelled like charbroiled dinners and cocktails and night air. Overhead, the clouds looked purple and blue, and they turned the sea purple and blue too. Nicco took my hand. We walked toward the edge of the water. The edge—it could be some metaphor, but it was just what we did.

A few days before, I'd told Nicco that Meredith had gone home sick. He didn't seem to believe me, but he left it alone. I didn't say anything about the scary fight or the paintings. Maybe Meredith had taught me a lesson about revealing too much truth, but maybe I also just didn't want to think about it for a while.

I slipped off my sandals. My feet sank into the sand, and I let the cold sea wash over my toes. Nicco kissed me and I tumbled into it. The cold didn't matter, because *IT* made a circle around us, and I was hungry and full at the same time.

"Big sparkle," I said, nodding toward the Cliff House. Even from there, you could see the candlelight on the tables, the flickering flames, the couples leaning in toward each other.

"Big night." He grabbed my hair and kissed me hard.

"Tie loosened like a weary businessman," I said when we broke away again. I scribbled in the air like it was something for his notebook. He had the knot of his necktie scooted down, the top button of his shirt undone. He had to wear a tie for certain catered events and he hated it.

"Who invented these stupid things?" he said. Then, suddenly, he whipped it over his head and tossed it, and a wave caught it and out it went. He didn't have a lot of money. It was a frivolous and funny thing to do, a playful moment, and it was just another thing to love about him.

"There it goes!" I laughed. It went farther and farther out.

"Bon voyage, tie. Have an awesome adventure." We watched it like a story. For a minute, it looked like it might come back riding on a wave, but no. It kept going.

"Send us a postcard, tie," I said.

"Safe travels, pal," he said.

The fog started to drift in. It got harder to see. We walked the beach. We didn't get far. I told you, that crazy feeling between us was everywhere. It was a current and a tide and every other force.

"Oh, man," he said. "Oh, man." My fingers were in his hair and up the back of his shirt. His hands were cold on my sides.

We stopped. Not for long. We started kissing again. He took my hand. He walked me toward a cove of rocks, a dark and hidden cove. It was sheltered from the wind, but probably not from the patrols who strolled the beach with their flashlights. We were near the ruins. You could think about how the ruins had been destroyed, but you could think about how they'd lasted, too.

We dropped to the ground. The sand was damp and hard, but who cared? My hands were on the bare skin of his hips, jammed down his black pants, and then I popped the button. Hands had DNA, a history of their own. They knew what to do from years and years of being hands. Tongues did.

"Syd, Syd, Syd," Nicco said. His breath was hot against my cheek. I forgot about being cold. "Syd, are you sure?"

I was nervous and a little scared, but I was sure.

"Yes. But I don't have anything." It felt crushing, that we'd have to wait.

"I do."

"You do?" What a relief, even though I had no idea how those things actually worked.

Nicco did, though. There was the funny smell of rubber, and then of us, and he lifted my hips and put his shirt under me. The ground was hard, and a shirt couldn't keep away the sand, and I tried to concentrate on the feelings, but everything seemed squeaky and badly fitting and my mind kept up a running commentary, like, *This is it*. And, *So that's what it feels like*, and, *I'm not sure, but I think it's over*.

He lay heavy on top of me, and kissed my neck and my face, and then we rose, and brushed off and got dressed. It was so foggy white out there now, it was just us in a strange, unseeable world. And even though right then kissing might almost have been better than actual sex, hands and crazy desire more physically awesome, I was happy, and I felt close to him. I felt different, but a larger different. I was glad we hadn't gotten caught. He held my hand. Our hips bumped as we walked. The fog had become so thick that I couldn't see three feet in front of us, but it seemed like a mystery, not a haunting.

He led me back to his van. It was a seventies-song cliché.

He set out a blanket, and we lay on the floor. We did it again much more slowly, and more of those songs made sense then.

Nicco drove me home. He was right, because sex did change things between us. I didn't want to go.

I told him this.

"Me neither," he said, and then I watched him drive away like I was some lovestruck heroine in a movie.

When I turned toward the house, I noticed that it was completely dark. I opened the door, and there was Max, waiting up for me like the worried mother I never had. He leapt on my legs and then dashed out to pee. He circled and circled and pretended to make a weighty decision and then just went on his same old bush he always went on.

There were no open guest room windows with nervous voices drifting down that night. I stood on the grass and let the moonlight shine on me. I felt longing, but it was the good kind of longing—a yearning for things that haven't happened yet. I was happy, in spite of everything that was going on at home. I was so happy that I picked up Max. I picked his big, huge self right on up. He seemed a little surprised yet patient about being suddenly off the ground.

"Oh, big, giant buddy. I love you, you big, beautiful beast," I said, and then I kissed his velvet head and set him down before I broke my back.

* * *

When I went inside the house, the little hairs on my arms stood up. That ghost—she blew her cold breath right down my skin. Something was wrong. I didn't know what yet, but I could sense a change. The alarm had been turned on, so Lila and Jake were asleep in bed, I assumed, but I felt a strange absence. An echoey space. Something, *someone*, gone.

The house was quiet except for Max's toenails in the kitchen and the slurp of him having a long drink of water, and the ticking of the clock in the White Room, and the roar of the sea outside.

The White Room pulled me forward. *Tick, tick, tick.* And then I saw what the absence was. I saw what was gone. The huge painting, *Crying Girl*, otherwise known as a *woman*, with her red lips and her finger wiping away that tear.

There was just a large, empty space on the wall. I could see the holes where the hanger had been.

I felt a curl of nervous fear. My mind tried to put pieces together, but I didn't have the pieces. I had the words from the night before, though. *Watching us. Stakeout. Prison.*

In the dining room—*Jacqueline*. Gone.

I went upstairs to the guest room. I was scared to push open the door. And then I did. I looked. Crates—gone. The whole room was empty.

There seemed to be only two possibilities. Either Jake had hidden the paintings, or the police, or whoever had been watching our house, had taken them, which meant they'd probably taken Jake, too. You know, off. Away. To jail.

I felt shaky and clammy. I started to panic a little. If that had happened, though, Lila would be awake, crying and hysterical, wouldn't she? Maybe Lila's friend Louise would be here too, her "crisis manager," who always showed up when there was a problem. I'd have gotten calls from Edwina, wondering what was going on. But 716 Sea Cliff Drive was still and silent.

There was only one way to know for sure if Jake had been carted off. I crept upstairs to their room.

I listened. It seemed so quiet.

My heart was pounding. After that horrible fight that night, anything seemed possible. I didn't know what I might find behind that door.

My hand shook. Lila's room was strictly off-limits. I suddenly thought of that scene in *Nefarious* when Lila's character goes to the home of her lover and his wife and sneaks into their bedroom, with plans to bludgeon them with a hammer.

I turned the knob slowly, slowly, slowly. I pushed the door open.

I peered inside.

Two lumps, two sleeping bodies. Lila on the far side, her blond head on the pillow, her breath raising and lowering the covers. Jake, closest to the door, the back of his head facing me, his body curved around hers.

The paintings hadn't been seized by police.

He'd hidden all those women, I realized. The crying ones, the faceless ones, the beautiful ones, the ones without mouths to speak, the ones who were only bodies. He'd hidden them so no one would know what he'd taken.

I hated him then.

I hated him so much. For the bruises and the paintings and his ownership of that house and more. Honestly, for a moment I wished I *were* Lila's character with that hammer in her hand, walking toward that bed.

CHAPTER FORTY-ONE

Exhibit 59: Sworn statement of Evan Dunne

Lila wore her sleeveless white dress, the one trimmed in gold around the neck and the hem. Her lucky dress. At least, that's what she'd called it the last time I saw her in it, a few weeks before, when she and Jake had gone out for dinner.

We were up early. She was driving us out to Nick's Cove for a preproduction table read of *Peyton Place*, her new project. Lila had insisted I go with her. I had no clue why. I thought maybe she didn't want me alone in the house with Jake.

Nick's Cove was a resort of seaside cottages perched next to the ocean, pretty much halfway between Sea Ranch and San Francisco. Most of the town scenes would be filmed in Sea Ranch, Lila said, because it was so charming and had dramatic views of the Pacific coast. They'd also use Highway 1, with its long stretches of high bluffs that fell straight into the ocean.

But Connie, Lila's character, and her daughter, Allison, would "live" at Nick's, in one of the cove bungalows.

They were doing the reading at the boat shack at the end of the pier at Nick's. We were supposed to spend the night afterward at the nearby Timber Cove Resort. This was the kind of thing Evan Dunne did, Lila told me, bringing everyone out for a first read in the actual setting of the film. Compared to where he'd done this before, Nick's Cove was nothing. For *Endless Kingdom*, the cast had met at the Neemrana Fort-Palace, a lush fifteenth-century fort built into fourteen tiers of a hill near Delhi.

Jade Arcadia, the girl from *Twenty Seasons*, was going to play Allison, Connie/Lila's daughter, and Terence Tate (*The Dubious Trent Darby* and *Constantine Valentine*) would be Michael, Lila's love interest. Those were the big names, but the whole cast would be there. I was nervous to meet Evan Dunne. I knew he was important to Lila, and important in general.

She was driving us herself, and this seemed strange. For long trips—and this one was over an hour each way—she'd usually hire a car service so she didn't have to deal with the stress of traffic. But that morning, not only did she drive us, she also took Highway 1, the scenic route. The road hugged the coast and had high, winding switchbacks. I clutched the handrail on those blind curves.

"Why didn't we take a car?" I asked. Her driving was making me nervous. That road was.

"I wanted it to be just us. We have hardly had any time

together since you've been here. Plus, *look* at this incredible panorama! Girls' road trip!"

It was beautiful, yeah, and we were alone, but I'm sure those weren't the only reasons she didn't hire a service. Maybe it was money. If Jake got arrested, it was all over. His financial help, that house, her entire career. Even the project she was working on that very day. A scandal like that could destroy her. *Us.*

I didn't want to talk about it, but someone needed to.

"Where'd they go?"

"Where'd what go?"

"The paintings. *Crying Girl. Jacqueline.* All the others."

"I didn't ask. It's not my business."

"Not your business? It seems very much your business. Why are you still with him after all this shit?"

"Baby, do we have to do this now? I'm stressed enough already. I'm trying to enjoy myself with you."

I was so exasperated. Beyond. *Tick, tick, tick,* my anger grew.

"Lila. You need to leave this guy. Everything about this is bad."

"*Baby.* I have it managed."

I could feel the slippage. The plates of the earth shifting and shivering.

I stared out the window. I shut my eyes tight on those blind curves. For a few miles, she tailed an old, slow camper with the license plate CAPTAIN ED, revving her accelerator obnoxiously, clicking her nails on the steering wheel until she could pass. I texted Meredith. She'd gone mostly silent on me since she left. There'd been a few brief texts between us, several ignored phone calls, the word *busy* used too often. I hope you're okay. I hope everything is all right with us.

No answer.

Please don't ignore me, Mer!

Nothing.

I texted Nicco. Big cliffs. It's as curvy as you said, and Lila's driving like a maniac. When we'd talked on the phone that morning, he'd warned me that it was a nail-biting road.

Big seat belt? he texted. Can't stop thinking about you.

"I'm driving here with *you*, so we can have some time together in this stunning place, and all you're doing is texting that *boy*."

"I'm texting *Meredith*." It was a lie, but among all the crimes happening right then, it was pretty small.

"Jake thinks you're too young to be 'involved.'" She made the sarcastic air quotes with her voice.

"Yeah, well, maybe he should concentrate on his own problems."

"'She's not a *child*,' I told him. I don't know why he's so *protective*." She glanced over at me, like maybe I did know why.

We drove the rest of the way in silence. Silence, except for the little sighs that told me how badly I was disappointing her. I didn't know what Lila wanted from me. Even she seemed to want me to be sexy and beautiful but not be sexy and beautiful. If I hadn't known better, if I hadn't been sure that mothers would never feel such a thing, I'd have thought that she was jealous.

* * *

The cottages of Nick's Cove were so cute—red, blue, white, and green, with their little decks hanging over the water. All of the fancy cars in front looked out of place.

Lila held my elbow. She was unsteady in her heels as we walked down the dock to the shingled boat shack at the end of the pier. Inside, the shack was rustic chic, all rough-hewn wood and open beams strung with lit white lights and charming multipaned windows looking out toward the sea. There was a stone hearth with a big drum stove, a canoe hanging upside down across the ceiling, walls hung with fishing baskets and floats. Two beautiful wood tables were shoved together. We were the last ones to get there, which was how she liked it. Everyone else was already seated in glossy red wood chairs around the tables.

Evan Dunne, well, you know what he looks like. Hair, which he was always pushing back, swooped down over one eye; a direct gaze; jeans and a sweatshirt that looked like he'd worn them for days. Signature high-top work boots that supposedly belonged to his father, the iconic director Reese Dunne. He was clearly impatient, since they'd been waiting, and so after the hugs and introductions, he moved two flat hands in a downward motion, as if he were quieting an orchestra, and the reading began.

It was exciting, really, to see these people and hear their voices making a story come to life. They didn't know what I did, though, that this whole project might be doomed. As soon as word got out about Jake, boom. Finished.

I sat in my red chair and listened. And as I did, I felt a creeping awareness. I started to feel sick. Connie was a bombshell single mother, the most desired woman in town, in a relationship with a dark-haired man who physically overpowered her. Allison, her teenage daughter, was naive. Pathetic. Alone and misunderstood, until she kissed a boy and was sexually "awakened."

I sat in that chair next to Lila feeling exposed. Humiliated. My face was red.

"She isn't six, she's sixteen," Terence Tate said. Michael and Constance were arguing about Allison.

"She's not *your* child, so what do you care? Keep it to yourself," Lila read.

It was our conversation. My humiliation turned to an ugly shame. I could barely breathe as I sat in that red chair. How could Lila do such a thing? How could she use me like that?

I dug my nails into my own hand. I needed to get out of there, but I couldn't move. I was a prisoner on an island, and the currents around it were too strong for me to swim to my escape.

"Your body looks incredibly young," Terence/Michael said to Lila/Constance. "For a woman of thirty-nine. How is that possible? You have breasts like a virgin."

"Close on: the hips of Terence moving against Constance," Evan Dunne read.

God, I felt sick enough to vomit. I shoved my chair back.

"Excuse me," I said to no one and everyone. I hurried out of the boat shack. I could hear Lila's voice and then laughter. She was making a joke about me fleeing, I was sure, but I didn't care.

I sped back down the pier, toward the restaurant at Nick's Cove. I found the bathroom and closed myself inside. I splashed my face with cold water. I stayed in there a long while. I felt this rage building. I don't know how to explain it, but it was building and building, the worst kind of rage, when you're as helpless as you are angry.

When I finally stepped back outside, Lila was there. Her arms were folded. She looked amused, not mad, which made me even more infuriated.

"Baby," she said. "Why did you run off?"

It wasn't the time or the place for this. "Why are you out here?"

"We're taking a break." I could see it was true—waiters were heading toward the shack with trays of oysters on the half shell and plates piled with french fries. The cast milled around outside. Anyone could tell by looking at us that this was a confrontation. I tried to keep my voice low.

"How could you?"

"I have no idea what you're talking about."

"The whole story. Me. You."

"Oh, it is not."

"Lila."

"I optioned it two years ago! There are *similarities*, that's all."

"You used me. You used what's happening to me."

"Baby, the book was written in *1956*. The film came out in *1957*. That was over sixty years ago! These aren't *my* ideas."

"Well, that's even worse, then, because it means nothing has changed."

"*What* nothing has changed?"

"This," I said. I circled my hand in the space between us, meaning her, all of it. Us. Men and women, women and women.

"Mothers? Daughters? That will *never* change. Never, ever, ever."

"You. The way you keep making yourself this *thing*. This *body*."

"It's my *profession*."

"*Why* do you do this? Why? It's like it's the only power you have! Like, they made you an object, so you see yourself as one." I shouldn't have blamed her. She probably never really had the chance to be anyone different from who she was. She'd only taken in every message she'd gotten, every message given for thousands of years, and swallowed them. God! That's how bad things were, that even the targets of this bullshit believed the bullshit. The vampire sinks his teeth into your neck, drains your blood, and turns you into another vampire.

Her face flushed. She looked pissed, but she was keeping her voice low too. "You don't know anything. I'm *here*. Do you know what that took? Girls now will never know what it was like. You'll never have the struggles I did."

She was right. But she was wrong, too. Because I did have her struggles. I did know what it was like.

We both stood there, silently fuming at each other.

Then, in her purse, her phone rang. She dug around for it, looked at the number.

"I have to get this."

"Fine, whatever."

She walked away, plugging one ear to hear better. She disappeared toward the front of the restaurant.

I made my way to a dock near the boat shack, one that lay flat on the water. I sat at the edge.

My own phone rang then. Meredith! I answered so fast. I was so glad to see her name there.

"I was worried you were going to ignore me forever," I said.

"I had my phone off. I was at the dentist," she said, but her voice sounded different. "I told you, there's been a million things going on."

"Are we okay?"

"Are *you* okay, that's the question."

"*Yes*, I'm okay. There haven't been any more fights. Please don't be mad."

"I'm not *mad*. I'm scared for you. For *a lot* of reasons." She meant Jake and Lila, but not just. She meant the way I'd had my hands on Nicco, too. The way I was so hungry when I was supposed to order the salad.

"I'm fine," I said. Now my voice sounded different.

"Well, I'm glad to hear it. Hey, I need to go," Meredith said. "My mom needs help unloading the groceries."

We hung up. My heart felt stricken and sad. When everyone returned to the boat shack to eat lunch and finish the read, I stayed where I was. I'd lost any appetite I might have had. I slipped off my sandals and took photos of my feet in the water, because this was me, drowning.

CHAPTER FORTY-TWO

Exhibit 60: Sworn statement of Jade Arcadia

Exhibit 61: Sworn statement of Terence Tate

I couldn't even imagine having to stay at Timber Cove for the night with Lila. But it turned out I didn't have to. After the read was finished and everyone filed out, Lila waved her arm and jingled her keys, indicating it was time to go. I could feel a new tension in the air. Evan Dunne seemed pissed. Terence seemed pissed. I could see it in their shoulders and jawlines as they walked down the pier side by side, talking. I wondered what had happened in there.

"Come on," Lila said.

I got into her car, and I folded my arms to make sure she knew I was still unhappy with her. My plan was to not speak to her all evening and excuse myself from dinner with the rest of them.

But then, when the other cars turned left to go north on Highway 1, Lila turned right.

"Lila. Wrong way."

She didn't answer. Maybe she was punishing me right back, silence for silence.

"What are you doing? They all turned left," I said.

"We're going home."

"What do you mean, we're going home? Ugh!" I exhaled in frustration. "Honestly, you don't need to make a big deal about this in front of everyone! You don't need to make some big *point* because we had a fight." God. How humiliating!

"You know, Sydney, everything isn't always about you."

This pissed me off. SO off. Everything about *me*? But then I got worried. "Why are we going home, then?"

"I got a call."

"A call."

"And I have to deal with it."

It was the kind of bad where you're too afraid to ask. The sky turned a blazing orange and pink, and then the sun dropped. Rapidly, the curved road was turning dark, and Lila was going too fast.

"Lila. Slow down."

She looked over at me, her face in shadows. "Hand me my purse."

"What do you need? I'll get it."

"Just hand it to me."

I did. She stuck her hand in, retrieved a pack of cigarettes and a lighter.

"Oh, great. Thanks for the cancer ride."

She ignored me. She lit one of the cigarettes while still driving. She inhaled, and then exhaled a long train of smoke, like an old movie star, older than her, from the days when people didn't know what those things did to your lungs. She cracked her window, and the cigarette hung out there and rode in the air like a nervous skydiver in the doorway of the plane, unable to make the leap.

The orange tip glowed, and her dashboard glowed, and her two headlights beamed into the black night. The only other lights were when a car came from the other direction. Then it was a sudden blaze of brightness, arcing around a corner. It was scary. You'd never even know that the sea was out there.

She edged over the line because she couldn't see. I was driving for her even though I never learned how. I was looking out for cars, my foot hovering over my imaginary brake. I didn't know why we were in such a hurry. And I still didn't know why we had to go home when that day was so important, when Evan Dunne was, when everyone was there and so much had been done to make it happen. But we were heading back so fast that it felt like an emergency. I watched the speedometer, the little red hand creeping up, up where it shouldn't be. My foot pressed hard to the floor. I watched the road, navigated the winding maze of black. I was sweating, and my palms were clammy. But she sped and she smoked and the toxic fumes hovered around us.

It wasn't safe anywhere. The car wasn't. She wasn't. Those curves weren't, and neither were the sheer drop-offs I could sometimes see, the straight-down plunges into the ocean. I stayed quiet, and I focused on the narrow highway.

"Lila, shit!" I said as a semi passed and our car shuddered and shivered from its speed.

"Would you relax?" she said. "I've been down this road a hundred times." Well, I was too terrified for metaphors then, but I see it now. And it was true, wasn't it? She *had* been down that road, with my father and Papa Chesterton and Roberto and Trace Williams. But she hadn't been down this exact road. Not with these particular curves, not with a darkness this deep.

I rolled my window down because I could feel the carcinogens eating their way into my healthy pink lungs. But I had to roll it up again. The strong wind coming in the car was another distraction, and I had to concentrate. I had to help her drive.

I was relieved when we reached the city. The traffic forced Lila to slow down, and there were no more blind curves. The dangers were clear, instead of horrible surprises that might come around a corner at any moment, like the highway version of an R. W. Wright novel. Still, she rode people's asses and sped through the lights as they turned from yellow to red. Might as well bypass the whole "caution" thing. *Yellow is just a suggestion,* I remembered Jake saying once.

She swerved into the drive of 716 Sea Cliff and didn't even bother going into the garage. The car ended up at a weird angle.

She yanked the parking brake and got out. I took my bag out of the back, but she was already inside. When I'd packed that bag, my big worry was what Evan Dunne and everyone else would think of my clothes. My mind had been on the heartache of being away from Nicco for a full forty-eight hours.

"I missed you, buddy," I said to Max, and scruffed his neck. But I was tense. I dropped my bag in my room. I expected fighting, so I wanted to get out of that house. I considered listening to Meredith and taking a flight home, but that would mean leaving Nicco. I pulled on a pair of shorts and a tank and a sweatshirt. I got my drawing pad and my pastels, because drawing was distracting, and it would be better than just sitting there. Maybe, too, I just wanted to remember who I was before I'd come to that place.

I crept down the stairs. I listened. They were in the kitchen. Lila's voice was full of emotion, but she sounded more scared than angry. She sounded like she was being careful. Maybe that's what you did after someone put a hand on you—spoke carefully, quietly. Or maybe she was just too afraid to be angry.

I listened only long enough to understand what had happened: The phone call she had gotten was from the FBI. *The FBI!* Well, you know this already. They called to ask questions about Jake and what she'd seen at the house, what she knew. They wanted her to come in to speak in person. They asked her so many questions that everyone at the read had to wait. Evan Dunne and the rest were pissed when she said she had to go.

"You don't answer anything!" Jake said. "You don't talk to anyone without a lawyer!"

He was mad, but she started to cry. "This could ruin everything," she said. And he kept saying, "It's okay, baby. It's okay, baby. It's going to be okay."

No, it wouldn't be. You had the foreshocks and then the shock itself. In 1906 the earthquake took just one minute to change the lives of thousands, and then the tsunami buried the Presidio, and then the fire burned for three days. And our great-grandmother, you know, she had to run.

I stepped quietly through the White Room, where the blank space of *Crying Girl* still called to me from that large, bare wall. I opened the doors to the beautiful patio overlooking the ocean. In the darkness, I took the 104 steps down to China Beach.

CHAPTER FORTY-THREE

Exhibit 62: Recorded statement of Sydney E. Reilly,
4 of 5

It was dark down on the beach, but it was a warm night. I could see our house on the cliff above me, but also the unfinished one next door. The frame was nearing completion, but there were no walls to contain you and no roof to shelter you. I walked until I was right in front of it, sat on a rock, and listened to the crash of the waves and then the *crickle-crickle* as the water retreated over the sand.

I set my drawing pad down beside me and called Nicco.

"You're home! A day early."

"Yeah, unexpectedly."

"Is everything okay? You sound awful."

"I don't know. Things are strange."

"What's going on?"

I still hadn't told him about any of this. Not the art, not Jake, not the man watching us, who I now knew was an agent with the FBI. "Jake. He's in some kind of trouble."

"Oh, shit."

"Large shit." Somehow this reference to our old joke didn't really work. It wasn't the time to joke.

"God, Syd."

I didn't say anything. I just watched the moonlight decorating the waves with diamonds.

"What kind of trouble?"

"Has to do with art."

"Art."

"He buys and sells it, but you know, I'm not sure if it's all . . . on the up-and-up." To put it mildly. I had no idea who he stole it from, or how.

"Oh, wow."

"It's bad."

"Oh, wow," Nicco said again. "I hope you and your mom are okay."

I liked how he said this. "You and your mom." It shoved away all of her fame and the money and the important people and this big crime and all the rest of it, and made it about what it *was* about, just me and my mother. Me and my mother, and what could happen to us.

"He's not a good guy."

"Do you need me to come and get you? You could stay here."

"Nah. I'm all right. Just sit here and keep me company."

"I can do that. Are we still on for day after tomorrow?"

"God, yes. I definitely want that."

"I wish I didn't have to work, or it'd be sooner. If you need me to, I can take time off."

"That's okay."

"And shit, my roommate's having a party. If we want to be alone, we'll have to go somewhere else."

"We'll go somewhere else." I wanted to be alone, all right.

"Where are you? It sounds like a hair blower."

I laughed. "It's the ocean. I'm down at the beach. Hair-blower ocean," I said. Something for his notebook.

"You'll be careful? The tide comes in quick. There's not much beach down there."

I knew nothing about tides. The way they could come in and swallow you up, the way that they always went out again.

We hung up. I hadn't even noticed, but he was right. Before I called, the water was out past a nearby group of rocks, and now the rocks were covered.

It was late, but I wasn't going to go in yet. I could see that the lights were still on in our house. I'd go back when everyone was asleep.

I picked up my drawing pad. It was funny, because the last thing I'd drawn was a still life of some flowers in a vase that we'd done in class. But life wasn't still, and this seemed like so long ago, and those flowers had nothing to do with me.

In those paintings, the women were bodies. The artists had held the brush and decided what to leave out. I'd never leave out the things that made a person human. I turned to a blank page.

And I sketched Nicco then. The way he'd looked when he was reclining on the beach that night in the fog.

I got lost in what I was doing. I wanted to capture him, the real him. The eyes were the hardest part.

And then I heard a shout.

"Sydney! For God's sake, what are you doing? Get the hell over here!"

Jake. I looked up, and I saw that he was right; there was reason for alarm. The tide had crept in. The sea had covered the space between the unbuilt house and ours. The water had reached our stairs.

"Jesus!" he cried.

"I'm coming!" I yelled. But I had to wade. The water was up to my ankles. When a wave came in, it splashed up my thighs, wetting the hem of my shorts. I could feel the pull of it, drawing me out.

Jake reached his arm toward me, and I took his hand. The force of the next wave was stronger than I imagined. His hand gripped mine hard. Even with the way I felt about him right then, I was thankful for it.

"Your mother was worried."

I doubted that. I doubted she'd even noticed I was gone. *He'd* noticed. His eyes were the ones that were always on me, even more than hers.

He yanked me up to the stair where he stood. The water still smashed at our feet.

"Do you know how dangerous it is out here? You would've had to climb back up." He pointed to the cliff. "Could you have climbed that?"

"I lost track of time."

He caught sight of my drawing pad. "What is that?"

I tried to flip it closed. "A study."

"A study, huh?"

I didn't say anything.

"I saw that. You think I don't know who that was?" He exhaled disgust. "Nice, you know. Real nice. The guy's dick hanging out."

What did it matter to him? Didn't he have bigger problems than me drawing a penis, for God's sake? "The women are naked in all those paintings."

"That's *art*. This isn't. You're lucky I don't burn that. You think that's what men want? Someone easy? Someone handing it over? Wrong. Men want a *lady*. You gotta respect yourself. A beautiful girl like you, Jesus Christ."

"I do respect myself."

"The way you're acting with that kid, it sure doesn't seem like it."

"What about *him*? Is *he* respecting *him*self?" Whoever said that about guys and sex? No one. Never.

"His job is to respect *you*." Jake was pissed. "If I see that kid again, he better watch his ass, that's all I can say. He better keep both eyes open while he sleeps."

We were at the top of the stairs by then. Jake shook his head and exhaled, stormed into the house, mad. He slammed the glass doors of the White Room, making them shudder.

I opened the doors again slowly, carefully. I crept upstairs without being seen or heard. I did that because he scared me. But I was mad, too. Really mad. I mean, first off, he was a bully-asshole-criminal. And second, Jake and me and sex— he didn't care about me taking a big step, or getting STDs, or using contraception. He was guarding my virtue, like my body and my spirit would spoil if I were touched. Like my body was *his*. To leer at and control. Well, fuck you, because it was mine, and I wanted it—the all-and-everything that any guy could have.

I was angry, you know. The kind of angry that makes you feel dangerous. Under my feet, the earth shook. I imagined how it would look when everything began to fall.

CHAPTER FORTY-FOUR

Exhibit 63: Sworn testimony of Detective Reese Craig,
2 of 2
Exhibit 64: Surveillance notes of Detective Reese Craig

The next morning, I called the car service. I wanted to go to City Lights again. I wanted to be with all those spines and words, where the signs in the windows read STAND UP TO POWER and THERE IS NO PROGRESS WITHOUT STRUGGLE and COURAGE IS THE TRIUMPH OVER FEAR.

I didn't want to be in that house, either, so I waited outside. And then I saw Shane.

For once, he didn't see me. He was actually inside the structure of that house, on the second floor. His back was to me. He held a large drill. He raised it above his shoulder, as if sinking that drill bit into wood were no effort at all. I watched his big shoulders, his powerful, strong forearms. I thought of all the times he'd looked at me and called to me.

I felt *compelled*. My heart started to pound like a fist on a door again. *IT* pushed me forward before I could even think it through.

I hurried over, because *need* makes everything suddenly urgent. Two of the other guys were out by the utility box near the street. If they saw me, I didn't notice, and didn't care. I stepped around rolls of tar paper and stacks of who-knows-what. I made my way across what would be the living room, and then I went up the stairs to where Shane was.

He didn't hear me. His back was to me. He was wearing goggles, and the strap was buried in his curly hair.

But then he must have sensed my presence, because he lowered the drill and turned around. When he saw me, he tossed his goggles off.

"Shit, you scared me. Hey, you."

I looked at him. As I said, he was handsome, really.

"What are you doing here?" He lowered his voice, raised one eyebrow like we were playing that game again.

I lifted my hand to his face. My hand was on his skin, and it was warm and I could feel his strong cheekbone under my fingers.

And then I gripped his jaw and turned it so that he looked at me. I mean really looked at me. It was so clear to me then: *IT* was not only about sex or fun or exciting stuff that might change me. What I wanted was larger than any of that. I wanted to be as full in the world as anyone else.

"Stop harassing me," I said.

He looked shocked. He grinned. He grinned like I was being cute, like I was being amusing, a playful little kitten.

"Stop. Harassing. Me."

"Hey. Hey," he said. "Let go."

I did. But not until he saw me first.

"If you don't stop this, I'm going to call the head of . . ." Shit. I didn't know. "Whatever company you work for. I'm going to call and file a complaint."

"I thought you liked it."

Did I? Had I? Was there part of it I liked? I didn't even know. Maybe I did the first time. But then I didn't. It made me nervous. Scared, even. But I was supposed to think it was a compliment. And if it didn't feel like one, what could I do about it anyway? Look at him, I mean. Look at his arms, his age, his shoulders. It seemed better to like it. Or at least, to not make a big deal out of it. To put up with it. To take it.

"I'm sixteen, you know. I'm just trying to have a good summer," I said.

"I thought you were in college."

"If I were in college, I still wouldn't like it."

"I'm sorry."

"I'm a real person."

"Hey, I'm sorry."

"Why is that so easy to forget?"

"Jesus, *okay*."

I wanted to say more. I had lots more to say. But I could hear the edge in his voice. He was getting pissed. We were standing on the second floor of that house in a place where there were no walls. How pissed could he get? Could he shut me up with a shove? He was the one who got to decide how this went.

I turned around. I felt his eyes on my back. I felt them boring into me, same as that drill. I didn't run or even hurry. It was so hard not to. But I didn't want him to know I was scared.

There still wasn't a handrail, and my legs shook as I went down the stairs. My little flowered purse bumped against my hip.

I stepped out of that frame, the bare wood bones of a future home. My heart was beating hard. My face was flushed. God, I was sweating like mad. I didn't feel victorious. The bigger victory would have been to not have to say it in the first place. But I did something necessary, you know. I made sure he knew it was my world too.

The car service was waiting for me out in front of 716 Sea Cliff Drive. I got in the back.

"Where to?" the driver asked.

"City Lights."

He met my eyes in the rearview mirror. "No prob."

My flowered purse sat in my lap. My hands were shaking so bad that I could barely get the seat belt into the buckle. Finally,

I fastened it. I was in the back seat. I wasn't behind the wheel. And I decided right there that the first thing I needed to do was learn how to drive.

At City Lights, I saw Agatha again. After Nicco, I realized that this probably wasn't some fateful coincidence. Likely, I'd just happened upon a person's routine.

She had her sun hat tied around her neck, and it hung against her back. She wore tan walking shorts with lots of pockets, and an old T-shirt with a large orange sun that said BIG SUR FOLK FESTIVAL. I pictured her with her narrow, bare butt and droopy boobs and her skin like fallen bread dough. I wondered what had led her to walking that beach naked. Or more important, not caring when she did. If I ever heard her stories, I was sure she'd have things to teach me.

She was in the travel section, like the time before. She had another book about Oregon under one arm, and she perused the shelves with her head at an angle in order to read the titles better. I wondered why she was so interested in Oregon—if it was a part of her past or of her future.

I snooped on Agatha, and then I tried to find the second Elena Ferrante in the series, but they didn't have it. The bookseller offered to order it. It would come in about a week.

"That's okay, I'll just look around," I said.

We are animals, and animals have instincts, I know. But what if instincts were just the ghosts of our own family history talking? Telling us their stories, whispering all the things they learned about vulnerability and danger, of bad stuff about to happen. Warning us, if it's quiet enough to hear them. In that bookstore, it was quiet enough. My instinct told me a week was too late. In a week, I wouldn't be there. A week might as well have been years.

CHAPTER FORTY-FIVE

Exhibit 65: Receipt, FTD

Exhibit 66: Sworn statement of Riley Latona, FTD
Delivery

Exhibit 67: U.S. Department of Justice/Federal
Bureau of Investigation subpoena issued to
Giacomo (Jake) A. Antonetti

The next morning, Lila was awake early again, but not for work. She was making little repairs to me. She was in the kitchen wearing her ivory satin robe and she was baking. *Baking!* Muffins out of a box, where all you do is add the egg and water, but still. Maybe she'd talked to Edwina, because they were my favorite kind, the poppy seed ones that Edwina made for me on Sunday mornings when I stayed with her for the weekend.

"Are you free for a few minutes today?" Lila asked, as if I were a titan of business with a packed calendar.

"Well, there was that meeting with the foreign heads of state," I said. "But I could cancel. Yeah. I'm free until tonight."

"What's tonight?"

I rolled my eyes because she should have known this meant I was hanging out with Nicco.

"Let's go to lunch," she said.

"Okay."

"Sutro's at the Cliff House."

I didn't know if this was some weird Lila move, because that's where Nicco worked. "Why Sutro's? You getting the dirt on Nicco?"

But she just looked baffled. And then, "Oh. Oh, right, I forgot." I'd told her a hundred times that Nicco worked there. "It's just close and you can't beat the view."

I shrugged. We wouldn't see him anyway, since he was working at his moms' store that afternoon. He'd laugh about us going.

The host sat us by the large glass windows. People stared at Lila, who was dressed all in tangerine. The restaurant was decorated in shades of white and gray, so she was a bright solar flare.

It was strange to see that place from the inside out, rather than from the outside in. From every angle, you could see the Pacific Ocean or Seal Rocks or the Sutro Bath ruins, looking different from that perspective. The waiter wore Nicco's familiar black pants and white shirt, and I pictured Nicco doing the same things he did, offering his service, describing the specials, gathering the wineglasses the moment he was sure we wouldn't need them.

We ordered crab sandwiches. I looked out at the ocean. In 1887 a schooner loaded with dynamite crashed into those very rocks and exploded, destroying a wing of the old Cliff House, right where we sat. Two more fires blazed here after that. History was everywhere, and you were looking right at it, even if you didn't realize it.

"Syd-Syd," Lila said. "I want to apologize. This whole summer . . ." She waved her hand around, indicating chaos. I didn't say anything, because *yeah*. Yeah, it had been. "And last weekend . . . it didn't even occur to me, you know, about *Peyton Place*. I didn't even make the connection, you and your budding romance with the boy."

"Lila, gross. 'Budding romance'?"

"You know what I mean! I didn't even realize the similarities. Maybe some part of me did, I don't know. So much is under the surface. I just don't *see* things sometimes."

That was for sure. Lila signaled the waiter. She changed her mind about the wine. Then she leaned forward, took my hands.

"Baby, I'm leaving him," she said.

"You are?" I was so relieved. So, so relieved.

"I don't know what this means for us, but we'll get through somehow."

"That's great, Lila. That's really great."

"I'm scared of him. And now he's gotten me involved in a terrible mess. . . ."

"I know."

"I had no idea what he was doing. I feel like an idiot. I thought he was a big, successful real estate man. An art collector . . ."

I didn't entirely believe her, that she had no idea what he was doing. But it didn't matter. It felt so good to hear her say that she was leaving Jake. Something was being *done*. I wish I could explain how beautiful she looked sitting across from me, and how wonderful it felt for her to be honest and real about her own mistakes. But even more than that, I wish I could explain what I saw in her eyes. What I understood. How she had hoped for things. How it was complicated, really complicated, for her to know how to get them.

"I'm going to tell him this weekend. I can't do it tonight because it's our *anniversary*, and he's got this fancy dinner planned."

"Oh, Lila . . ." I groaned. But I didn't know about any of this. I didn't know how you sometimes didn't say the important thing because of an anniversary or a birthday or because it was Christmas or Valentine's Day, or his mother had just died, or his cat was sick, or he'd been nice or had paid the check or had just helped you or was about to.

"After that, I promise. I just need to wait this out. He'd kill me if I did it tonight."

Of course, she didn't mean that literally.

The Lamborghini was in the driveway when Lila and I got back home. You didn't keep regular office hours when you were a real estate tycoon–slash–art thief.

Max greeted me like I was the parent coming home after his night with a mean babysitter. I could feel his jazzed tension, and his ears were back and he was yawning a lot and kept jumping up even though I told him to quit. Jake sat in the White Room on that white couch. In front of him, on the glass table, there was an enormous bouquet. It was the size of a pup tent. White lilies, white orchids, white roses. It was stunning, very Lila, no expense spared.

Her face lit up when she saw it. But like this whole story that I'm trying to tell you right now—it was not what it seemed.

Because Jake was seething. It didn't make sense. If he had bought these for her, he'd be pleased, seeing her beaming like that. But no. He looked murderous.

"I thought these were from *you*," he said before she could even set down her purse. "For our anniversary. Fucking bastards."

"What?" Lila was having trouble understanding too.

"The guy handed me the flowers, and I signed for them."

Inside that bouquet was a subpoena for all of Jake's business records. They'd tricked him into taking it. Score one for the FBI.

Before I left to meet Nicco, I tapped on Lila's bedroom door to say good-bye. She was getting ready. She wore a glittery gold dress, but she was barefoot. She hadn't put on her heels yet. She smelled good. I heard the shower running.

"You're still going, huh?" With Jake's legal troubles deepening by the minute, I thought their plans might change, but no.

"He's in a *mood*." Lila rolled her eyes. She held her lipstick, twisted it upward, the red ready to meet her mouth. But her hand trembled. It gave me an awful feeling in my stomach.

"Maybe you shouldn't go."

"That's what I said, but he's made all these arrangements."

"You don't have to," I said.

"It's fine. You look pretty."

"Thanks." I was wearing the flowered sundress we bought that day at Paige. "You do too."

"Love you, baby," she said, so of course I said it back. Those were the rules.

"Love you."

"At least they're going out," I told Max. "It'll be okay. You can just kick back with a relaxing bowl of water and a nice dinner of brown crunchy stuff."

I swear, he looked doubtful.

That awful feeling in my stomach came with me as I stepped out the front door of 716 Sea Cliff Drive. And then the ghost leaned in close and tried to speak. I couldn't hear her, but I felt her cold, forever presence, and I shivered.

CHAPTER FORTY-SIX

Exhibit 68: Blue wool blanket, 90" x 90"

Since Nicco and I were only going to Baker, I walked.
There were no good places to be alone. Nicco's roommate was
having a party at his place, and so all we had was his car and
the beach.

I hurried to the end of the street, took the stairwell to the
shore. I could barely see the steps. The sun had set, and the fog
was already drifting in. It sounds like one of Lila's films, the
fog some moody metaphor or bad omen, but I can't help the
way it was. When I reached the bottom, the beach looked like
it was filled with floating apparitions.

"Boo," he said. And then arms went around my waist. Hands
pulled me close.

I let out a cry. "Goddamn it. Don't scare me like that."

"I didn't want you to have to walk down here alone. It's so hard to see."

"It's creepy. But beautiful."

"You are." He pulled me to him. His mouth was already on mine.

"Hey, thanks a lot," I teased when we pulled away. I socked his arm. "Creepy but beautiful."

"Only beautiful."

It got crazy hot, fast. Mouths and mouths. Need. And here was another reason he was right about how sex changed everything, because who even wanted to joke around right then? Who cared about talking? I mean, telling each other about your first-grade teacher and your dreams for the future wasn't *this*. It was nice and great and important, but not *now*.

It was just Nicco, and Nicco's dark curls and dark eyes against the white of the night. He'd brought a blanket this time, the one I remembered from his bed, the woven blue one. We walked away from the parking lots, toward the darker end of Baker, toward China Beach, but we didn't get very far. We were holding hands, and hands moved up arms, and then he turned and then I did, and his body was against mine, and we were drowning in it again.

"I wish we could go to my van, but the patrol car was right there in the parking lot," he said.

"Is there nowhere in this city you can park a—"

"Come *here*."

We were down on the sand. Somehow, the blanket had gotten under us. I didn't even notice him spreading it out. We were kissing for a long time, trying to slow it down, because slow was maybe better. My sundress was shoved up, and his shirt was off. The stupid sand was getting everywhere in spite of the blanket, and, God, Baker was always colder than you remembered. A wind picked up, and the fog swirled, and it was so eerie, and the mist from the sea blew up and dampened my skin.

"God, we're getting soaked," Nicco said. His hand was on my hair. He moved it down and cradled my face. "Mist on eyelashes." Something for his notebook.

"Did you feel that?" I asked. Because, oh, no. That wasn't mist. It was a drop, a big fat drop, landing on my bare shoulder.

"Noooo," he groaned. Because, yes, there was another. And another. He stood up and so did I. He shook out the blanket and put it around me. "I didn't even know it was supposed to rain! We'll take our chances in the van."

"Wait," I said. "I've got an idea."

"I like ideas. I love ideas."

Oh, God. Why did I say it? Why?

"No one's home."

"Wait. Are you sure?"

"Yeah. They were getting ready when I left."

"No, I mean are you sure you want to go there?"

"Very." Very, because there was no ghost voice then, was there? No terrible warning, knocking. I couldn't hear anything over how I was feeling. Want was louder than anything else. "Look, the tide is out, and I can practically see our stairs."

"Shortest distance between two points is a line," he said as the rain started to fall harder.

We ran. My hair was soaked and so was his, and I could see that his clothes were getting soaked too. I wanted to take all that stuff off. Cold bodies in warm sheets—oh, it sounded amazing. I wondered what it would be like, him in my bed, where I'd so often thought about him. I was nervous about going there, but I did quick mental calculations. We wouldn't be there long. Lila and Jake always stayed out really late.

We reached China Beach as the tide crept in. It did come in fast, so fast. We stood at the bottom of the 104 steps. We paused, and I saw Nicco's profile, the way he looked toward the house above us. You could see it up there, even in the fog.

Nicco was reluctant. God, maybe *he* heard the voice, warning.

"Come *on*," I said. "It's fine, I promise."

"Yeah?"

"Kiss," I commanded, and then he did, and that settled it.

"Jesus," he said. "What *is* it about you?"

We ran up the stairs. I still had that blanket around my shoulders. Halfway up, he caught me on the landing. And it was raining hard now, windy, enough that the wind whipped around those old mansions, but it didn't matter, because it would be warm soon. We could just let the rain soak us and feel what it felt like to be in that storm together.

I laughed. He pressed me against the wall. The blanket fell

off my shoulders, and his hands pulled the top of my sundress down, and as I shoved my hand down his shorts, my laugh wound its way up, up, up to 716 Sea Cliff Drive. Up the rest of those stairs, to the dark patio, where Jake sat brooding.

Nicco ground his hips against my hand, and then I didn't want anything between us, so I took my hand out. I could feel the rain on my bare skin. I could feel Nicco's mouth on my neck, and the rain and the wind and the fog and I was lost. Too lost to hear those footsteps, but not lost enough to feel the instant terror when I heard that roar.

"What the FUCK is going on here?" Jake shouted.

Oh my God—the panic! Shit. Shit!

Nicco broke away from me and struggled to pull on his shorts and I was trying to get my dress back up, and Nicco was shoving that blanket at me so Jake wouldn't see me there, half naked.

"I . . . I . . ." Nicco was bending and shoving and buttoning. He could barely speak.

"Get the fuck out of here. GET. THE. FUCK. OUT. OF. HERE."

"I'm sorry. I'm sorry!" Nicco's voice shook.

"I'M GOING TO FUCKING KILL YOU!" Jake was tearing down the stairs. He was almost to the landing. His shirt was open, and now he was getting drenched too. His face was twisted in rage.

"Sir, I'm sorry. . . ."

"Go," I said. "Go."

"I can't leave you with—"

"Go! I mean it!"

Nicco hesitated. I gave his shoulder a little shove. And so he turned. He turned and ran down those steps and then he was gone.

"Look at the little pussy, running away!" Jake said, with the singsong of a playground bully. But then, when he reached the landing where I stood, his voice turned vicious. "You little slut. Look at you." He grabbed a handful of the blanket and shoved me backward.

I clutched the blanket to my body. I felt so ashamed.

"I can't even deal with this. This is crazy. This is OUT OF CONTROL."

Well, he was right about that.

"I'm sorry," I said. "I'm sorry."

"Sorry," he spit. "You *disgust* me. Get inside." He put his hand around the back of my neck. I felt his fingers on my skin, pressing, and they felt bad there, where Nicco's fingers had just been. Jake was leading me upstairs by the neck, and he was being rough, but it was his skin on mine that felt the worst.

"Jake," I said. My voice was soft. He stopped and he looked at me then. He looked right into my eyes. The rain beat down, and he held my eyes as he always did. I wasn't sure what I saw there, I wasn't sure what he was going to do next, but I could feel his breath on my face, breath that smelled like some kind of alcohol. "Let me go."

He dropped his hand. And then he whirled away from me

and stomped back up those stairs. I felt so humiliated, but I hated him too. I hated his big, blocky head and his horrible, meaty hands and his money and this house and everything about him. I *hated* him. He repulsed me.

I put my hand to my neck where Jake's fingers had been. I realized that my heart necklace was gone, lost somewhere in the night, the chain broken. I began to shiver. I was shivering so bad that every part of me was trembling. I didn't know what to do. I wanted to run back down those stairs. To follow Nicco and never return. What would have happened then?

Something else. Something different.

CHAPTER FORTY-SEVEN

Exhibit 69: Miyabi Birchwood chef's knife, 8",
stainless steel blade, wood handle

That blanket was heavy and dragging, wet with rain, and so I dropped it outside. Through the big doors, I could see Jake inside, the back of him, flying up the stairwell to Lila's room. I saw the glass on the table next to me, empty of its brown liquid, his chair knocked over from rising with fury.

The shouting from Lila's room had already started. *You let her run around!* Jake yelled. *You're not her* father! Lila yelled back. *You're raising a slut,* Jake said, and then there was the sound of a slap. And then him again: *Goddamn you!*

This fight, the last one, it wasn't about Jake's crimes or the FBI or stolen paintings. It was about me. Me, and whether or not I belonged to myself. Her, and whether or not she did.

I'm leaving you! Get out of here!

It's my house, you stupid bitch. You think you'll leave me? You'll never leave me.

Thuds, crashing. Screaming. Her screaming. Max ran in circles downstairs, whining, trotting half up the stairs and down again.

I had to do something. I felt in my pocket for my phone.

But it wasn't there. It wasn't there! Where was it? I had no idea. I ran outside to look on the patio, but no. It could have fallen out of my pocket down at the beach when we were on the blanket, or while we were running, or on the stairs. It could be anywhere. I remembered the security system, that button with the little red cross that meant *emergency*. I ran to the box on the wall and pushed and pushed and pushed the button.

And then came a scream like I'd never heard before. A primitive sound. A terror sound. I grabbed Max by the collar and practically threw him into the garage and I shut the door. I didn't know if help was coming. I couldn't wait for it if it was, because it might be too late by then.

I was in a panic. I didn't know what to do. Something. Something! I would scare Jake—that was my plan, if you could call it a plan. I went into the kitchen. I grabbed one of those knives. One of those fancy kitchen knives stuck on that magnetic holder.

And then I ran upstairs.

I did.

On the stairwell, I saw that poster of Lila on the ground, the glass broken as if a fist had gone through it. I ran to their room. The door was open, and I saw Jake with his arm raised. He was coming at her. I saw a flash of black. I thought it was a gun, maybe.

"Stop it, stop it, stop it!" I shouted.

Lila looked at that knife and screamed. "Baby, no!" She grabbed the knife from me. And as Jake charged toward her, she thrust out her hand and the knife went in. God, *into* his body! His eyes looked at us both in shock. Blood started to . . . just seep through his shirt. I shut my eyes. I turned away, put my head in my hands in horror and confusion, but not before I saw the expression on his face. Disbelief. *Betrayal. How could you?*

My head was turned away, but I heard it, the crashing stumble backward, the hard thud of his landing.

And then Lila began to sob. "Oh my God, oh my God, oh my God. I didn't mean to. I didn't mean to."

I looked. She was on her knees, next to him. She was stroking his forehead. Blood was pooling beneath him, soaking the hem of her satin robe. He didn't look right. His eyes didn't. A terrible sound was coming from his throat.

"Baby, help me here!" Lila craned his neck back, breathed into his open mouth. Her hands and arms were all bloody and it didn't look real. Nothing seemed real. It was like an R. W. Wright movie, the blood, the body, the girls, but the one girl was frozen; she just stayed frozen for way too long, and the body didn't get up again—it just lay there.

"Baby, what am I going to *do*?" Lila was crying. She was

pleading. "You've got to help me. Please, you've got to help me."

She stared and stared into my eyes. And even through the cold distance of being frozen, even through the unreality of the film playing, I knew what she was asking.

An ambulance arrived, and then the police. There was a sudden swirl of lights and people, and the house was full of cops and attendants. A different van came, and Jake's body was taken outside on a rolling stretcher, and Lila's attorney, Bill Greer, suddenly appeared.

It was all a spinning mass of confusion, but when Detective Don Chambers leaned toward me and said, "Sydney, can you tell me what happened?" it was clear what I was supposed to do. I *was* guilty anyway. I felt guilty. I'd wanted and I'd taken and now I was getting punished, like the dirty, slutty girls in the R. W. Wright books. I'd been hungry, and hungry was wrong and bad, and now look. That fight had been about me, and I had gotten that knife, and I didn't listen hard enough to the ghost when she'd tried to speak. I would help Lila, just like she asked me to.

"Sydney, can you hear me?" Detective Chambers asked. His eyes looked into mine. I wasn't sure if my heart was beating or not.

"I didn't mean to do it," I said.

CHAPTER FORTY-EIGHT

Exhibit 70: Sworn statement of Nicco R. Ricci
Exhibit 71: Photos of decedent's body, decedent's face,
*   decedent with and without measurements,*
*   surface under decedent's body*
Exhibit 72: Crime scene sketch
Exhibit 73: Sworn statement of Dr. Jonathan Martin,
*   medical examiner, City and County of San*
*   Francisco*
Exhibit 74: Sworn statement of Detective Don
*   Chambers, City and County of San*
*   Francisco*

Well, you know this already. You saw those pictures,
too. I was suddenly in different clothes. My flowered sundress was gone, and I was in shorts and a T-shirt. There were
so many cars outside, and people—press, photographers,

strangers. There was the flash of camera lights, the spit and sputter of police radios, sirens, and there were cameramen, and onlookers snapping photos with their phones. I rode to the station in a police car with Lila. We sat in the back. She held my hand, as if we were in this together, but we weren't, not really. As soon as I'd spoken those words and as soon as she'd let me, we weren't.

I had no idea what time it was. Detective Don Chambers was there again, and the police chief, too. I sat with Detective Don Chambers in front of a table of recording equipment. For hours and hours and hours I told my story. And then I said it again. *I didn't mean to do it.*

Lila appeared much later, clinging to her attorney. She said something like, *Baby, you'll have to stay here, but only for the night.* A woman came and led me down a corridor, to a holding cell with iron bars. It had a cot and a toilet and a sink. I had to remove my shoes, and the guard had to look under my clothes for weapons, and she brought me tea and a blanket and I looked right into her eyes and I repeated that lie. *I didn't mean to do it.* Any dreams of *IT,* of largeness in the world, were gone, gone, gone. The summer had been life changing, all right, but in the way an earthquake was, and now I saw only rubble.

I sat on that bed and it wasn't real, how I'd just been with Nicco in the rain and now I was there. I thought about Nicco and Meredith and Carlos and me on that tour of Alcatraz, and it seemed like a million years ago, because I was a different person now. I was older. The night had made me older.

I would never be Lila's baby again. Anyone's baby. And that was right and good, because I wasn't one, and hadn't been one for a long while.

My father had arrived sometime in the night, and by morning, so had Edwina. *I didn't mean to do it. I didn't mean to do it*, I said. I was taken to an all-white room with a shower, a toilet, a high, high window, and another window in the door, from which I could see the faces of the other girls trying to see mine. My father moved like he could make stuff happen. There were new attorneys. *I didn't mean to do it.* I started to believe my own story. It almost seemed like it had really happened that way. My father spoke in the loud, certain voice that some people use and others listen to. And Lila leaned on his arm.

Here is what you know. Here is what you saw: horrible headlines about Lila and me. Images of 716 Sea Cliff Drive— the orange stucco exterior, the maze of the stairwell, a body being rolled out of the front gate. That clip from *Nefarious*, again and again. My Academy yearbook photo, where I smile sweetly in that blue sweater. Somber people dressed in black on a sunny day, standing in a half circle as Jake Antonetti was put into the ground.

And then: new headlines, about ninety-four-year-old Doris Brawley, who'd shipped multiple crates of precious artwork to Giacomo (Jake) Antonetti but never got paid. You heard the interviews with the Brawley family—how Jake had every excuse. The pieces were gifts from the Brawleys. They were stolen by delivery drivers. The workmen at the storage facility mistook the art for building supplies and pilfered them. You heard that *Aphrodite of Knidos*, a marble statue from the fourth century B.C., had vanished. You watched as FBI agents eventually recovered the 46" x 46" *Crying Girl*, by Lichtenstein; the oil on canvas *Jacqueline*, by Picasso; *Female Torso*, by Kazimir Malevich; and four drawings and two paintings that were originally attributed to Willem de Kooning, though the authenticity has since been challenged. Other works came out of that warehouse too, origins yet to be determined. You heard the word *fraud*. It was such a true word. It was such a perfect word for big, important men with lots of secrets.

You heard about all that other stuff of Jake's they found too: a pile of guns and ammunition; expensive gifts from Lila, including a Rolex watch; and a trove of photos of naked women, from Lila's age to mine. There were reasons, many reasons, to feel *uncomfortable* without knowing why.

You also saw those pastel courtroom drawings from the coroner's inquest, held to determine the cause of Jake's death. You saw sketches of Lila on the stand, raising her hand and swearing to tell the truth. Me, doing the same. You saw photos of hundreds of pieces of evidence, from a picture of Lila and Edwina and me in Mexico, to aerial views of 716 Sea Cliff Drive, to the damage Max had done in the garage that night. You read that I had gotten the knife to scare Jake and that he had fallen into me as he charged forward. On every news channel and entertainment show and media outlet, you heard that "I didn't mean to do it."

And then you saw what the grand jury had decided: justi-fiable homicide. The district attorney would not be pressing charges.

But you would never see or hear what I saw and heard. When I closed my eyes, if I wasn't replaying images of Nicco and me that night, or Jake spitting those words *You* disgust *me*, or Lila thrusting that knife into Jake as he lunged toward her, or Jake's confused expression before he fell, or the blood inch-ing up the hem of Lila's robe, I was hearing Detective Don Chambers, who came to speak with me again before the hear-ing. *It doesn't make sense. The story is too pat. The guy wouldn't just walk into a knife. The fingerprints on the handle were smeared, like maybe on purpose. . . .*

I would hear him say those same things again and again in my mind. Again and again, I would shrug.

I would say, *Lots of things don't make sense, but they happen anyway.*

CHAPTER FORTY-NINE

Exhibit 75: Ivory satin robe belonging to Lila Shore

Before I could go home, there was another hearing, this time to determine who would be my guardian for the next two years.

The judge, the Honorable Joan K. Fuller, asked whether I preferred to live with my mother or my father.

My grandmother, I'd said.

The judge's orders included these requirements: I would study with a private tutor at Edwina's home. I would see a psychologist twice a week. Lila and my father would not be allowed to see me more than one day a month. When the judge said this, my father only glanced at his watch, but Lila let out an excruciating cry. It felt like claws ripping me in two halves: before and after.

* * *

Three weeks after that awful night, when I could finally go home, Edwina and I headed to the Fairmont, where she'd been staying. She'd chosen it for a particular reason, and when she swiped the key, that particular reason jumped all over me like I was the returning soldier home from the war, which I pretty much was.

"Max. Max, Max, Max." I buried my face in his fur. I've never been so happy to see someone in all my life.

"Ugh, that damn dog," Edwina said. "What a nuisance." But I could tell that they'd formed their own bond. She'd brought his old dog bed from home, and she'd chosen a hotel that not only allowed dogs, but also welcomed them, with dog treats and a minibar with a bowl, a blanket, and toys. I'd see Edwina drop her hand and trail her fingers so he'd come by for a pet.

Max—well, he was also traumatized that night. In his panic to get to me, he'd scratched and chewed that garage door so badly, it had to be replaced. His collar had caught on something, and the tags had been ripped right off. I understood his terror. I understood his desire to protect.

"I've missed you so much," I told him.

My phone had been found in the cove where Nicco and I lay, ruined by rain, and held as evidence. Edwina had already bought a replacement and set it up, and when I turned it on, there was all my old stuff, as well as a flood of new texts and voice mails. Meredith, Ellen, and even Meredith's dad had called. Hoodean, Cora, and Lizzie, too. There were multiple calls from Coach Dave, a message from Ms. Fiori, my art teacher. And Nicco. And Nicco, and Nicco, and Nicco. Frantic calls that night and the next day. Cautious messages in the days after that.

I didn't return any of the calls. Not then. Not for a long while. I felt ashamed and full of horror that Meredith had to get back on that plane to testify at the coroner's inquest, and that Nicco had to too. They had to get up on that stand and swear to the truth. I couldn't bear the thought of seeing or even talking to any of them and saying that lie straight to their faces: *I didn't mean to do it*. I couldn't bear to hear what they said or did or felt on that stand, while I was in that white room with the window, being rightly punished. I loved Meredith and her family, but I had broken and lost so much more than the necklace they gave me. And Nicco—well, he'd finally seen the bad person I truly was. I was dirty and dark and guilty, and maybe always had been. It was better if I kept my darkness away from all of them.

Before Edwina and I flew back to Seattle, I had some unfinished business. Lila had already moved into another rental in Sea Cliff, a much smaller and older house, but not far from 716. How she could be anywhere near there, I didn't know. Those roots, probably.

In the new place, boxes were piled everywhere, since she was still unpacking. Right then, Lila was deeply in debt, though this would change when *Peyton Place* was released. Of course, it would become a huge hit, especially because of that courtroom scene, where Constance and her daughter, Allison, have a tearful reunion after the murder of the abusive, lecherous Lucas Cross.

The new rental might have been much smaller than the old house, but it still had the same view. You could still see that bridge, and the headlands, and the sea, and I could still smell the ocean. The shipwrecks and fires and quakes that had happened right out there still haunted from her own backyard.

"Baby, thank God!" Lila said. She hugged me. She had my favorite things set out in the kitchen—the Beecher's macaroni and cheese, those Asian pears I always liked. I wouldn't be eating any of it, though.

We took our iced tea into the living room and sat on the white couch, surrounded now by tan walls. I could barely sit there, remembering Jake on those same cushions, fuming over the huge bouquet the FBI had sent. Somewhere in those boxes was that smiling, staring doll too. The one passed down from woman to woman in my family. I hoped she never got out.

Lila took my hands and looked deeply into my eyes. "There are just so many *words*," she said.

But there were only a few necessary ones.

"I'm here to say good-bye."

"Good-bye for *now*. You'll be here for Christmas, of course."

No.

I was leaving that place. I didn't yet understand everything that had happened. I only knew that there'd been a fire and that our lives had been destroyed, though, this time, no one had run out holding only a baby and a photo from a wedding to a cruel man. All of it was gone, and I was glad. Maybe that woman, the one who fled, had been the ghost who kept trying to tell me so many things I needed to know.

Lila held my hands and I looked into her beautiful eyes, and right then I was still confused about why I had helped her, why I had lied for her. I thought it was because that night felt like my fault, and because she was my beautiful and helpless mother, and because Jake had hurt her, and because she needed me. I thought it was because I was trying to give her what no one else ever had, real love and devotion. I thought it was because she'd had it harder than me, so maybe I owed her a debt that I could finally pay and never have to pay again, and because it would be easier for both of us if she didn't suffer. I thought I'd lied for her because I was her object but she was *everyone's* object. Because her beauty and her body were her power, but that wasn't all I had, or all I was. Because, well, maybe I just plain wanted her to love me.

And while all these things are true, I now know there was another reason: When you're a toaster and the lever is pushed, you toast.

Edwina and I said good-bye. I asked the driver to take us past 716 Sea Cliff Drive. But I didn't want to see our old house. I wanted to see the one next door.

After three weeks, more walls had gone up. The place

looked more defined. It looked more like the house it would become. A frame—it could be a good thing if it held you rightly and properly. But this one was as hazardous as ever, with high places and no railings. It was still uncovered, exposed to the elements. The rain would still pour in, and the fog would still loop and wind through the beams. All the stuff in there wasn't entirely sheltered yet.

It had a long way to go before it was done.

CHAPTER FIFTY

Exhibit 76: Flowered sundress belonging to Sydney E. Reilly

Exhibit 77: Photo of enlarged blood-splatter pattern on sundress

I finished school a year early. What else was there to do? After one awkward meeting at Cupcake Royale with Meredith and Hoodean and Cora, I didn't see friends. My former life at Academy belonged to someone else. Even cupcakes did, honestly. So instead I studied. The rain dripped down the windows.

I visited Dr. Mann, with her auburn hair and looped scarves and kind eyes. Twice a week, I'd sit on the couch next to the table with the Kleenex box and the little clock, and I'd talk to her. Dr. Mann would listen, or gently suggest new thoughts, helping me to put the puzzle together. We untangled the knots of Lila and those paintings, and Nicco, and my own desire, and mothers and fathers, going back years. But I didn't tell her the truth about what happened that night. I still kept the secrets. I felt too ashamed about being an object to admit it out loud. I couldn't say that yet.

The deep need I had for an exciting *IT* that summer had burned to the ground. Now something else was rising in its place. It wasn't about being seen and noticed anymore. Or about a guy or an event that might magically arrive to make me different and somehow larger. This *IT* was about becoming full in the world and in my body and in my own self, already large by the fact that I existed at all, larger still after the things that I'd survived. Now, in the early-morning hours when the lake was still glass, I'd go down to Lake Union Crew and take out a scull. I'd row and row. Those legs in that boat got stronger than they'd ever been. I had to learn to set the boat on my own, using only the stability of my own body.

And I learned how to drive.

One day I got a text. It was a photo. Just that. The image was the back of a big guy in motorcycle leathers, a red bandanna on his head, tattoos up his arms. In one hand, he carried a little red trike.

I smiled.

Big dude, little bike, I texted back.

It looked bigger in the Craigslist ad, Nicco responded.

Hey, I have to get off and walk when I go up hills too, I typed.

Then came this: I haven't forgotten you.

I decided to drive out to see him after my "graduation," which Edwina and I celebrated with a little cake she baked from a Duncan Hines mix. Her gift to me was a Subaru with a million miles on it, because that's what everyone in the Northwest drove, and because it had room for Max. Also, for all of my stuff that was now in the back.

"Look at you in there," Edwina said as she stood in her driveway, arms folded, to see me off. "You look like a beautiful young woman."

A changed young woman.

"You drive carefully, now," Edwina said.

"I'll keep it under a hundred," I said, and she scowled.

Flying would have been easier and faster, but I couldn't take an airplane. I couldn't sit in first class, looking at magazines that might have Lila's picture in them. And I didn't want to step foot in the arrivals section of that airport, imagining Jake hugging me. I needed to get there a new way.

When we pulled up into the Lands End parking lot, Max started jumping and whining and scooting all around because he remembered. He remembered that place, and his favorite parts of it too, I was guessing—the running so fast, the other dogs, the great and stinky dead stuff. Before I could even get him on the leash, he shoved out of the car and sped off.

"Max! Get back here!" I called, but it was no use, and who could blame him.

It was late afternoon, and the fog had cleared and the sky was the bright blue of early summer. Max galloped toward the shore like a racehorse, but it was clear that it wasn't just the beach that he remembered. He spotted Nicco way before I did, and now I could see Max in the distance, greeting Nicco like he'd been counting the moments until he could see him again. From that far away, I could only see Nicco bending toward the big guy's neck, giving him a good scruff. But then Nicco waved, and I waved back.

He walked toward me as Max leapt at his side, bumping into him on purpose in a show of dog love. When Nicco got closer, it was so astonishing, because he still looked like himself. There were those eyes again, and there were those black pants rolled up and his white shirt unbuttoned and his tie loosened. My throat got tight with emotion. The then-and-now of it crushed my heart, and as he took me in his arms, I could have broken down crying, but I didn't.

He gave me a sweet kiss.

"You," he said.

We walked. We talked nothing-talk—Carlos, his moms, his classes at College of Marin. It was safer that way. I felt so full of feeling, I could barely speak.

Our shoes were off, and we were on the soft part of the

sand where your feet sink a little. He stopped. He rubbed my arm. "Syd."

His eyes were full of the questions I couldn't answer. I hoped he wouldn't say it, but he did. "I keep hearing, you know, that maybe you weren't really the one—"

"I can't," I interrupted. "I can't."

"Okay. It's okay."

I wanted to break his gaze, stare out at a tanker in the distance, but I didn't.

"Big lie?" he said finally. It was our old game, but his eyes looked worried, and his voice was gentle.

I shrugged.

He took that in. "Fuck. I'm sorry this happened. I can't imagine. God, I feel so bad about that night."

"*I* am," I said. "*I'm* sorry." My voice cracked. I was trying so hard not to cry.

"But there's lots I'm not sorry about."

I smiled, because I wasn't sorry about those things either.

He took my fingers, and we walked again. We climbed the rocks and then hiked the path all the way to the labyrinth. We circled the maze. I could see the treasures people had left at the end—the shells, and feathers, and smooth, colored glass.

At the center, Nicco took my chin in his hand.

"Middle kiss," I said.

"Love instead of seashells," he said.

I could barely look at him. My chest ached with emotion. I was feeling everything, all over again. We headed back. It was the golden hour, just before sunset, when the sun turned everything a glowing yellow. We stood in the ocean and cupped our hands in the water and let it fall on our arms and legs to cool off. My legs in that boat, my legs that had wrapped around Nicco's waist—they felt so different from the legs that now stood in the sea.

"Ready?" he asked.

Our plan had been to go back to his place. Being with him was the only good part of last summer, and I wanted it again, or I thought I did. Dr. Mann had helped me understand how badly I didn't want this to be another R. W. Wright novel, where the girl who has sex gets punished forever. I didn't want that ending.

But it turned out there would be a different ending altogether. Even though I'd driven all the way out there, and even though I'd told him I would stay with him a few nights, and even though that was what we were both expecting, I realized I'd changed my mind. This would be an ending where I listened to myself and used my voice, no matter what the world said back.

"Nicco." I could barely speak.

He turned to look at me. God, those eyes.

"I can't," I whispered. My chest felt like it was caving in from grief and love and every large feeling.

"Oh, no." He put his hands to his heart as if it had just broken.

"I'm sorry. I thought I could, but I can't."

"I get it."

"It all feels like too much right now."

"It's okay."

We were there by the water's edge. Damn it, Max was trying to fetch another dog's Frisbee. My throat was tight with tears. And then a sob escaped, and I put my palms to my eyes to stop it, but there was no stopping it.

Nicco put his arms around me. We just stood there, the surf lapping our ankles. When we separated, Nicco's own eyes were filled with tears, and his shirt was damp and wrinkled from mine. He kissed my forehead. And then he pulled his loosened his tie over his head and tossed it in the water.

"Have a great adventure, tie," he said. His voice cracked with emotion.

"Send us a postcard, tie," I said as we watched it drift out.

"Don't be gone forever, tie," Nicco said.

CHAPTER FIFTY-ONE

Exhibit 78: Recorded statement of Sydney E. Reilly,
5 of 5

I still believed that Agatha had things to tell me. About how she'd carried that body through her life all these years. About how she'd become free enough in the world to let her body be what it was. I couldn't imagine all the stories she carried in those wrinkles and sags, stories of feeling beautiful and hideous, of feeling insecure and vulnerable, proud and strong. I'd never get the chance to talk to her. So I just let her tell me something else. A direction I should head.

Before I'd left for California, I'd rented a small house in Oregon, near Portland State University, where I'd be going to school in the fall, and that's where I went next. After I moved in, I would advertise for a roommate, since Edwina was worried about me being lonely, and since I liked the idea of making new friends. Right then, though, I was driving down Highway 101 with an old friend sitting upright in the passenger seat. He liked the window rolled down.

"We could play the license game if you could talk," I said. His hair blew in the wind. His nose tilted up, taking in every magnificent smell.

"Your conversational skills could use some work," I said.

But this wasn't true. He always told me the most necessary things. And he was the best listener anyone could ask for.

Just outside the city, I stopped to get gas at an ARCO station. A man filling his tank next to me leaned over to catch my eye. He asked me if I had a boyfriend, and then told me to smile, and when I turned away, he said, *I know your type.*

And then, in a park in Ashland where I let Max run around a bit, another man hovered near the bench where I sat. He stood too close to me and tried to make eye contact. He had one hand in his pocket, and I didn't know what he was doing or about to do.

He made me nervous. Uneasy. I pretended to talk on my phone so he'd go away. When he didn't go away, I had to leave. *I* had to leave.

When I got back to my car, I felt pissed. The world hadn't changed and this made me so angry. It was the same as it had been for hundreds and hundreds of years, and this filled me with fury. I was angry at the paintings of women who were only bodies, who had faces with blank eyes and no mouths. I was angry at R. W. Wright, and his sexy, punished girls, and men who leered, and boys who grabbed, and the gaze, the gaze, the gaze. I was furious at dick flashers and violent men, the frauds, the thieves. I was pissed at how beauty was some highly prized commodity—sold and sought and viciously envied, made to feel shameful. Pissed at the guardians of your virginity who were just as much creepers and controllers as creepers and controllers.

And I was furious at mothers who encouraged you to be sexy but not have sex, and *ladies' man* fathers, who flirted with waitresses and treated you like another unseen girl, because who were you supposed to be, then? The you in the middle of all this. The hopeful you, the wanting you, the you with dreams, the unsteady you, the you that wants to feel everything but isn't allowed to, who doesn't know what to make of this mess, and how could you?

"Goddamn it!" I said as I sat in that car. Max looked worried. He had reason to be. "This here is some worrisome shit," I told him.

I gripped the steering wheel of the old Subaru. And right there in that parking lot in Ashland, Oregon, I made a decision, because our eyes do see, our mouths do speak, and we are not objects. I am not.

It wasn't a decision that would change the whole world. I doubted I could do that. But the women of my family, going back generations—we'd been told lies about ourselves that we believed, and we'd even gone on to tell each other those same lies. I could maybe put an end to that particular plotline.

* * *

I got to my new place and settled in a little. Edwina had done the Edwina thing and sent a bunch of furniture, which had already arrived, along with my few boxes. I used a hammer and a drill and I hung pictures and shelves and curtains. It was a jumble of stuff, but it didn't matter. It takes time to sort things out.

After a week or so, I went to the thrift shop I saw downtown. The store smelled like dusty old things that haven't quite given up hope. I hunted around. I looked through used board games and radios, paperbacks and stereo speakers. And then I found one.

A tape recorder.

The recorder on my phone wouldn't work for what I had in mind. And this was a double-awesome find because it still had the batteries in it, and when I pressed the button, the little spindles moved in a circle, just as they were supposed to. I found an unopened package of tapes, too, circa what, 1997? Who knows.

"Look!" I said to Max when I returned to the car. "Retro."

He panted his regard.

"I know, huh? It's hard to believe all the shit that's still around."

Back at the house, I opened the screen door to the yard, which was one of the biggest reasons I chose the place. Max needed a yard. Out on the grass, there was an old lawn chair from the previous tenants. I unfolded it and sat down. Max ran around and sniffed every bush and dandelion.

"You still can't tell anyone!" I yelled to Max as he lifted his leg on a rhododendron.

I wasn't sure what I was going to do with these tapes when I was done. Maybe I'd put them in a box in the closet with all the stuff from the hearing. Maybe I'd let someone listen to them. Maybe I wouldn't. Maybe I would someday, but not yet. I didn't know. It didn't matter. The important thing was this: The truth is something you have to tell yourself first.

I settled into that low-slung lawn chair and set the recorder on my knees. I took a deep breath, because the truth might be ugly and hard, but it is necessary. And then I began the story that you—you, whoever is listening—are hearing now.

It's a story that was years in the making. *Eons* in the making. It's a story that went back and back and back. It's a story I didn't want to live anymore.

I pushed record. The little spindles spun.

I spoke.

"I had a bad feeling, even before I left home," I said.

Acknowledgments

Boundless gratitude to my incredible editor, Liesa Abrams, who brought her own passion and heart and history to this book, and to my agent, Michael Bourret, who's changed my life with his talent, intelligence, and extraordinary guidance. Love and my deepest appreciation to everyone at S&S, as always—Jon Anderson, Mara Anastas, Chriscynethia Floyd, Anna Jarzab, Caitlin Sweeny, Michelle Leo and the whole fantastic Education and Library team, Sara Berko, Laura Eckes, Alissa Nigro, Elizabeth Mims, Christina Pecorale, Christine Foye, Emily Hutton, Victor Iannone, and Leah Hays. Hard hugs to each of you.

Forever love and thanks to my family, which now so beautifully includes Erin, Pat and Myla, and our best buddy Max. And to my John, Sam, and Nick—I've said it before, but no amount of times would be enough: You are the joy and the meaning and the everything.

Turn the page
for a sneak peek at *One Great Lie*.

Lucchesia Sbarra, poet.

Published Rime, *and possibly another volume, both lost.*

(1576–unknown)

Picture it—the exact coordinates where Charlotte's life will change and never change back: a table in the Seattle Public Library. On it—the book *Biographical Encyclopedia of Literature: Sixteenth Century.* Above—an angled ceiling of enormous glass panes, which makes the library feel like a space colony of the future. Just ahead—yellow escalators and green elevators, shades of disco-era neon that sometimes give Charlotte a migraine.

Now picture Charlotte herself—her long dark braid is over one shoulder. She's wearing a sweatshirt, zipped all the way up, which looks kind of goofy, but who cares—she's always cold. She's trying to write a report on a long-ago female Renaissance poet Isabella di Angelo but can only find information about the guy everyone already knows about, Antonio Tasso. There's tons and tons of stuff about Tasso and his poetry. But all she's been able to unearth about Isabella di Angelo is this one fact, repeated again and again. Charlotte's brown eyes stare down at it: *Tasso's longtime paramour. Paramour*: old-fashioned word for someone Tasso had sex with.

Charlotte's good friend Yasmin is across from her, studying for her macroeconomics test and sucking on sour apple Jolly Ranchers. Yas loves those. Whenever she leans over to talk to Charlotte, her breath is a great burst of fake-apple sweet. Charlotte's boyfriend, Adam, is there too. He sits to her right, his knees touching hers under the table, the sleeves of his hoodie pushed up to his elbows. He's always touching her like this, like she's his lucky rock, or like he's worried she'll run off if he doesn't hang on.

Nate sprawls in the chair next to Yasmin. They've been together since sophomore year, and Nate has stopped working out, and he has a little splootch of belly over his stomach, and he's on his third day in that Kurt Cobain T-shirt, and this bothers Yasmin because he doesn't seem to be trying anymore. Also, his pits have a slightly tangy odor, which is a constant problem for Yas. It's the end of spring quarter, right before break, and Charlotte and Yasmin have serious stuff to do, because they're perpetual overachievers with lots of AP classes, and graduation is coming. Charlotte's got this term paper, which is going nowhere, and Yasmin's final is going to be brutal.

Adam and Nate are just fucking around, though. Nate made a triangle football out of a note card, and Adam has his hands up like goalposts, and they're flicking it back and forth and making whoops of victory and *Aw!*s of defeat, and they're basically being way too loud for a library. A guy with a big beard and a backpack scowls at them. A little kid stares, wide-eyed, like they're a riveting puppet show, maybe wishing he could get away with stuff like that.

"Guys, *stop*," Yasmin says. "Show some *maturity*." She sounds like her mother right then, Charlotte thinks. Yasmin's mom is very serious, and always on her case about her grades even though she gets straight As. But Charlotte wants them to knock it off too. She and Yas are both the polite, anxious sort of people who worry about getting in trouble. She wishes she weren't, but she can't help it.

Nate tries to grab Yasmin's butt, and she pulls away, annoyed. Charlotte looks up to see if the librarian is watching.

And that's when it happens: Charlotte's eyes scoot in a fateful arc, from Nate's hand on Yasmin's butt, across the space of the library, stopping just short of the librarian's desk, because there it is, that flyer. It's posted on a noticeboard hanging on the wall by the bank of escalators. She's not sure why she didn't see it before, because the words practically call out to her now, which is a cliché, but true.

Anything about writing calls out to her, though. Short-story contests, ads in the *Stranger* for writing classes, articles online. New notebooks, packages of pens, fat blocks of printer paper. Anything that has to do with writing has drawn her since she wrote her first story, "The Land of the Mixed-Up

Animals," when she was seven. Wait, no. Anything about writing has pulled her in probably since she was five and read this line in *Where the Wild Things Are*: *That very night in Max's room a forest grew.* Is that beautiful or what? Words were forests to explore in your very own room, warm tents to hide in, and magic cloaks that transformed you. *I'LL EAT YOU UP!* Max shouts to his mother, so words also let you be what you wished you could be—impolite and bold, someone who could talk back and get into trouble and not care.

After that book, even when she was that little, Charlotte would run to her room to madly scratch out some idea, and since then, piles of *stories* grew, her own forest where she could be wild. Her mind started to be a writer's mind, with ideas constantly falling forward like an annoying wisp of hair you have to keep pushing aside. She stumbled on a secret: writing was a place she could be honest in ways she couldn't in real life. And after that incredible discovery, all the sentences were roads leading to something *meant*, and all the ideas she'd urriedly scratch down were doorways to her future. She never wanted to be a veterinarian, then an astronaut, then a scientist, like most kids. Only a writer. And that report she's working on, about that poet from way back in the 1500s? Isabella di Angelo was a great-great-great-(too many greats to count)-grandmother on her mother's side, so, see? Isabella's existence is *proof* that writing is in Charlotte's *blood*.

A lot of people (okay, her father) don't take her and her writing seriously. He acts like she's making pictures with macaroni and glitter. But she has the will and intention of an artist already, even if she's young and has a lot to learn. She's making art *right now*, like you do when you're an apprentice, and so is her friend Rebecca (photography), and Dara (painting), and if you don't think so, you're wrong, Charlotte's sure. Her biggest dream: to say something that *says something*. How great would it be, to be one of those young writers you hear about, published ridiculously young? Her own photo in an artistic black-and-white on a jacket flap—can you even imagine it? She can. She does. She believes it can happen. She *wants* it. She can feel that want like a fire inside. No, that's a cliché, too, and you're supposed to avoid those, if you're a writer. But the point is, it burns like a passion does.

Charlotte rises from her chair. "Hey," Adam says. He reaches out to tug the tail of her sweatshirt to bring her back to him. He thinks she's mad at him for being obnoxious in the library. But she just wants to see that flyer. From there, she can only read the words *Aspiring Writers*.

Up close now . . . Wow. It's advertising a new summer study abroad program, one you have to apply for. It looks expensive. Very. So, no way. It's in Italy, on a private island, La Calamita, across the water from Venice. She's never even heard of that island, and Italy feels like a planet in another cosmos. There's a photo of a villa. Her family could never afford that.

But wait.

In smaller print: *Scholarships Available*.

Her heart actually speeds up with thrill-fear. But then,

she sees another daunting phrase: *College Students*. She isn't one now, but she will be in the fall. Does that even count? She'll be enrolled. Technically, she'll be one, right? There's nothing about age, but, God, she'd probably be the youngest one there. This gives her an anxious whoosh of intimidation. She spins the rings on her fingers like she does when she gets nervous.

There's also a romantic, grainy photo of a Venetian canal, with a gondolier guiding his boat under a bridge. It's a basic shout of *Venice*, but who cares. It's not corny or unoriginal to her. Not at all. It feels like fate. She's in that library right this minute studying Isabella di Angelo, and Isabella di Angelo lived and died in Venice way back in the 1500s. Her mother's side of the family was there for eons until her grandma moved to the US as a little girl. What are the odds? It feels like an offering, meant just for her.

Charlotte's never even been on an airplane. A place Venice that is so hard to imagine, it almost doesn't seem real—a postcard place. But now, look. She's actually are touching the glossy paper.

She removes the pushpin and takes the pamphlet down to examine it more closely. And that's when something even more stunning and astonishing and terrifying and marvelous occurs, because inside the fold is Luca Bruni's photo. She knows this photo; of course she does. It's the one where he's straddling a chair, his thin shoulders leaning toward the camera, his long arms folded. His hair is kind of a mess, and his nose is a mountain on his narrow face, but his dark eyes look right at you, *into* you.

Luca Bruni! Holy shit, Luca Bruni has a summer abroad writing program in Venice!

It's incredible. God. God! He's one of her favorite writers ever. Just the thought of him gives Charlotte that very particular reader's pleasure, a sigh mixed with a thrill. Just the thought of him also gives her that particular *writer's* pleasure, a sigh mixed with awe. Under his image, there's a small paragraph with his bio, but who needs it? Who doesn't know him? He's known all over the world, a celebrity, the way only the tiniest handful of authors are.

As she stands in the library holding the pamphlet, Charlotte's heart begins to thump in double-espresso time. Above her is the futuristic ceiling, and all around her are words, old words, new words, words from when Isabella di Angelo walked the stone streets of Venice in 1573. But more importantly, Luca Bruni stares up at her from that pamphlet, and two shelves over and four shelves up are some of the most beautiful words she's ever read. She can lead you right to it, Luca Bruni's shelf.

The words inside *A Mile of Faces* are so beautiful. The words inside *Under the Sudden Sky*, *The Tide of Years*, *The Forever King*, and *The Glass Ship* (oh, especially that one) are beautiful too. All of Luca Bruni's work is beautiful, and powerful, and meaningful, and raging, and funny, and soul-crushing, and life-changing, full of blood and bone shards and heartbeats. And in his interviews, Luca Bruni himself is powerful, and meaningful, and raging, and funny; arrogant, and tender, but sometimes cruel, too, full of blood and bone shards and heartbeats.

This is what she knows more than anything else as she stands there, clutching the pamphlet, her chest filling with hope. She knows this without a doubt: Luca Bruni's words—they will shatter you.

There's something she doesn't know, though. Not yet.

His words will shatter you, but so might he.

Amedea Aleardi, poet.

Little is known of her life, and most of her work is lost.

(Dates unknown)

Charlotte feels some sort of determination, an iron core of it, rise in her body. A challenge, petrifying but exhilarating. This is what a dream feels like. An engine cranking up, a sky that stretches on and on. She replaces the pushpin, but not the pamphlet. It's wrong to take it; she should just write down the information, but she's already feeling proprietary and competitive. The fewer people that apply, the better.

Yasmin raises one eyebrow. They stare at each other, a meaningful stare full of paragraphs. Charlotte has looked into Yasmin's eyes since they sat next to each other in that horrible algebra class in the ninth grade, when Mr. Shattuck would scream and throw the whiteboard eraser at anyone who talked. Charlotte would get bad, bad stomachaches in that class because she can't stand it when anyone yells. It scares her, when you're as good as you can be but still get screamed at.

After that, she and Yas were forever friends, same as two soldiers in a trench.

Charlotte flashes Yas the pamphlet before tucking it into her backpack and zipping it up tight. Yasmin gives a slow nod of acknowledgment and grins. They know each other so well. Besides, Yas understands going for the impossible. She's trying for a summer internship at NASA.

"Totally," Yasmin says. It's an entire pep talk in a single word. Sometimes all you need is just one other person to believe along with you.

"Score!" Nate shouts, and pounds the table with his fists.

It's the kind of beautiful Seattle day that makes people wear shorts and take the tops down on their convertibles even though it's too cold, if anyone's honest. Which also means it's a day where everyone in the city heads to Green Lake. After they leave the library, Charlotte sits on a blanket with Adam at their favorite spot on the grass, near the boat rentals. Yasmin and Nate run across the street to Starbucks. She and Adam are alone, aside from a million people at the park, so they kiss, and Adam sneaks his hand up her shirt.

They've been together since the fall when Adam and his dad moved here from Portland. Right away, she was drawn to the moody, brooding loner-ness about him, like she was light and he was dark, so together they were a full rotation of the Earth. He was so different from Owen Burke, her boyfriend during sophomore year, student body treasurer, tennis team captain, someone who would never step on a crack, just in case. Nope, Adam had shadings of her first serious crush, Jake Kerchek, eighth grade—the same piercing eyes and mop of hair, only Jake was slightly cruel (he made fun of her for being in orchestra) and mostly ignored her, except for when they were lab partners, where she did most of the work.

Charlotte probably has some messed-up draw to darkness, who knows, but Adam plays the guitar and he's really good, and she loves that. He has that curly brown hair, and he's thin, and she likes that, too, or rather, she likes the way his jeans just lay on his hips as if they're balanced on a hanger. She was attracted to Adam in ways she was never attracted to Owen Burke, and when she had sex for the first time in Adam's bed when his dad wasn't home, she didn't feel like she'd lost her virginity or anything else. She felt like she'd gained something: a secret, like the hidden, zippered compartment of a suitcase that makes it larger.

Now Adam's tongue is slipping into the corners of her mouth, and his fingers are wriggling under the elastic of her bra. Usually, Charlotte loves kissing him, loves her skin on his skin, but she's distracted. She's thinking about what story she should write to submit with that application. Something strong, something Luca Bruni will relate to. Most people probably know him from that TV series they did of his book *One Great Lie*, but then again, *A Mile of Faces* is the one everyone studies in high school or college, the one that his fans always name as their favorite. It isn't Charlotte's favorite, though. It's great, but

The Glass Ship is *hers*. She feels ownership about it like that. Same as you do when you love a song from a band that no one's really heard of yet.

She's pretty sure *The Glass Ship* is Luca Bruni's most personal and biographical book too. It's just a guess, but a lot of details match the ones from his childhood—a sad, silent mother; an abusive, absent father who left them alone and poor in the village of Arquà Petrarca to go work in the US. Luca Bruni's depression and mood swings, present forever after that.

Charlotte has the (ridiculous, childish, okay, but so what) feeling that if he knows *The Glass Ship* is her favorite, he'll be pleased with her, like she can see something about him that other people don't usually see. Maybe she should write about her own loneliness, since the ache of it drips off the pages in *The Glass Ship*, or about her silent, absent father and angry mother. He'll feel a connection to her maybe, like she feels to him.

"Char?" Adam pulls away and looks at her. Ugh! This sounds awful, since his hands were up her shirt, but she sort of forgot he was there, and now he's noticed. That pamphlet in her bag is what she feels desire for right then, not Adam. She just wants to get home and get started.

"Yas and Nate are coming." It's true, thank goodness—Nate's holding the cardboard tray, and Yas pretends to stick a finger down her throat from seeing them make out. It's a good excuse—Charlotte doesn't want Adam to see the secret plan in her eyes. He's always worried she's about to break up with him. It's like she's his whole world, and she doesn't want to *be* a world. She wants to be *in* a world. She wants to tromp around in it, explore it, own it. Plus, darkness is tiring sometimes. In her mind, her life has already changed, gone beyond Adam; she's somewhere in another country, and the sun is hot, and boats slide through the waters of a canal, and words are everywhere. Written, spoken, taught; genius words, beautiful words, hanging like ripe lemons from a tree.

That night before dinner, Charlotte has her laptop open. She should be working on her report, but she isn't. One: That report is becoming impossible and frustrating beyond belief, because Isabella di Angelo seems to be forgotten by everyone but her mother's family. Two: Well, on one tab, there's the website for Luca Bruni's program. A hundred times already, she's looked at the images of his villa on La Calamita, the words *La Calamita* a lyric in her head. On another tab, there's the application for the scholarship, and on another, the blank page of a new document. It's utterly empty except for her name and address in the upper left corner, and a blinking cursor.

That cursor insists. *Hurry up, hurry up. I'm waiting,* it says, again and again, and Charlotte kind of hates that cursor, but she kind of loves it too. It has the tick of a clock. Clocks are pressure, but they also say, *You better get going and make the most of life.*

A warm and buttery smell comes upstairs from the kitchen. Her mother, Adele, is back from work at Dr. Denton, DDS's, where she scrapes and sprays and peers into the dark caverns of mouths, handing tools to Dr. Denton before he asks, anticipating his every fucking need. Those are Adele's words. *All the dirty work of the dentist for a fraction of the pay!* Downstairs, she bangs pans around. The pans sound mad. Adele sounds mad a lot, even when she's not talking. Charlotte feels guilty at that sound, really guilty. She's gotten so good at guilt that she feels it whenever *anyone* is displeased or upset, or when she's been a disappointment, or hasn't given someone what they want. She should go down and help, but mad isn't exactly inviting.

In the room next door, Charlotte's little sister, Ella, plays some boy-band music. Adele yells for Ella to turn it down. This same scene has occurred at least twelve million times over the course of Charlotte's life already. Marvin, their Jack Russell terrier, lies on Charlotte's bed, snoring and farting as he sleeps.

"Oh, Marv," she says, and waves her hand.

It's silly to even start on a story. Dinner will be ready any minute. Still, Charlotte's dying to get to it. Instead, she fills in the easy parts of the application, the basic name-and-address stuff. Suddenly, Marv shoots off the bed, a dog rocket, barking his head off, racing downstairs as the front door opens.

"Hey, guys!" her father yells.

Charlotte hears him trudge up the stairs. *Trudge*—it's the exact right word, her writer-mind says. Her father has been gone for a week, but aside from Marv, no one dashes over to greet him because this is usual life. He's a traveling salesman, though Charlotte only sees the traveling part. The sales part is a bit of a mystery. She's not even exactly sure what he sells. Something to do with cellular technology. The wireless something-something that connects to the other something.

"Hey, Dad," she calls.

Through her half-open door, she can see him in her parents' bedroom. He loosens his tie. He heaves his suitcase onto a chair and unzips it, retrieving his toiletry kit. Most of the time, he keeps his suitcase packed. Now, he disappears into their bathroom, and Charlotte hears a flood of peeing and then the opening and shutting of drawers, as if he can't find things. When he returns after a trip, he seems weary and distracted and uncomfortable—lost, even. Their house is the hotel in a foreign city, and his real life is elsewhere. He spends a lot of time reading things on his tablet and makes very little conversation, like he's waiting at the airport and they're strangers he doesn't want to make eye contact with, in case they start asking him where he's from.

When Luca Bruni writes of loneliness, when he says his heart has a hole that the wind whistles through, she knows just what he means.